TIMELESS LOVE

"All we have is today," Leonardo said. "No, we don't even have today. All we have is this moment."

Sara was lost in thought. "I believe what you say may be true. The simple fact that I've traveled through time tells me that I've been wrong about many things. But the one thing I do know is that I can't stay here."

"You mean you won't."

She stared into his eyes and her lip quivered. "That's not fair."

He saw her struggling with her emotions and felt a stab of guilt. "No, it isn't fair and I apologize." He smoothed the hair back from her temples, gently kissing her forehead.

She melted easily into his embrace while he rained soft kisses down her cheek, finally claiming her lips. Over and over he kissed her until, with a soft moan, she pressed herself against him.

"There is one thing that would make you stay here," he whispered into her hair.

"I don't want to leave my family . . . my father," her voice was barely audible and he could tell her resistance wore thin.

"None of that would really matter if you were in love."

"Love?" she repeated the word and it resounded in his head.

"If you loved someone, you would want to be with him wherever he was. Don't you think that is true, Sara?"

"Yes," she whispered as he kissed her again.

YOU WON'T WANT TO READ
JUST ONE—KATHERINE STONE

ROOMMATES   (0-8217-5206-5, $6.99/$7 99)
No one could have prepared Carrie for the monumental changes she would face when she met her new circle of friends at Stanford University. Once their lives intertwined and became woven into the tapestry of the times, they would never be the same.

TWINS   (0-8217-5207-3, $6.99/$7.99)
Brook and Melanie Chandler were so different, it was hard to believe they were sisters. One was a dark, serious, ambitious New York attorney; the other, a golden, glamourous, sophisticated supermodel. But they were more than sisters—they were twins and more alike than even they knew . . .

THE CARLTON CLUB   (0-8217-5204-9, $6.99/$7.99)
It was the place to see and be seen, the only place to be. And for those who frequented the playground of the very rich, it was a way of life. Mark, Kathleen, Leslie and Janet—they worked together, played together, and loved together, all behind exclusive gates of the *Carlton Club*.

Available wherever paperbacks are sold, or order direct from the Publisher. Send cover price plus 50¢ per copy for mailing and handling to Penguin USA, P.O. Box 999, c/o Dept. 17109, Bergenfield, NJ 07621. Residents of New York and Tennessee must include sales tax. DO NOT SEND CASH.

RENAISSANCE MAN

Diane Bernard

Zebra Books
Kensington Publishing Corp.

http://www.zebrabooks.com

ZEBRA BOOKS are published by

Kensington Publishing Corp.
850 Third Avenue
New York, NY 10022

First Printing: April, 1997
10 9 8 7 6 5 4 3 2 1

Printed in the United States of America

*To my husband, Bernie, a true Renaissance Man
who helped me conceive this story and
was my inspiration throughout.*

One

Sara was to remember that first Saturday in October as unusually cool with a strange, low-hanging mist curled in the pines like a road leading somewhere else.

They had been driving forever and she was half afraid they might be lost. Had she been alone, she would not have cared. But glancing over at her fiancé, she saw a look of intense concentration on his face. It had taken weeks to persuade Roger to accompany her to the Renaissance Festival and now they had spent the entire morning trying to find it. Her scribbled directions were sketchy.

"Where in the hell is this place?" Roger asked, irritated.

"He said it was north of Houston. We turn right at Magnolia, go over the railroad tracks, then left."

"We did that."

"He said it was just up the road."

"I love it when Texans say, 'just up the road.' Dallas is 'just up the road.' "

Roger was from Pittsburgh and, although he'd lived in Houston ten years, he'd never really naturalized. He still thought of Texas as a foreign country.

Ignoring him, Sara rolled down the window and took a deep breath of air. It was a beautiful day to be lost. They passed cattle grazing contentedly in verdant meadows. Roadside stands displayed the last of the summer's produce and overhead, the leaves had just begun to change color. In Sara's imagination, they drove into another world far away from the stress of a big city. Here, life moved at a slower pace as if time was not relevant.

Roger, intent upon reading all road signs, noticed none of these things. He gunned the engine of his Porsche, passing pickup trucks and tractors as if they were standing still.

Finally, in the midst of the pastoral landscape, flags waved and towers beckoned in the distance.

"There it is. The Renaissance Festival!" Sara sat on the edge of her seat.

"Out in the middle of nowhere," Roger muttered, pulling into the parking lot. "And it took us half a day to get here."

"Roger, you're going to love it." Sara had heard nothing but good things about the Renaissance Festival. Everyone loved it.

"I really needed to work today." He raised an eyebrow and put on the parking brake with great ceremony as if to impress her with the sacrifice he'd made.

She gave him an impish smile. "But you don't want me to think you're a workaholic."

"That's right." Roger squeezed her hand.

Sara studied him, thoughtfully. "After we get married, will I ever see you?"

He laughed. "Occasionally on holidays." Then at her dark look, he shook his head. "Sara, right now the company is in bad shape. Thank God Sam had the presence of mind to bring me onboard. Otherwise, I think Carlyle Chemical would be bankrupt."

Sara's eyes widened. Her father had started the company with only ten thousand dollars twenty-five years ago and built it into a thriving business. "But I thought an investor offered to buy the company for five million dollars?"

"That was last year, before your father's stroke. Ben should have taken the offer. Instead, that was the first of many bad decisions made before he went completely downhill."

Sara winced. Although his paralysis had disappeared, Ben

Carlyle had lost his ability to communicate. Once a brilliant classical scholar, his garbled speech sounded like the incoherent ravings of a maniac. Doctors had thrown up their hands and said he would never be the same. Sara had been unable to accept this prognosis, always believing that her father would recover. But after a year, she'd begun to have doubts. Ben could no longer run Carlyle Chemical and no one else in the family could take his place. As an English professor at the University of Houston, Sara had no head for business. And her brother Sam, who'd been sales manager, had been over his head as acting president. In desperation, Sam had enlisted the help of his friend, Roger Latham. Gradually, Roger had bought into the company and now owned thirty percent. Sam had been only too happy to turn over the reins to a Harvard MBA. They all had.

Until this moment, Sara hadn't realized how much they depended on Roger to save the business. "We're very grateful to you."

Roger took the compliment in stride. "You know I'm glad to help." Painstakingly, he unfolded a sun screen across the windshield and came around to get Sara. Her mood dampened by his words, she nevertheless allowed him to thread his arm through hers possessively as they walked to the entrance.

Recent rains had battered marigolds along the fence and mud puddles dotted the pathway. Overhead, clouds threatened more rain, but now the air was crisp and clear, redolent with the scent of pine.

"Good day, Milady and Milord." A Yeoman Warder, dressed in red tunic, ruffled hat, and tights, boomed out a greeting.

"Don't tell me everyone is in costume," Roger scoffed as he escorted Sara through the gate.

"Yes, isn't it wonderful? We have to get into the spirit, Roger," she giggled, pulling him toward a clothing store.

"I won't wear a pair of tights," he warned, following her into Glynnis's Closet.

Minutes later, Sara emerged wearing a red skirt and a white blouse and apron. Black slippers and a black woolen cloak completed her ensemble.

In the end, Roger refused to wear a costume, and Sara had to admit that the Renaissance clothing was too bulky for his stocky frame. But he was a good sport and his smile told Sara that he approved of her purchases. The white blouse revealed a creamy expanse of bosom, and a black bustier cinched in her small waist.

"You could have stepped off an Elizabethan stage," he told her.

"I'll take that as a compliment," she laughed.

The festival grounds comprised some fifty acres devoted to games, booths, and taverns. Strolling minstrels, knights, jugglers, barbarians, giants, witches, and gypsies entertained the visiting gentry. They took their time, walking slowly, stopping at almost every booth. Roger tried his arm at archery and sampled a flagon of Guinness beer. People milled around them with painted faces and Renaissance costumes. The atmosphere was lighthearted and bawdy, exactly as it must have been hundreds of years ago.

At lunch they sat on a vine-covered bench, dining on roasted turkey legs and cider. Afterwards, they stopped to listen to a woman play the Celtic harp, then watched a jousting match.

Sitting beside Roger, Sara felt happier than she had in a long time. Roger was like the white knight who galloped onto the field—a savior come to save the family and Sara. Shy and withdrawn as a child, Sara had been her father's favorite. They'd shared a love of languages and books. When Ben became involved in business, Sara devoted herself to learning. Books took her father's place and she continued to go to school until there were no more courses. She hadn't intended to get her doctorate; it just happened.

Over the years, she built an academic wall separating her from the real world where she led a safe, cloistered existence. Other than a brief affair with a history professor, she'd met few men, and those had been awed by her credentials.

She thought her life was perfectly fine until Roger simply walked in and staked his claim. Only then did she realize what she had missed—the love of a dynamic and forceful man. Something primal in Sara responded to his male dominance and she had been swept away by his proposal.

A loud cheer from the crowd signaled the end of the contest. The White Knight had been victorious. As they walked away from the tournament, hand in hand, Sara thought how lucky she was.

"Do you want to get your fortune read?" Roger suddenly asked when they passed a gypsy's caravan, "to find out when our wedding will be?"

Sara smiled wryly. "Maybe later."

Roger frowned. "We've been engaged for two months now and every time I mention the wedding, you have another excuse. Sometimes I wonder if you really want to get married."

"Of course, I do," she said. "I just want to enjoy being engaged for a while." Her light kiss was intended to pacify, but she knew she couldn't put him off forever. She told herself it was too soon after her father's stroke. Too soon after their engagement. Too soon. She just wasn't ready to set a wedding date.

They stopped at a jewelry display near a craftsman's stall and Roger bought her a pair of amethyst earrings.

A voluptuous woman with vivid blue eyes and dark hair tied in love knots held the mirror while Sara put on the earrings. "They become you, dear," she said, "but be careful. Stones like these have special powers."

"Powers?"

"Amethysts recall the past," she said. "Many psychics

wear them. They find out all sorts of things." She smiled at Roger, who immediately looked away.

Sara couldn't decide whether it was the woman's words or the touch of the stones against her skin, but she immediately felt a strange warmth spread through her body.

The woman continued to stare at her as Sara turned to leave. "Have a nice day," she called after them.

"I hope you don't believe all that nonsense," Roger said with a chuckle. "I'm always amazed at what people will do to make a sale."

Smiling, Sara shook her head, and the stones touched her skin. Despite Roger's words, the eerie feeling crept down her spine and stayed. It was still with her hours later when they stopped to have a drink.

At three o'clock, the Black Boar Tavern wasn't very crowded and they found an empty table near the back, away from the smoke. Roger bought them large glasses of mead. The honeyed brew was delicious. Suddenly thirsty, Sara downed her glass and asked for more.

Roger ordered another round.

Halfway through her second glass, Sara became dizzy. The room spun, faces started to merge and her head throbbed. Passing her hand over her eyes only made things worse. It was like she was watching a movie in slow motion.

"I think I need to find a bathroom," she said, rising to a shaky stance. She managed to drape her purse over her shoulder, but the effort exhausted her.

"Are you all right?"

"I feel a little dizzy. If I splash some water on my face, I'll be all right."

"Don't be long. I'd like to head back soon."

Roger's words were drowned out by loud laughter and the music of a minstrel. Sara wove unsteadily between the tables to ask the bartender where the ladies' room was.

A woman tended the bar with a white blouse and corset

similar to Sara's. "The ladies' room is through that door."
She pointed to the back of the tavern.

She retraced her steps, almost stumbling over a chair before she finally opened a door. The door led outside. *Was
this the right way? Where were the bathrooms?* Sara wondered fuzzily. Perhaps they were at the side of the building.
Her head spun and she almost fell down concrete steps.
Hiking up her skirts, she walked around in a dazed circle,
finally tripping over the root of a huge oak tree. There she
collapsed, unable to move.

The amethysts lay against her cheek sending warmth
through her body. Touching the stones, she thought of the
saleslady's words. *Special powers.* There was an energy
there. She could feel it.

Her own energy was simultaneously draining away. Little
flashes of light brightened the pine trees. Lightning. A slow,
growling thunder followed. Soon it would rain. *I have to
get back,* Sara thought. But she was tired, so tired.

She thought if she could close her eyes for a moment,
she'd feel better.

Then she might remember what she was doing here. . . .

A sound awakened her.

She'd fallen asleep with her head cradled awkwardly by
a tree root.

"Oh, God," she said aloud, jerking her head up. "Roger
will be furious."

Sitting up, she shivered. The temperature had dropped
and it was suddenly very chilly. Pulling her cloak around
her, she took a deep breath and gagged at the smell of raw
sewage. *A pipe must be broken,* she thought, *or something
is wrong with the bathroom. Bathroom!* The word rang a
distant bell in her mind.

The tavern door opened and a woman appeared with a
bucket. Squinting, Sara thought she looked familiar. She

wasn't the bartender. Instead, she wore her dark hair pulled atop her head like the saleslady in the jewelry booth where they'd bought the earrings. *What would she be doing here?* Sara thought hazily. She was about to speak when the woman emptied the contents of the bucket not far away. Then she went back inside.

Sara gagged. The foul smell hung in the air. Obviously, something was wrong with the plumbing, but this was ridiculous.

Staggering to her feet, Sara leaned against the tree. Then she recalled feeling dizzy in the tavern and taking the wrong door to the bathroom. How could she have fallen asleep? How long had she been there? And where was Roger? Why hadn't he come looking for her?

A glance at her watch told that only fifteen minutes had elapsed. Roger would still be waiting for her inside. But something was not quite right. Judging by the sun, it was early morning. How could that be? Had she been here all night? Impossible. Roger would have found her. Unless he'd gotten angry and left.

The bright, early morning sunlight made her squint. Obviously, her watch was wrong. Perhaps it needed a new battery.

She imagined Roger's reaction. He might not understand. *She* didn't understand. As much as she hated to admit it, she'd obviously gotten drunk and passed out. She had all the accompanying characteristics—headache, wooziness—there could be no other explanation.

Stalling, she picked up her purse and pulled out a compact. Her reddish-brown hair hung in frazzled clumps. Quickly, she brushed it and applied lipstick, then noticed that one amethyst earring was missing. Glancing around, she saw no sign of it. But that was the least of her worries now. She felt sure Roger had left by now. She would have to call him from the tavern.

Stepping gingerly around the liquid excrement, she rehearsed various things she might say. "I don't know what happened, Roger. I fell asleep. I just didn't feel good. Oh, shit, I guess I just got drunk and passed out, Roger. I'm sorry."

Arriving at the door, she noticed there weren't any steps. *Why aren't there any steps?* Did she dream she fell down concrete stairs? Another wave of nausea came over her and she decided to sort it all out later.

The door hung slightly askew. The handle was nothing but a rope threaded through a hole. Driven on by the horrendous smell, she jerked the door open and stepped inside.

Despite the fact that it was early morning, it took her eyes a few moments to adjust to the cave-like atmosphere of the tavern. Lit only by a few sputtering candles, the darkened room was empty except for two men who were apparently having breakfast. Roger wasn't there. He had left. Sara's spirits fell. How could he just leave without her?

The woman from the jewelry booth cleaned a table nearby. *Busy woman,* Sara thought. One of the men called her to him.

"Sophie," he said.

When she sidled over, he whispered something in Sophie's ear, then swatted her on the bottom. She whirled around, lashing him with her wet rag. "G'wan with ye," she said.

The two men thought that was terribly funny.

"Excuse me?" Sara threaded her way through crude tables and benches to the woman. Her feet crunched on what she thought might be crusts of bread and bones. Bones? She looked down at the floor and saw animal bones. *This place has gone a little overboard,* she thought. The health department would be shocked.

On closer inspection, Sophie looked different from the saleslady. Though her hair was dark and her eyes the same vivid blue, her clothes were now dingy and worn. Perhaps she'd had a bad day.

"Don't you remember me?" Sara asked.

"Nay and I've a good eye for faces."

"I bought some jewelry from you. Amethysts."

The woman eyed Sara speculatively. "If ye know the Black Boar, ye know I only sell food and ale, but none of what you may offer. I expect you'll want to ply your trade elsewhere."

"My trade?"

"Ye're a whore."

Sara's mouth dropped open. "Whore! You say you don't know me yet you openly accuse me of being a prostitute?"

"Well, look at ye're red skirt. It's clear enough what's on your mind."

Sara rolled her eyes. "I can't believe this. Surely you're joking."

"I'm not, and this is a decent establishment. Be sure of that." She spoke with a Cockney-British accent and, though she resembled the jewelry vendor, this woman was much more authentic. She could have stepped straight out of a Shakespearean play. Sara wondered where the festival director found all these unusual characters.

"I'm sure this is a decent establishment, but you could clean it up a bit."

"Clean. What'dye think I'm doing? Now you'd best be off. I'll have none of your sort here." She turned Sara firmly around and gave her a little shove toward the back door.

"Oh, no. I'm not going back out there again. You need a plumber."

"A what?"

"A plumber. Apparently a sewer line is broken."

"A plumber?" the woman repeated. She turned to the two men who had been smiling at Sara. "She's looking for a plumber."

"A plowman?" one of the men suggested.

"Mayhap a palmer," his companion amended.

Sara held up her hands. "No, actually, I'm looking for a

man named Roger. Roger Latham. He was here earlier. Did
you see him? He was sitting right here when I left. I want
to talk to the manager!"

The woman stepped closer to Sara. "Have you lost your
senses, girl? Ye're lookin' at the manager right here, Sophie
Winborn. And no one named Roger has been in today."

"But I know this was the place. Is there another tavern
nearby?"

Sophie's eyes narrowed. Clearly, she'd lost her patience.
"Are you from the country then that you don't know where
ye are?"

"I'm from Houston," Sara informed her "That's a pretty
big town."

Sophie studied Sara, reflectively.

"Roger must have driven back without me. If I could
find a telephone, I could call him in his car." Sara's words
rang through the empty tavern and sounded strange, even
to her.

Something was wrong. Terribly wrong. Three pairs of
eyes stared at her earnestly. Were they playing tricks on
her? Or had they worked at their jobs too long? Any minute
she expected them to break out in laughter.

But they didn't. Their expressions were solemn, unchang-
ing.

"You must be lost, dearie. Perhaps you'd like a draught
of ale," Sophie suggested. Despite her red skirt, she'd taken
pity on Sara. But the look in her eyes only made Sara more
nervous.

"Thank you, but I must get back to Houston this afternoon. I know there are buses that go back and forth . . ."
It was as if she were speaking a foreign language. Sara
looked from one person to another, desperately trying to
explain. It was no use. Their eyes followed the words, the
gestures of her hands, but they did not understand. Not a
word.

A tight knot formed in Sara's stomach. *Damn Roger for*

leaving her here alone. Anything could have happened to her. She could be dead, dying. Or worse.

"Well, I think I'll just go look for a bus or something." Sara's voice was shaky. They thought she was absolutely crazy and at that moment, she wasn't entirely sure they were wrong.

Shrugging, she crunched past them to the front door which was exactly like the one in back. Glancing over her shoulder, she saw that her audience stared at her as if she were some sort of apparition. She managed a feeble smile and pushed open the door.

"Oh my God!" she exclaimed, looking out into the street. Everything had changed.

Blinking, she looked again. Instead of the Renaissance Festival, she gazed out at an actual town. Few people were about. A woman in drab clothing walked by, carrying a water jug. A man drove a wagon, filled with sacks of grain. Several children played in the street. Again the putrid smell assailed her senses when someone from an upper story threw out another pail full of excrement.

This was not Texas.

She was not at the Renaissance Festival.

Sara was somewhere else.

Apparently, she had lost her mind completely. She'd hurt herself when falling and was now hallucinating.

"Perhaps you'd best come back in and rest. What is your name, dear?"

Sara turned away from the open door to find Sophie standing behind her. "Sara. Carlyle."

Sophie thought for a moment, then brightened. "Ah, Lord Carlyle. You must be his daughter. His name is well-known hereabouts. Pray, forgive me if I spoke amiss. I mistook your dress. Please sit for a while." She led Sara to a bench. Then, bustling back behind a crude wooden counter, she retrieved a pitcher of ale. She poured the liquid in a flagon and brought it to Sara. "Drink this. It'll take the chill off."

Sara thanked her and took a long drink. It was bitter, but satisfying in a way.

"She's of the gentry, no doubt," Sophie said over her shoulder to the men. "I could tell that right off."

The men nodded and Sara smiled weakly. Things were steadily getting worse. Finally, she knew she had to face her fears and ask some hard questions. "Sophie, what day is this?" Sara asked.

"Day?"

"Yes, you know, Monday, Tuesday, Wednesday. What day is it?"

"Let me see," Sophie counted on her fingers. "Saturday is Market Day, then the Sabbath. The next day would be wash day—Monday. That was three days ago so this would be Thursday." She smiled proudly.

All right, Sara thought. *It's Saturday in Houston and Thursday here.* Wherever *here* was. "What year is it?"

This was a hard question for Sophie. She just didn't know. She asked the two men and they conferred.

"It is the Year of Our Lord fifteen hundred and thirty," one man said.

"Must be more than that, Will. Cristina died in fifteen and thirty. It's writ in the church record. And it's been two autumns at least," his companion corrected.

Sophie took a consensus. "Year of Our Lord fifteen and thirty-two or three." She shrugged as if Sara might choose one or the other. Sara felt a terrible sinking sensation in the pit of her stomach. They weren't playing a game and they weren't acting. They were perfectly serious.

Could it be true? Could Sara have somehow gone back in time? No, it was impossible. She had temporarily lost her mind. That thought was even more disturbing. Either way, she was in deep trouble. Surely there was some explanation, some plausible reason for this whole thing.

Sara shook her head sadly. "I've got to get back," she murmured.

"Your man Roger will come for you," Sophie said.

"No, I don't think he can," Sara said.

"Then your father will send someone else for you."

"No, you see, I can't talk to my father."

"Oh," Sophie nodded, "you've had a dispute. Well, you're welcome to stay with me until you can arrange your return."

"Thank you," Sara said, weakly.

"You'd best hide her when the guard comes through," Will said.

Sophie sighed. "Those ruffians. They wreak havoc in the place every time they stop. I thank the saints they don't come often. But have no fear, you'll be safe here."

Safe? How could she feel safe when she didn't even know where she was? Tears welled in Sara's eyes and coursed down her cheeks.

Sophie planted her ample form next to Sara and put an arm around her. "Poor love, you can stay here as long as you like."

Sara shook her head. "But I don't even know where I am."

"The Black Boar Tavern."

"No, I mean what town?"

Sophie clucked soothingly. "Why, you're here in Todd Mission, down the road from the King's palace."

"What king, Sophie?" Sara asked tentatively, fearing the worst.

The question drew a hearty laugh from all three of them, but Sara couldn't even manage a smile at their chorused answer. "Henry, of course."

"I guess that would be Henry the VIII of England."

"England. To be sure."

Two

Sara waited expectantly for her world to right itself. It did not. With trembling hands and racing heart, she was forced to accept her situation, but she kept wondering why and how it had happened. Was it possible to go back in time or was she imagining the whole thing? If this was all in her mind, surely she would have created a better place, omitting the dirt and the lingering smell of sewage.

To maintain her sanity, she continued to believe that this was all a bad dream from which she would awaken. Three times she retraced her steps from the back door of the Black Boar Tavern to the tree. There she stood and prayed that the nightmare would end. Closing her eyes, she tried to project herself back into the future. If she had gone back, she should be able to go forward. But nothing happened.

Discouraged, she trudged back inside. More customers drifted into the inn, drawn by the smell of stew simmering over the fire. Sophie busily supplied them with ale and bread filled with the greasy liquid ladled from the caldron. Red-faced and panting, Sophie could not move fast enough.

"Can I help, Sophie?" Sara offered. It was the least she could do to repay the woman for her kindness.

Sophie pointed toward the counter. "The bread is ready to be put on plates and filled with stew," she said.

Sara obtained plates from the crude cupboard. As she poured the steaming mixture into hollowed out bread, hunger pains knotted her stomach. Dipping beneath the fat, she sampled the stew. It was delicious. Later she would have a bowl, but now she judiciously spooned it onto plates and delivered them to waiting tables.

The men stared at her. Several winked or made crude comments. Sara ignored them.

"It's your skirt," Sophie whispered as she hurried past. She handed Sara a worn apron that partly obscured Sara's red skirt. "It'll have to do for now," she said.

Farmers, townspeople, and travelers continued to crowd the tavern until shadows slanted through the narrow windows. Sara glanced at her watch which now registered three forty-five. If her watch was correct, only fifteen minutes had elapsed, whereas in Todd Mission, England, eight hours had already passed. Were they not besieged by more customers, she might have stopped then to consider that time was different here. She soon understood, however, that Sophie's life did not allow for a moment's reflection.

Though she was at least ten years older than Sara, Sophie worked with the energy of a much younger woman. Since she ran the tavern herself, she had no choice. With blue eyes and dark, curling hair, Sophie did resemble the saleslady at the Renaissance Festival. But Sara judged Sophie to be twenty years younger than the other woman. At this hectic pace, Sophie would soon catch up with her. Frown lines already creased the bridge of her nose and her constant grimace bespoke a hard life. In another time, Sophie would be a fading flower. Here, she would wither and die at a much younger age.

During a brief period when the tavern was empty, Sara cleaned tables while Sophie started more stew to simmer for the evening meal.

"We must be prepared. Tradesmen will return from Hampton Court at dusk," Sophie said.

"Hampton Court?"

Sophie frowned and shook her head. "The King's palace.

They say he's brought his new bride there. Queen Anne Boleyn."

Sara shuddered. "Poor thing."

The older woman arched a brow. "Poor thing, indeed. She has everything she could want."

"Not for long," Sara said.

Sophie gave her a puzzled look, but Sara knew she couldn't explain. For a brief moment, she wondered if it were possible to change history. Her thoughts were interrupted by the arrival of more customers and she was too busy to think of anything else.

The day flew by and Sara wondered how Sophie had managed alone.

"Me man died last year," Sophie explained, "and, since I can't afford wages, I've been hard put to make do. I'm obliged for your help."

"I owe you a debt for taking me in. Otherwise, I'd have nowhere to go," Sara smiled.

"I'm glad of the company," Sophie confessed. "I wouldn't mind if you stayed for a while."

Later, some travelers took an upstairs room for the night. Sophie was elated and, after the last dish had been washed, the caldron scoured, and the tables cleaned, she and Sara had a mug of ale.

For the first time, Sophie noticed Sara's watch. "What is that?"

Sara held it up for inspection. "A watch. It's supposed to tell the time and date."

Sophie's eyes narrowed. "Where did you get such a thing?"

Sara hesitated. "My father gave it to me." This was true, but she hesitated to elaborate.

"It looks magical to me. You're not a witch, are you?"

"Don't worry. It's not magic. I don't even think it works."

Taking a drink of ale, the older woman leaned toward Sara. "Tell me about this Roger again."

"Well, he's good-looking. Light hair, blue eyes."

Sophie winked. "So, there's the problem. You have your cap set for him."

"Yes, I'm going to marry him."

"Against your father's wishes, I expect." The older woman blew a dark curl from her forehead.

Sara spread her hands on the table. Upon Roger's orders, she had put her diamond engagement ring in her purse. "You'll be a walking target for thieves," he'd told her. She now studied her ring finger. "Actually, my father doesn't know that I'm engaged to Roger."

"I thought as much. A young girl such as you shouldn't go against your father's wishes."

Frowning, Sara recalled the time when she tried to tell her father of her engagement to Roger. She'd shown Ben Carlyle the ring and said she was going to be married. He had flown into a rage, one of the worst they'd seen. Later, when Roger arrived, her father was still obsessed and screamed at them. It was then that Roger had suggested they put him in a rest home. She had protested and since then, nothing more had been said.

Sara shrugged and shook her head. "I tried to tell my father, but he doesn't understand anything these days."

"Well, I know. I ran off from my own father when I was but thirteen. It was that or be thrashed to death," Sophie confided.

"He beat you?" Sara was a little shocked, but realized in this age morals were much different.

"Aye, he had a foul temper on him."

"Where did you meet your husband?"

"Right here. I worked as a serving wench. He was a much older man, but willing to marry me." She sighed and shook her head. "It wasn't much better, for he beat me too. But when he died, he left me this tavern. I mean to turn a profit from it and I will, too."

"I'll help you until I find Roger," Sara promised.

Impulsively, Sophie threw her arms around Sara. "You're a Godsend, you are. But my advice would be to forget this Roger and send to your father. No doubt, he'll be worried."

No doubt everyone in her family would be worried, Sara thought grimly. But there was nothing she could do.

That night, she slept on Sophie's bed, a wooden box with an uncomfortable straw mattress. Straw poked through the coverlet and rats skittered along the floor. But Sara was too tired to care. She understood how people could develop total indifference to their surroundings when their wits were dulled by exhaustion. She wondered if that would happen to her, but fell asleep before she could think of an answer.

The next day sped by quickly, filled with back-breaking work—scrubbing, cleaning, and serving food. Forced to make the best of her new life, she worked alongside Sophie. She endured the smells and trips to the outdoor privy only by dousing herself with a vial of cologne she carried in her purse. Finally, she strapped the purse around her waist so that she could reapply the scent when it began to fade.

At the day's end, Sara glanced at her watch and noticed that only forty-five minutes had elapsed since she left Roger at the Renaissance Festival. Of course, her watch was wrong. Or had time lost all meaning here?

Sara knew Market Day had arrived when there was a sudden influx of tradesmen and customers. Since no one had a calendar or a clock, there was no other way to tell. Cut off from the world as she was, she could only *feel* the difference in days. It was as if she'd lost her other senses.

People in Todd Mission operated instinctually. Sara imagined that if a dust storm or an eclipse suddenly blotted out the sun, they might get up on a different day and come into town with their wares. Market Day would thus be renamed or changed because no one would notice. But it wouldn't really matter.

The atmosphere of this day, however, was decidedly different. Townsmen were jovial and expectant as if something exciting were about to happen. Their enthusiasm was infectious and Sara felt her own spirits rise.

Mid-afternoon, Sophie touched Sara on the shoulder. "Why not go visit the stalls for a time? Fresh air will do you good," she suggested. "The market brings many people to town. Who knows, someone might have seen Roger."

Suddenly, it occurred to Sara that Roger may be searching for her. He, too, could have fallen through what she'd come to regard as the "black hole" of the Renaissance Festival. If so, he might be wandering around as lost as she was.

"Yes, perhaps I'll find Roger." Filled with new hope, Sara turned to leave.

"Here's three pence for ribbons." Sophie caught her arm and pressed coins into her palm. "The rest is for you to buy what takes your fancy."

Sara thought of the twenty-dollar bill she had in her purse, but doubted that people here would know what to make of it. "Thank you," she said, hurrying out the door.

The late afternoon sun filtered through gathering clouds as Sara made her way to the market stalls at the center of town. Makeshift cloth awnings protected the goods while vendors, like carnival peddlers, hawked their goods to passersby. Several women raised their eyebrows at Sara's red skirt. She paid no attention. By now, she had adopted a dismissive attitude and adjusted her apron to cover the skirt.

A rabbit's warren of stalls were closely packed with one practically on top of another. A man sold piglets next to a woman offering fine piece goods. An apothecary and a miller were side by side, one measuring herbs, the other grinding barley or some other grain. The smell of meat en brochette and fried grain patties mingled and hung in the air. Except for the claustrophobic closeness of unwashed bodies, it was not unpleasant. In fact, there was a certain festive air about the patrons who milled about, stopping to look at one booth or another, much like the Renaissance Festival.

Thinking of home, Sara sighed deeply. Trying to forget her problems, she browsed through multicolored ribbons hung across a string. Next to the ribbons, a collection of trinkets—thimbles, earrings, and brooches—caught her eye. Perhaps she would buy Sophie a present, she thought.

"I would have a word with you, fair maid." A deep, commanding voice drew her attention.

She turned to find a tall, swarthy-looking man standing behind her. From the look of his costume, boots, and sword belted over his padded doublet, he was a soldier. Sweeping off his plumed hat, he bowed gallantly.

"Yes?" she said.

"If you are not already occupied, I'd like to secure your services for the afternoon," he said. His breath smelled foul and his smile revealed a crooked row of yellow teeth.

"Services?"

He looked exasperated. "I have but a limited amount of time, so I would have my sport without your good humor, miss. I think you'll find I pay very well."

"Pay? For what?"

"I pray you, don't make me beg for it. I'm not in a good humor."

"I think you have mistaken me for someone else." Sara started to turn away, but the man grabbed her by the arm.

Pulling her along with him, he strode through the marketplace.

"Let go of me!" she shouted, trying to wrench her arm free.

"Feisty wench." His mouth curved into a cruel grimace. "I like a spirited girl."

It was the damned skirt, Sara thought with rising panic. "Stop! Or I'll scream," she warned.

He shook his head as if he didn't believe her, then, dragging her with him, he ducked into a nearby tent. A family of gypsies was selling rugs and crudely woven tapestries. Accosting the patriarch, the soldier held a hurried conference and tossed him a money pouch. Immediately, the gypsies disappeared, leaving them alone.

Sara was petrified. He wasn't much taller than she, but the man's arms were made of steel.

Throwing Sara down on a rug, he began divesting himself of his clothes.

"Don't do that. Please, stop!"

He frowned. "What? Good woman, I'm providing you with your livelihood."

"I'm not a whore. I bought this skirt by mistake." She tried to wiggle away, but he caught her and threw her back against the ground so hard, she couldn't breathe for a moment.

"Raise your skirts, wench." He gave the order like a military command. He was nude from the waist down and his erect penis jutted forth from a mound of dark curls as if in salute.

At that moment, Sara kicked him in the groin. "Go to hell!" she hissed as he doubled over in pain.

Rolling over quickly, she sprang to her feet and raced out the door. The gypsies, standing outside, smiled and waved at her as she passed.

Sara ran past the booth with trinkets where she had hoped to buy a gift for Sophie. She ran past the ribbon seller, past the apothecary and did not stop to take a breath until she had left the market far behind her. Her breath came in ragged gasps now. Still, she hurried along the street to the tavern. Now and then, she stopped to look around and prayed she was not being followed. Finally, she rushed inside the Black Boar. There, she collapsed crying in Sophie's arms.

"There, there, what's the matter?" Sophie clucked like a mother hen.

"A man. A soldier tried to rape me," Sara choked out.

"Rape?" Sophie shook her head, bewildered.

"He tried to make love to me without . . . without my consent."

"Ah, well, it's the red skirt, then. If only I had another, I would give it to you."

Sara sobbed, tears running down her cheeks. "He was awful. Smelly and so ugly."

"Ay, many of them are," Sophie nodded, sympathetically.

Depositing her charge on a stool, Sophie gave her a mug of ale while Sara confided the details of her escapade. They had only a short time to talk before more customers arrived. But Sophie promised to get some dye from a weaver on the following day.

"A black skirt will put an end to your troubles," she nodded.

Evening approached and Sara calmed. Then, just as she finished serving a group of men, the same soldier walked in, followed by an entire platoon.

Sara's heart leaped to her throat and she tried to dart out of the room. Unfortunately, he spotted her at once and charged over.

Sophie stood nearby. "That's the man," Sara whispered. "What can I do?"

"God's Bones, it's the Captain of the King's guards!" Sophie exclaimed.

"Is this your girl?" the captain demanded of Sophie.

"Well, I . . . yes, she's working for me." Sophie's voice was a hoarse croak.

"She insulted me today!" he bellowed.

"Oh, beg pardon, sir. I'm sure she meant no harm. She's from the country—"

"If she were a man, I would run him through. But since she is a woman, I'll be lenient."

Sophie's hand flew to her mouth. White-faced and trembling, she was so terrified she could hardly speak. "Please allow me to make amends."

"She is under arrest. No one insults the Captain of the King's guards."

"That's ridiculous!" Sara spat out. "You can't arrest a person for insulting you. It's against the law."

A feral smile cut through his dark face. "Woman, I am the law hereabouts, and you will respect that."

"If you're the law, you're a poor excuse for it," she said, then turning quickly, she darted through the crowded room. The soldiers came after her, but she thought if she could get away, she might find a place to hide. Slipping out the back door, she ran straight into the arms of two soldiers waiting behind the tavern. "You will come with us," they said.

This is it, she thought. *Now, he will kill me.* How strange it would be to die in another world where no one would mourn her and no one would think to bury her. Here, a whore would be thrown into a common grave, but not before she was tortured first.

The soldiers took her roughly by the arms and dragged her to the front of the tavern. Sophie stood in the doorway, wringing her hands, unable to help. "Please sir, have mercy!" she cried.

The soldiers ignored her.

Sara was forced onto a waiting horse and her hands tied behind her back. Sophie stood watching, helplessly, but the two women exchanged an unspoken message of love before the soldiers took Sara away. She thought if she lived through this, she would come back and repay Sophie for her kindness. But now, surrounded by twenty men, Sara's prospects looked dim indeed.

Leonardo Brazzi was having a bad day. He had designed an exquisite mural for the King's great hall, entitled *Morality*. It was an allegorical representation of the Pope being stoned by Satan and his henchmen while a hierarchy of angels looked on in helpless abandon. The subject had caught Henry's attention especially now, since his recent break with Rome. He'd defiantly taken a new bride after the Pope had denied him an annulment to Catherine of Aragon.

Leonardo had no real sympathy for the nobility, and thought it monstrously unfair that wealth should have been dispensed to such a foolish group. They had no occupation other than playing tiresome political games. Leonardo, however, was in the fortunate position of being able to move quickly over to the winning side. If tomorrow the Pope commissioned him to do a mural of Henry being stoned by Satan, he'd gladly comply. Providing the price was right. As far as he was concerned, both men were pompous asses and, at the moment, he was furious at Henry.

Anxious to finish the great hall, the King had his men working round the clock and there was chaos all around. Leonardo was used to painting in quiet refectories or in his own workshop in Florence. Never had his thoughts been so continually interrupted. There was so much banging, hammering, and even singing that he could not think. He complained. Henry, having nothing yet to show for his advance, gave him a thorough tongue-lashing, forcing the artist to angrily retreat to his chamber. Now, however, he had completed the mathematical calculations he needed. He knew exactly the position of each figure and had begun to sketch, but the noise drove him outside for a few minutes' peace.

Walking along the canal, Leonardo had to admit that Hampton Court was a beautiful palace. Henry had done well to take the place away from Cardinal Wolsey. Now with the new queen in residence, it promised to become a showplace. Though Leonardo was not too fond of the English, he had to admit they had a certain style.

Picking up a stone, he skipped it over the dark greenish water and watched it drop to the bottom. He had been in England for two years, originally commissioned by the Archbishop to paint a mural at Canterbury. There he had met the King who, impressed with the project, immediately secured his services when he learned that Leonardo spoke English perfectly. He could have his Italian artist and communicate with him, too. At times, his knowledge of English had proved to be detrimental to Leonardo's creativity. Henry liked to be on top of everything, kept abreast of progress. This had a smothering effect on the artist, because much of Leonardo's time was spent thinking. Kings did not think. At least, not often.

"I see nothing on the wall but white gesso," the King had complained.

"There is nothing to see yet, Your Majesty," Leonardo retorted.

"Why not?"

"Because I am now calculating where I should place each of the seventeen figures."

"And how long will that take?" Henry asked. "I want the mural to be finished when the great hall is completed."

Exasperated, Leonardo tried to reign his explosive temper. He had to constantly remind himself that Henry was a king, not a huge pig with small blue eyes. "I cannot say exactly when I shall finish my calculations. But when they are completed, I can begin sketching in the figures. I assure you, Sire, that it will be splendid."

Leonardo wasn't sure he had convinced the King, but he had bought himself a little reprieve. He had to have time to think. Each time he began a new project, he was overwhelmed by fear. The vast, empty space beckoned, but could he fill it with something meaningful? Again? This commission at Hampton Court might crystallize his reputation if it were done well. His stomach knotted with anxiety. Could he draw from the well again to bring forth something truly magnificent? His aesthetic sense would not allow him to leave anything less than perfect. For, while Henry might not be a true connoisseur, others would see the mural in the great hall and someone would remark on its quality. It was the responsibility of artists to think of the future and the legacy left behind.

He took in a deep breath, then shivered. He longed for Florence and hoped one day to return in glory. However, at present, he vacillated. He would just as soon leave the project as it was.

Retracing his steps, he crossed over the moat and prepared to enter his chamber. But he halted when the King's guard arrived. There was a scream followed by a great deal of commotion among the soldiers. The gate guards hurried over. Disgusted, Leonardo shook his head. Soldiers were barbaric. All they did was eat and drink excessively then mount women or horses, whichever was at hand.

Turning, Leonardo saw that the Commandant had a woman and was dragging her to the guard house. This did not surprise him, for it happened regularly. He did wonder why the Captain of the Guard would make a show of such abominable behavior.

Suddenly, the woman put up a spectacular fight, kicking and throwing punches. Leonardo could not believe his eyes, nor could he tear his gaze away from her. Even from a distance, he could tell she was stunningly beautiful, not at all the common wench he would have expected to see. Reddish-brown hair flowed over her shoulders in glossy waves and the high color on her fair skin was dazzling. Just then, she launched a punch at the captain and kicked his lieutenant in the groin.

Leonardo had to suppress a laugh when the lieutenant fell upon the captain and the captain on his sergeant. They all collapsed down like a row of pins. With the speed of a cat, the girl wriggled through their grasp and ran across the bridge, directly toward him.

"Help me! Help me, please!" she cried out.

Eyes the color of sherry wine implored him, and he was momentarily stunned by her beauty. At that moment, he would have moved heaven and earth to save her. But the guard was right behind her. Before he could make a move, they dragged her away, kicking and screaming.

He knew what they would do to her. The Commandant would have his fill of her, then he would pass her around to his comrades until they too had tired of her. Then they would cast her out, probably in the dead of winter and she would surely perish.

Compelled by her eyes, he followed the soldiers. Too absorbed by their task, the soldiers did not notice him. The Commandant flung her into his quarters and with a wink at his officers, went in after her.

There was little time and Leonardo knew he would have to work fast. Casting about for some means of distraction, he saw a wagon loaded high with straw, hitched to an ass. He darted into the forge nearby and for the price of a coin, he secured a few embers for his brazier. Carrying the iron scuttle, he walked by the wagon and as he passed, he flipped an ember into the hay. With his kerchief, he placed another beneath the animal's harness, then he slipped out of sight and waited.

In only a few minutes, fire erupted in the straw and, braying loudly, the ass bolted. The poor animal tore around in a frenzied circle until the cart overturned near the Commandant's quarters.

Half-dressed, the Commandant threw open his door and charged outside, sword in hand. The door stood open and Leonardo ducked in quickly.

The girl cowered in the corner, her blouse ripped open to her waist. His gaze rested on the creamy swell of her breasts and he momentarily forgot his purpose. When she glared at him, defiantly, he whipped off his hooded cloak and tossed it to her.

"Cover yourself and come with me."

For a moment she didn't move, and he wondered if she were wounded. But shock had slowed her reflexes. She gained a shaky stance and simply stared at him.

"Hurry, we must leave before he returns," Leonardo urged.

Suddenly galvanized into action, she snatched his cloak and threw it around her. Outside, the fire had spread to the officers' quarters and they had set up a bucket brigade. As she bolted toward the door, he caught her arm. "The stable. I will follow you there."

In a flash she was gone.

Leonardo hurried out behind her. A split second later, the Commandant accosted him.

"You there. Did you see a wench run by just now?" he shouted.

Leonardo thought for a moment. "Yes. She went that way." He pointed in the opposite direction. "She can't have gone far."

The Commandant charged after her while Leonardo hurried toward the stables. *Would she be there? Had someone else accosted her on the way?* he wondered.

Minutes later, he entered the stable. The stablers were outside, drawn by the fire. Frightened by the commotion and the smell of smoke, horses turned nervously in their stalls. Leonardo clucked soothingly to them as he made his way through the building. His eyes adjusted to the dim light, but he could not find her. Discouraged, he realized they'd caught her.

Turning he retraced his steps. Then a small shaft of light drew his attention to a far corner. The hood had fallen from her head and a wealth of burnished copper framed the pale oval of her face. Scarcely daring to breathe, he moved closer, half afraid she might suddenly disappear. Was this the same woman he had seen moments ago fighting with the Commandant? He had thought her a hellion, a beautiful wildcat fighting for her freedom.

He was wrong.

Here, haloed beneath a luminescent arc was an utterly perfect angel.

Three

"Hold it right there, cowboy. Don't come a step closer."

He didn't understand the words, but her meaning was clear. "It's all right," he said, holding up his hands. "I want to help you."

"Why?"

Her question caught him off guard and he had to think for a moment. He really didn't know why he felt so compelled to help her. "I don't know, but I dislike the Commandant. He is a barbarian."

She stood and brushed the hay from her and pulled the cloak around her. "As far as I'm concerned, everyone here is a barbarian." She shook her head and light glowed in her amber eyes. "You hear so much about the Renaissance Man. He's supposed to be some sort of ideal. God, I've even told my students that. But you know, I'm beginning to believe that written history is totally bullshit. If I ever get out of this cesspool from hell, I'm going to write a book!"

Leonardo thought he understood the language, but he had never heard the King's English spoken in this way with such feeling. Color flooded her cheeks, wedging angles of soft pink into the glossy pearl skin. Magnificent. If only she would hold that pose.

"So lovely," he murmured aloud.

Loud shouting outside drew his attention back to their dilemma. "We should go," he urged her. "They mustn't find us here."

He took her hand, but she pulled away from him. "Not so fast. Help me put a saddle on one of these horses and I'll be on my way."

He looked at her aghast. "Steal a horse?"

"Don't worry, I know how to ride," she assured him.

"That will do you no good. You'll be dead within the hour if you steal a soldier's horse."

"Then where can I hide?"

"I will take you to my chamber. Then we will decide what to do."

Grasping her arm, he pulled her to the stable door. "Wait, how do I know I can trust you?"

He shook his head. "You talk too much. Come."

The fire was out, Leonardo noted. Occupied with getting the remains of the cart out of the way, the soldiers did not see Leonardo and Sara slip by. Keeping to the shadows, they meandered along the side of the guardhouse to the moat in front of the castle. Sara drew the cloak tightly around her, and they passed the gate guard with only a nod.

Once they had cleared the bridge, Leonardo breathed a sigh of relief. Inside the courtyard, they turned right and hurried to his apartment beneath the stair.

Turning the key in the lock behind him, he collapsed onto a stool. He gestured to the bed. "Make yourself comfortable."

"Comfortable? Here?"

Suddenly irritated, he rose. He'd just risked his life for this woman and she acted as if his chamber was a pigsty. "What did you expect, Madam? The queen's apartments?"

Sighing, she sank down on his bed. "I doubt they would be much better. I just want to go home."

She was quite outspoken for a woman, and her accent was strange. "Are you very far from home?"

"Apparently."

He brought his stool over and sat facing her. "What is your name?"

"Sara. Sara Carlyle."

It was a beautiful name and seemed to suit her exactly. "What were you doing with the Commandant? He's a very distasteful man."

"I was trying to get away from him. He thought I was a . . ."

"Whore?" Leonardo supplied.

"God, I hate that word." She shuddered, filled with righteous indignation.

He gazed deep into clear amber eyes beneath arching brows. Though her features were fine and elegant like those of a noblewoman, she was dressed like a common harlot. She saw him staring at her skirt and gave an exasperated sigh.

"Look, I bought this skirt because red is my favorite color. At least, it used to be. Now I think if I ever get out of this mess, I'll never feel the same about it."

She stared vacantly with a forlorn expression that was exquisitely beautiful. Leonardo quickly retrieved paper and pencil, then returned to his stool. Long fingers worked the stub of his pencil in a circular motion across the paper. She turned to regard him solemnly.

"I don't believe this," she said. "You're an artist."

"Yes."

She nodded, tightening full lips into a straight line. If he could only capture the wealth of changing expressions he saw in her face, he thought. He worked quickly, but now a dimple formed in her cheek, then her mouth curved upward in a wry smile.

"I suppose you're going to tell me your name is Leonardo."

"It is," he smiled. "But how did you know?"

"A wild guess," she said. Closing her eyes, she shook her head. "The nightmare keeps getting worse. What else can happen?"

Suddenly her eyes dissolved into liquid sherry, brimming

with tears. Completely entranced, Leonardo was pulled into a vortex of feeling he'd never experienced before. With some effort, he concentrated his effort on finishing the sketch. He gave it to her.

"Very good. Actually, it's really good," she said, studying it. "Is this what you do? Portraits?"

Her question brought him into the present moment. "No, I'm painting a mural for the king. In fact, I should be in the Great Hall now," he told her.

Hurriedly, he gathered supplies into a satchel while she sat, watching him. At the door he turned.

"You will be safe here. Do not leave." When she didn't answer, he hesitated for a moment, then closed the door behind him.

Looking around the dingy apartment, Sara thought she'd exchanged one bad situation for another. This artist was certainly much nicer than the Commandant. Handsome in fact. However, she did not relish being at anyone's mercy. Though she was grateful for his intervention, she had absolutely no intention of staying here until he decided to come back. She had to return to Todd Mission. Immediately.

Tiptoeing out of the chamber, Sara found herself in a darkened corridor. Since the main gate was perilously close to the guard house, she had to find another exit. Drawing the cloak around her, she darted out into the wide courtyard, trying to look as inconspicuous as possible. She was halfway across when she saw a guard approaching. Quickly, she ducked through a gate leading to another hallway. The place was a maze, she thought.

She passed servants and two noblemen deep in conversation. No one noticed her. Then as she rounded another corner, an imperious female voice accosted her.

"You there!"

Sara froze, hardly daring to look up. When she finally did hazard a glance, she saw an elegantly dressed woman at the top of the stair. "What is your name?"

"Sara." Her voice was a hoarse croak.

"All right. This girl is in need of assistance straightway."

A serving girl staggered down the stair laden with two heavy trays. Sara sprang to help her.

"There we are," the noblewoman said, then turning she disappeared into an upstairs apartment.

"I am obliged," the girl said, breathing a relieved sigh. "I feared I would fall and break my neck."

"Isn't there anyone else to help you?" Sara inquired.

"To be sure. There are usually three of us, but she has the other two running this way and that."

"The queen?"

The girl's blue eyes widened, "Are you new here?"

"Yes, I just arrived."

"Oh, then. That's the queen's lady-in-waiting, Lady Jane."

Sara nodded. The next Mrs. Tudor. Lady Jane Seymour certainly had a way about her.

She hurried along with her tray, trying to keep up with the nimble girl. If she had to do this every day, she would be in great shape, she thought.

"Where are we going?"

"The kitchen, of course."

Sara gasped at the size of the kitchen. It was at least fifty feet long with three gigantic fireplaces. In one hearth a loin of beef roasted. Next to it, ten fowls rotated on a revolving spit. In the third were giant black cauldrons hung over the fire on hooks. Savory smells permeated the room and a warm, comforting feeling surrounded her like a womb.

"Oh, it smells wonderful." Suddenly Sara realized she hadn't eaten since early morning.

"There's not but bread for us," the serving girl said with a shrug.

At the end of the kitchen, the wall was gone. Workmen were plastering over a framework of timber further down a darkened corridor. They set their trays on a table and the girl jerked a thumb toward the new addition.

"Cardinal Wolsey's kitchen was not near large enough for King Henry. He wants more space and a serving place. I told me mum we could put our whole village in this new one," she laughed.

Before leaving, the girl pointed out an exit. Sara picked her way through the debris in the new serving place and out a doorway. Walking down a narrow passageway, she passed by a game court. It resembled a tennis court. Astonished, she paused when two men in bulbous Renaissance-style tunics entered the court. With strange-looking rackets, they danced comically around the court batting at a black ball. Sara couldn't suppress a giggle. Limp-wristed and ungainly, they looked as if they were trying to net a butterfly.

A ball whizzed off the court and rolled onto the ground in front of Sara. Without thinking, she reached to pick it up. It was much heavier than a modern tennis ball. No wonder they had so much trouble, she thought.

"What are you about, wench?"

Startled, Sara dropped the tennis ball. A guard stood so close she could smell his fetid breath. "I . . . I . . ."

"You were thinking to steal the ball, eh?"

"No. What would I want with that ball? It's way too heavy anyway."

The guard observed her with a strange look on his face. "You'd best come with me. We'll see what the Captain of the Guard has to say."

In the Great Hall of Hampton Court, the workmen were having their midday meal. The smell of sawdust and plaster permeated the room, but at least it was quiet for a change.

At one end of the hall, Leonardo ran his finger over two large wooden panels, testing each one to see if the gesso had dried. One felt slightly damp. The other was ready to paint. Taking his preliminary drawings from his satchel, he studied them a moment. Then using a combination of punching holes through the paper and sketching, he produced a faint charcoal outline on one of the gessoed panels.

While he worked, his thoughts turned to the woman in his chamber. *What would he do with her,* he wondered. He couldn't keep her for long. Just long enough to give her something to eat and send her on her way. Of course, he felt sorry for her. Obviously, she was lost. What he didn't like was her imperious attitude. She was certainly in no position to put on airs or give commands. When he returned to his chamber he would set her straight on a few things.

Two laborers appeared with their dinner and a pail of beer. Sitting on a bench nearby, Leonardo overheard their conversation.

"They say a witch is loose in the castle," one man said to the other.

Leonardo felt the little hairs at the back of his neck bristle.

"A witch!" the other man exclaimed. "Things are bad enough as it is. How came she here?"

"The Commandant."

"Aye me. He dips his wick in too many different wells. One day he'll lose it," his comrade said.

"That's so. And it would be well deserved."

"But what of the witch? How does she look?"

"She's fair, skin like milk, and hair of copper."

Leonardo's head jerked up at this. Could she really be a witch? No doubt, she'd bewitched the Commandant. He felt that he himself might have fallen under her spell.

"And they can't find her you say?"

"No, but 'tis clear she has her magic working already. A cow died last evening. And three ravens were on the lawn this morn. All in a row."

"God's Bones, we'll be none of us safe in our beds until they catch her."

"Aye, it's true enough."

Leonardo couldn't concentrate. The lines he now drew were crooked, uneven, and looked nothing like his sketches. Then he realized his hand was shaking. He might be harboring a witch. Hastily, he replaced his utensils and sketches in his satchel, all the while telling himself to be calm. Though he'd never actually seen a witch, he was convinced they did exist. There were many forces at odds in the world and a man couldn't be too careful. He walked by the workmen, who were too absorbed in their conversation to notice him.

As he hurried back to his chamber, he considered his options. He could throw her out. Then she would surely be tortured or killed. If he kept her, he ran a terrible risk of being caught himself.

It was a terrible dilemma, but he had his livelihood to consider. He couldn't very well throw all care to the wind. Witch or no, she was liable to wreak havoc in his life.

As he approached his chamber door, he considered what he would say. He would be polite. He would offer assistance where possible, but she had to go. Taking a deep breath, he walked in. Then looking around the room, his breath left him entirely. She was gone, vanished. Dematerialized into thin air.

Sara shivered as the guard urged her down a chilly hallway. Leonardo was right. She should have stayed in his chamber. Now she couldn't imagine what the Commandant would do when he saw her again.

"I have no quarrel with the Commandant," she pleaded. "I've only just come to the palace to work as scullery maid."

"Oh? Well you were far from your duties where I found you," the guard countered.

"I was only taking a bit of air."

"Indeed. Well, we'll see about that."

It was no use. The man was bent on doing his duty. They passed by the kitchen, but now the smell of the roasted meat only made her nauseous.

"Who did ye work for in the kitchen?" the guard asked suddenly.

"I forgot her name," Sara hurriedly answered. "She's a large woman."

His expression of disbelief unnerved her, then his grip tightened on her arm. Sara felt the last reserves of her energy drain away. Branded as a whore, she was soon to be tortured, then probably killed. Was this some kind of cruel karmic joke? Had she traveled through time only to end her life here? It seemed a cosmic exercise in futility. She would have much rather been hit by a car.

The guard hurried her along, squeezing her arm in a painful grip. Tears welled in her eyes. How she wished she could see her father one last time.

After he'd gotten over the shock of her disappearance, Leonardo congratulated himself. Good riddance, he said. He washed his hands in the basin, then carefully replaced his paints and brushes on the easel nearby. With a relieved sigh, he realized that he had nothing to worry about except completing Henry's mural.

He busied himself about his chamber for some time, then decided to get something to eat. He whistled a cheerful tune, but in the back of his mind was the woman's face—the sherry-colored eyes, the white, white skin. Try as he might, he could not stop thinking about her. He only wished he had been able to paint her portrait. At least once.

On his way to the kitchen, he looked for her in the shadows, stopping to peer in every dark corner. He told himself he must make sure no one had abducted her in his absence. He felt a certain human responsibility for her, and that was why he carefully scrutinized each person who passed. But she was not about. There was not a trace of her. No doubt, she had simply disappeared.

According to the Ordinances of the King's household, everyone was entitled to a quantity of wine or beer daily. As the resident artist, he also received bread and cheese. Occasionally, there was extra meat or stew if he desired. Having no desire to be as corpulent as the King, Leonardo ate sparingly. Sometimes, he even forgot.

Arriving late for the noon meal, he received only a portion of beer and some bread. The cook gave him a scowl of disapproval. But bowing low, he kissed her hand and thanked her. She tittered behind her reddened hand.

For some reason he took an alternate path back to his chamber, doubling around through another passageway. Then crossing through the courtyard, he heard someone behind him and turned. His heart stopped. There she was! The hood of her cloak fell back and auburn hair spilled into her eyes as the guard dragged her to the front gates.

Torn by differing emotions, he stopped. He knew he should forget her, continue on, have done with it. But he could not. Some irresistible force propelled him forward.

He ducked his head down, and he appeared to be lost in thought, unaware of anyone else. All of a sudden, he careened into the guard, splattering his entire ration of beer in the man's face. Quick as a flash Sara darted away while Leonardo effused apologies. By the time he had wiped the man's face with his kerchief, they were alone in the courtyard.

"What in blazes!" the guard sputtered. "What became of that wench?"

"Wench? What wench? Look here, I am sorry. I've soiled your clothing."

The guard elbowed Leonardo away. "Take care, man," he cautioned. "There's a witch loose in the castle." The guard looked around blearily, then charged off in the opposite direction.

Leonardo spent a few minutes gathering up the remains of his meal, then hurried to his chamber. Cautiously, he opened the door.

This time she was there.

She sat curled on the end of his bed, panting breathlessly like some small forest animal who'd just escaped a hunter. Her cheeks were bright red and her eyes were awash with tears. Again, he was so awed by her that it took him some time to find his voice.

"Are you all right?" he asked.

"Yes, thank you," she said, softly. "I'm indebted to you, and I don't know how to repay you."

Her voice had lost the hard edge he'd heard before. It was softer now, almost musical. The words, humbly spoken, were feather-light as if blown to him on the wind. He fairly floated over to the bed. Sitting on the opposite end of the cot, he regarded her solemnly.

"You do not have to repay me," he said. "But you are in great danger here."

"I can see that. Everyone in this castle is insane," she informed him.

He frowned.

"I mean, except for you," she quickly amended.

He acknowledged her exemption with a brief smile. "You must promise to remain here until I decide what is to be done."

"I will," she promised. "I am sorry to have caused you so much trouble."

Her lips trembled, and he could see she was terribly frightened. Suddenly, he was frightened, too. Now that he'd rescued her again, he had no idea how to keep her safe. The guards were all alerted. If they were caught, they would both be killed.

Her eyes beseeched him, drawing him into twin pools of liquid amber. Hair the color of summer smoke laced with strands of copper and gold caught the late afternoon light.

She must be a witch, he thought. No normal woman could look this way. Instantly, he knew the Commandant's reason for abducting her and his fury at losing her. Any man would feel the same.

With an unconscious movement, she pushed the cloak back and her blouse gaped open, revealing the creamy whiteness of her breasts. The quick rise and fall of her breathing drew his attention. Even if he had wanted to, he could not tear his gaze away.

"I am not a whore," she whispered.

If not a whore what then? A witch?

He moved closer, pulled unresisting into her web. He knew he risked great peril coming this close to a witch. Once she had him, what would she do? What did witches do once they had cast their spell? Men had lost their wits around ordinary women, but a witch like this could drive a man completely mad. Eyes like hers could easily torture him until he perished in agony. Transfixed by her beauty, he stared at her in wonder.

It might just be worth it to die in her arms.

Four

Sara studied the man who sat opposite her. Long, coppery hair almost touched broad shoulders and the stubble of a light beard sprinkled his cheeks. When he moved closer, she was struck by his clear green eyes. They were the color of a stream she'd seen once in west Texas—deep and unfathomable. He'd said his name was Leonardo. He was not Da Vinci. Da Vinci had never looked this good. Besides, this man was much too young and the great master had never traveled to England. Even so, she was curious about his name.

"Have you ever heard of Leonardo da Vinci?"

He smiled. "He was my teacher when I was very young. He is much revered in Florence. I was called after him."

"You studied with da Vinci?"

He nodded.

"He was one of the greatest minds of all time."

He frowned, puzzled. "You know of him?"

"Everyone in the world knows about him."

Leonardo pursed his lips and gazed at her, thoughtfully. "How?"

Sara shrugged. "Oh, I don't know. Books, movies, computers." All this tumbled out before she could catch herself. Immediately, she saw he did not understand a single thing she'd said. She shook her head. "Never mind."

He narrowed his gaze. With one swift movement, he picked up her hand and studied her palm, turning it over, touching her fingers. With the tip of his thumb, he rubbed her pale fingernail polish.

The warm touch of his hand created a peculiar sensation in the pit of Sara's stomach. There was so much energy there, just in his fingers. He ran his hand down the soft skin of her arm, then touched her cheek. The spot burned as if he'd left a mark there.

"You're not a peasant. Your hands bespeak a life of ease, yet you dress as a whore. Who are you and where do you come from?"

"I've already told you, I am not a whore." Sighing, Sara realized that sooner or later she would have to confide in someone. Her instincts told her that this man might comprehend her dilemma. In any case, things couldn't get much worse. Taking a deep breath, she began. "I am from another time," she said.

"Another time? I don't understand your words."

"I'm not quite sure I can explain what happened. I was attending the Renaissance Festival in a place called Houston, Texas. Somehow, I fell through a porthole and I actually seem to be living in another time, you see. In your time."

"In my time?" he repeated.

"Yes. We refer to this age as the Renaissance."

He shook his head, not comprehending.

She tried to think of the Latin, but was too agitated. "You are living in the Year of Our Lord Fifteen Hundred and Thirty-three. In other words, 1533."

He seemed perplexed. "I am living in 1533 and you are not living?"

Exasperated, she wondered if she could make him understand. "Yes, I'm living here now, but I need to get back to my own time."

Throughout her explanation, Leonardo watched her closely, trying to make sense of what she said. "You say you are not from this time." She nodded. "What time are you from?"

"I was born in what we call the twentieth century, in the year 1969. But it is now 1996, some four hundred years later than your time."

His eyes widened. "Are you mad?"

His question unnerved her, but anyone would think she was crazy. "I don't believe I am, however, if I don't find a way back, I'm sure I will be. I am telling you the truth. I can prove it." Taking the purse from her waist, she emptied the contents on his cot. There were car keys, lipstick, a hairbrush, a perfume atomizer, a small bottle of fingernail polish remover, two bottles of polish, and a felt tip pen. A black billfold contained a driver's license, checkbook, credit cards and a twenty-dollar bill. Looking at her belongings gave her a small measure of comfort. They were a link to her past and proof that she wasn't crazy.

Perplexed, he looked through her belongings, picking up each item and examining it. He held the twenty-dollar bill up to the light, then discarded it. What finally convinced him was the material of her dress and the rubber soles on her shoes. Retrieving his tablet from the easel, he made notes, then carefully inspected her as he would a laboratory specimen. He studied the fillings in her teeth, her college ring, her watch, her smallpox vaccination, but he was most fascinated by her shoes.

"What is this material?"

"Rubber. We use it to make tires for cars and all sorts of other things."

Of course, he did not know what a car was so she drew him a crude sketch. As excited as a small child, he insisted upon knowing how it ran. She did her best to draw a gasoline engine and a diagram showing how it worked. He was completely absorbed. After studying her drawings, he sat back down on his stool.

"This is not magic?"

She shook her head. "No."

"I only hope you're not a witch," he said.

She sighed. "You must believe me. I'm an English professor at a university with family and obligations back in Houston. I have to return. Won't you please help me?"

Leonardo frowned, lost in thought. The more he learned about this woman, the more fascinated he was. Not only was she beautiful, but she was full of information. He could never tire of listening to her.

Most astounding was her explanation of how she arrived here. *Was it possible to travel in time?* he wondered. His own explorations into science had convinced him that the universe was more vast than anyone imagined. In dreams, he had envisioned men flying through air, through space. But he'd not considered the possibility of traveling through time. He was intrigued by the very idea. Folding his arms across his chest, he smiled. "I will help you."

Sara had held her breath, awaiting his decision. "Oh, thank you," she said. Relieved, she impulsively hugged him, then pulled away, embarrassed. It struck her that he was the first person she'd met here who didn't smell bad. Leonardo exuded a warmth mingled with the odor of paint and linseed oil that combined to make an attractive, old-world fragrance.

Leonardo pulled up his stool and sat, lost in thought. He'd taken a terrible chance by harboring this woman in the first place. Now he'd agreed to help her travel through time and had no idea what that would entail. It could be dangerous. If anyone learned of his complicity, he would lose his head.

Even more dangerous was the information she'd brought with her. Though Sara intrigued him, he continued to be baffled by what she said. The idea of time travel set his mind turning in several different directions. If she had been living in another age, while he existed in this age, then it was possible that time was not linear or sequential. That might mean that events in two separate time periods could be occurring simultaneously. He was so overwhelmed by the thought, he could take it no further. Besides, he still had many questions. "What do you think happened to bring you here?"

"I wish I knew."

"Perhaps you angered someone—a magician or sorcerer."

"I don't think so. I really believe there was a mechanism of some sort. Probably something very simple if we can just figure it out."

"Mechanism?"

"Yes. Just as there's a mechanism that powers an automobile, there is something that made me travel through time."

Leonardo studied her, thoughtfully. She had an intelligent, inquiring mind. He'd never met a woman who thought logically and he was even more attracted to her. "You are correct. In every question lies the answer."

"But we can't find the answer here. I must return to Todd Mission. Will you take me there?"

His gaze again drifted down the curve of her neck to full white breasts, barely covered by the gauzy material of her blouse. What would it be like to make love to this woman from another time? Would she be like other women? He took a moment to imagine the warm press of her lips on his. Her skin, he already knew from taking her hand, was soft as down.

"Please. You're my only hope." She looked at him, expectantly, waiting for his answer.

Reluctantly, he drew his thoughts back to the present. "I will take you to Todd Mission. But I cannot take you now. I have no money. I must complete a portion of the mural before the King will advance me more money. When he pays me, I will hire a horse and cart."

Sara's shoulders sagged. "How long will that be?"

He shrugged. "I can't say. I have just completed the calculations and sketches. The King is angry because there is nothing on the wall."

Sara chewed her lip. "I'll help you."

"You? Are you an artist?"

"No, but I've studied art in school."

He frowned. "You've studied art, but you are not an artist?"

"I've studied art history. Many different techniques have been developed over the last four hundred years and I can help you if you'll let me. The work will go faster if there are two of us."

Leonardo considered for a moment. Her expression conveyed an assurance that astounded him. Her voice and mannerism indicated that not only could she help him, but he might learn something from her. His instincts told him that this woman was far superior to any other woman he'd ever met. Yet, she frightened him a little. He really didn't know what or who she was.

Shaking his head, he started to say no. But even as he formed the words, he could not utter them. *Beware,* he cautioned himself. *She could turn on you and rip your heart out.* He was not afraid of taking risks. In fact, he'd lived his whole life on the edge. Allowing his inner conscience to take control, he paid no heed to his fears.

Though he'd never worked with another person, it now sounded like a good idea. There would have to be restrictions. She would not, of course, touch a brush, nor would she have any real say in the design. Still, she could be useful. "I'll think about this," he said, laying his tablet aside.

"Good." She smiled as if it were already decided.

Somehow he felt he'd lost control of the situation, but he tried not to let that show. He made a pretense of straightening up the apartment, then his stomach told him it was time for the evening meal. Since he had eaten nothing all day, he was suddenly quite hungry. "I must fetch us something to eat. You will remain here," he cautioned before leaving.

"Yes, I promise."

After he left, Sara explored the cell. Small and cramped, it contained only one bed, chair, table, and stool. In the corner stood an easel on which was a piece of linen crudely stretched over boards, several vials of oil, and numerous small paint pots and mixing bowls. To the side was a wooden palette and brushes of all sizes. Curious, she inspected the brushes and found them quite different from their modern counterparts. Some had stiff bristles, while others were soft animal hair, tightly bound with cord and pulled through reed stems.

Next to the easel were rolled canvases. She unrolled several and, to her astonishment, saw finished portraits, landscapes, and a still life. All done in oils, they were brilliantly executed and could have hung in a museum. This Leonardo was also a great master. Why had she not heard of him? Had he died young? Had someone else taken credit for his work? Am eerie feeling settled in the pit of her stomach as if she were about to make a world-stopping discovery.

Her heart beating rapidly, she continued her exploration, wondering what else she might encounter. To the side of the wooden table was a satchel containing dozens of rolled up parchments. Taking out a few, she carefully unrolled them on the table, but was disappointed to see pages of written script that she could not decipher. The strange feeling was still with her when she unrolled another parchment and saw detailed computations for some sort of machine. Completely absorbed, she didn't realize Leonardo had returned.

"What are you doing?"

Startled, she released the parchment suddenly. It rolled up and fell onto the floor.

"Oh, I'm sorry." She smiled. "I was curious about your work."

Angry, he advanced and snatched the parchments away from her, returning them to his satchel. "I do not allow anyone to see these," he admonished. "If you are to remain here, you will have to respect my privacy."

Sara was ashamed. Remembering the age and the fact that brilliant men were customarily subjected to ridicule, she immediately understood his concern. "Please forgive me. You are the only friend I have. I did not mean to take liberties. I simply wanted to understand you."

His green eyes crinkled and he laughed. "No one understands me. I don't understand myself."

"You are a very gifted artist. That much is obvious."

"That much is not obvious. The King simply wants his wall covered. It is much more socially acceptable to secure the services of a Florentine artist than an English craftsman, but I doubt Henry would know the difference."

"I would," she said.

The corner of his mouth worked into a grin. Sara took it as a sign that the compliment pleased him. "Modern artists don't paint as you do," she continued.

Pushing papers aside on the crude table, he set down a basket containing a bottle of wine and a bowl with a thick wedge of cheese. "They don't? How do they paint?"

Sara shook her head sadly. "I know one artist who fills a machine with paint, aims it at a huge canvas across the room and splatters paint all across it." She demonstrated the procedure.

Leonardo was aghast. "What can he get from that?"

"Nothing. A lot of paint on a canvas. They call it modern art."

He hit his head. "Painting is so much more than the paint. Many have the innate desire to create, and painting is one means to express that desire. The form that expression takes is most important. There is a relationship between each step, much like the relationship between two people. It takes time. It takes much work and dedication, and in the end, it becomes something truly intimate—a gift from the soul of one to another . . ."

He stopped, realizing he had begun to philosophize. Sara stared at him in awe. His face held a golden glow as if lighted by some inner fire that danced in his green eyes and flared his nostrils.

"Go on," she said. "I like what you're saying."

His laugh revealed straight white teeth, then the smile faded. "Enough of painting. Let's have something to eat," he ordered.

He broke off pieces of bread and placed them on the table. She wondered if the table was clean, then pushed the thought from her mind. That was the least of her worries.

From his belt, Leonardo retrieved a dagger. Unsheathing it, he cut the cheese. Afterwards, he replaced it. He searched the room and found two odd-shaped cups that still bore the dregs of the last meal. With a cloth, he wiped them clean and poured the wine.

The cheese had a pungent, tangy taste and the crusty bread was stone baked, much like bread she bought at a Houston health food store. The wine was not as good, although after the second cup, she didn't mind it.

"I have brought you clothes," he said, reaching into the basket. He handed her a green jerkin and black tights. "If you are to be my assistant, you must look the part."

He tossed them to her, then turned his back so she could change. While she donned her disguise, Sara suddenly realized she was sharing quarters with a perfect stranger. Though he had agreed to help her, he must have some motive for doing so. What would he ask in return?

There was only one bed. For a brief moment, she fantasized sleeping next to him. It was too soon, she knew that. Even so, the thought sent a surge of passion through her body, forcing her to take a deep breath. She tried to focus on the present moment and finished dressing. "Where did you get these?" she asked. "The tights actually fit."

"I borrowed them," he smiled, mischievously. "The lad looked to be about your size."

She stepped out to model her new ensemble and the artist observed her, critically. Her body, which had hinted at perfection before was, in fact, an exquisite work of art. Long legs, outlined by the tights, gently curved over an enticing, rounded bottom, then into a small waist. The green jerkin offset the earthy color of her reddish hair and brought out amber highlights in her eyes. He could only stare at her in awe, wondering if he could capture her beauty on canvas. Then, as she moved toward him, his objectivity failed. He suddenly felt uncertain. Differing emotions clouded his critical vision. She was more than a model with splendid proportions. She was a flesh and blood woman. Her mere presence in the room changed the atmosphere. The solitary cell was alive with feeling, charged with a new and vibrant intensity.

"Well? What do you think? Will I fool the Commandant?"

If he is blind, perhaps, Leonardo thought.

On Sara, the green jerkin looked more like a small dress that came almost to her knees. Beneath, she wore her own white blouse and discarded the red skirt forever.

Leonardo smiled and shook his head. "I believe it will do if you wear a cap over your hair and stay clear of the Commandant." It wasn't the Commandant that worried him now. He had to contend with his own feelings.

She returned his smile and their eyes locked. In that moment, something passed between them—an electrical current, an unspoken message. He took a step toward her and she waited, breathlessly. *For what?* she wondered. *A kiss?* He stopped, uncertain, but the longing was there in his eyes.

She looked away then, relieved. At the same time, she felt a little deflated. His lips were so inviting, but she pushed her feelings aside. She would not allow herself to become involved with this man. For her, he could only be a fictional character, like someone out of a history book. Once she returned to her own time, he would disappear. He would be dead. The thought made her sad, but she forced herself to think about her priorities.

The light faded and Leonardo lighted candles. She knew it would soon be time for bed. Then what? Through the open window came the soft, soothing sounds of a lyre accompanied by a man's tenor voice.

Sara stood at the window and though she couldn't make out the words, she sighed, enraptured. "Who is that?"

Joining her at the window, he brought her another cup of wine. "The King's minstrel. He plays at Henry's table every night."

"How lovely."

He took a drink of wine and smiled at her. "You are lovely, Sara."

Sara could feel the color stealing across her face. It had been years since she'd blushed. Suddenly shy, she lowered her gaze. He made her feel both strange and wonderful. They drank their wine in silence, staring out into the night.

"It is time to sleep," he said, finally. "You can take the bed. I will sleep on the floor."

Glancing around, she saw no blankets or pillows. Then from a peg near the door, he retrieved his cloak and settled it on the floor next to the bed. Settling onto the cot, Sara thought she would never get used to straw mattresses. Then she imagined Leonardo lying next to her and the discomfort disappeared. Perhaps, under the right circumstances, she could get used to things here.

Wrapped in his cloak on the floor, Leonardo wondered why he'd been so gallant. The stones were hard and the chilly air crept into his bones. Earlier, he could have taken her into his arms. She waited for him to kiss her, but he'd hesitated, then the moment was lost. None of the reasons he now gave himself seemed valid. It was simply that it was too much too soon. For the first time in his life, he was completely overwhelmed by a woman.

A soft moan escaped her lips. Propping himself on one elbow, he strained to see her. *Was she all right? Was she comfortable?* In the darkness, he strained to see her. Sara had turned onto her side and drawn her legs up like a small child. She was cold. The pose struck him as symbolic of her situation—a stranger in another time. If what she had said was true, her world had disappeared and she was alone here, isolated from all she knew. It would be enough to drive anyone mad. He wondered how he would fare in her world.

She looked so small in the cot by herself. Like a lost child, she had curled up into a little ball. Life here would be hard for her. Could she exist long under circumstances so foreign? Touched by her plight, he resolved to help her. But first, he must keep her warm.

Rising from the floor, he slipped into the bed beside her, pulling the cloak over them. She did not move or acknowledge his presence even when he drew her close into the circle of his arms. Pressed against her small, delicate body, he felt a comfort he'd never known.

Light streaming in the narrow window slits awakened Sara. She felt Leonardo's warm breath in her hair and turned to look at him. In sleep, the fiery intensity had been tempered into a boyish innocence. She thought he must have been a beautiful child. Afraid to wake him, she did not move. Instead, she nestled into his embrace, thinking how good his body felt. His arm lay on her stomach and long fingers splayed almost touching her breast. She wondered what it would be like to be touched and caressed by those long artistic fingers.

He stirred and, as if in answer to her unspoken question,

the sleeping fingers grazed the tip of one nipple. An unexpected surge of passion shot through her. *Good God!* she thought. If one accidental touch could affect her so, what would happen if they made love? A swift pang of guilt interrupted her reverie. She was engaged to be married and shouldn't have these thoughts—these delicious, enticing thoughts.

Mornings with Roger were never spent languishing in bed. He was up at six every morning, off to the gym before work. Even weekends were scheduled. Sara had thought all men were like Roger. Until now.

A loud shout from the guard right outside made Sara flinch.

"The guard is changing. Don't worry. You're safe here." Green eyes gazed into hers as he pulled her into the circle of his arms.

Held firmly within his embrace, Sara did feel safe for the first time since this nightmare began. A warm sense of security made her tranquil and content. Lying close to him was all that mattered at that moment. The world, any world, could go on without them. It was an odd thought to be so timelessly locked in a feeling that all else faded away.

Then he kissed her. With the touch of his lips on hers came the dramatic realization that their mouths were perfectly matched. As if carved from the same material, they blended in something more than a kiss. When his tongue probed deeply between her lips, she freely relinquished a part of herself that she'd never given to anyone. Welcoming the honeyed taste of him, she drew his passion in with a wild, unbridled torrent of feeling.

A loud knock on the door startled them. He leapt out of bed, leaving her bereft and longing. Fires lighted all through her body now smoldered. For the first time, Sara thought she'd had a taste of real passion—the heart-stopping, mind-blowing kind. Though people sang and wrote about this elusive feeling, she never believed it really did exist. But she'd experienced more emotion in one brief encounter than she had in an entire lifetime.

As she gazed across at the man who stood at the door, she was truly frightened at the emotions surging through her. It was just a kiss.

But oh, God, what a kiss!

Five

"The King has summoned me," Leonardo said, running fingers through his tousled hair. "His royal ass doesn't usually waken this early," he muttered, trudging over to the table. A frown creased his forehead and Sara could tell he was preoccupied. Retrieving an ewer from its place by the wall, he set last night's cheese aside and poured water into the bowl. He took off his jerkin and full-sleeved shirt, then began to wash. From a small pouch on the floor, he took a crude razor and soap. From what Sara could tell, shaving was more like scraping off the morning's growth of beard.

Fascinated, she admired his muscled back. Though slender, he had the well-honed physique of an athlete, contradicting her image of the sedentary artist. Unlike the pale, pasty complexions of the English, Leonardo's skin exuded a ruddy glow of health and now glistened as he rubbed himself dry with a rag.

He turned to her, suddenly with a worried look on his face. "Do not leave the room while I am gone. You can be sure they are still searching for you."

"What would happen to you if they find me here?"

"We could both lose our heads."

"Oh." She shuddered, pulling the covers up, protectively.

He approached the bed and, folding his arms across his chest, he studied her a moment. "If you are to be my assistant, make yourself useful while I am gone. Organize my brushes and paint. Then put them in the valise by the table.

The mural sketches are beside the easel. Collect them and place them with my paints. After that, you may straighten the room."

His voice and manner were like a cold dash of water on her face. All business now, he ordered her about like a servant as if the intimacy they'd shared earlier meant nothing.

Slipping on his full-sleeved shirt and jerkin, he was on his way out the door.

"Wait a minute," she called after him, but the door slammed shut, cutting off her parting comment. "I'm not your servant," she muttered to herself.

Leonardo took the long way, walking north along the King's tennis court and huge kitchen. Workmen were everywhere, creating dust and confusion. Cardinal Wolsey's huge mansion was not large enough nor sufficiently grand for Henry. A king had to have a palace, after all. Nothing, it seemed, was too bizarre or extreme. Like a spoiled child, Henry indulged his every whim.

After having spent two years in the country, Leonardo had to admit that the English knew how to live. Never had he seen so much gold, silver, and jewels displayed with such arrogant abandon. Henry VIII wanted the world to take note of his wealth and power. But for all his posturing, the king was a fat pig. Had he been born a commoner, Leonardo mused, his porcine face and small, beady eyes would have been openly ridiculed.

The path wound around through the gardens and he took in a deep breath of crisp air. It would be winter soon and the thought of spending another damp, chilly season here filled him with sadness. He yearned for the warmth and serenity of Florence. Were it not for this commission, he would leave tomorrow. Then he thought of Sara. How long could he harbor the girl until someone noticed. She might cost him his employment or worse—his head.

He hesitated, lost in thought. Two days had elapsed since he'd last spoken with the King. Why did Henry wish to see him again so soon? A cold chill crept down his spine. Had Sara's presence already been detected? If so, what would he do? He could not hand her over to the Commandant. By now the man would be angry enough to kill her, but not before torturing her first. He shuddered to think what might become of her. He could not even imagine another man kissing her. Shaking his head, he realized there was only one course of action. He would take Sara away as soon as possible. But penniless and with no friends at court, Leonardo did not know how to accomplish this feat. Yet.

The sudden warmth of the sun overhead reminded him that he could delay his audience with Henry no longer. He turned around and walked quickly back through the palace. Filled with apprehension, he approached the King's chamber.

A short time later, Leonardo was ushered into a crowded room, filled with fawning courtiers vying for the sovereign's attention. He made his way through the perfumed dandies to bow before his sovereign. The King, ensconced in his chair of state, sat on a raised dais.

Dressed in full regalia, Henry looked splendid in a gold brocade jerkin over a green satin doublet, slashed and puffed. He wore a scarlet bonnet with a halo brim. At the moment, he was having his short reddish beard trimmed while one particularly irksome courtier prattled in a high-pitched singsong voice.

"He has not been loyal in the past and it would not be in Your Majesty's best interest to continue patronage—"

"Beg pardon," Leonardo interrupted. "You summoned me, Your Majesty."

Offended at the artist's interruption, Guy Lemontaine looked up. His sharp features contorted with anger. "What impertinence! I was speaking of something very important. I beg to continue, Majesty."

"It's all right, Guy. We'll speak of it later. Now, I would have a word with my artist."

"As you wish, Sire." With a haughty glance at Leonardo, Guy retreated back into the room.

"Now, Leonardo. I toured the Great Hall yesterday and it is near completion. As you know, my laborers are working by candlelight to see that it is finished. Yet there is no mural. I want to see something on my wall."

"But Your Majesty, I plan to start painting right away."

"Today," Henry said without a smile.

"Today? But I am not ready."

Henry sighed and drummed fat fingers on the arms of his chair. "I don't want to force you to paint by candlelight. But I must see progress right away, else I shall suspend your pay indefinitely."

Leonardo winced. He was already out of money. Clearly, Henry had the upper hand and was about to squeeze it around the artist's throat. He bowed, acquiescing. "Of course, Sire. I wanted to make sure everything was perfect before I began. However, I see no problem with starting immediately. I have an assistant now who will help me with the work."

Henry nodded, indulgently. "Where is your assistant?"

Leonardo hesitated. "He's in my quarters. It's very cramped, but he's been sleeping on the floor."

"I'll have another bed sent round."

"Thank you, Your Majesty. Another stool would also be of use."

"Very well. Tomorrow, I expect to see something magnificent."

"You will, Sire. You will," Leonardo promised.

He bowed and backed away from the King directly into Guy Lemontaine. The courtier roughly pushed him aside. "Have a care, you ignorant fop," Lemontaine hissed.

Color flamed in Leonardo's face. "Ignorant, am I? I am

not so ignorant that I don't know a fool when I see one. Get out of my way."

Lemontaine grabbed his sleeve, but Leonardo shook him off and stalked out the door. In another place, the altercation would have erupted into a duel, but here in the King's chamber such behavior would be inappropriate. However, even after leaving, Leonardo could feel the man's anger and was aware that he had made an enemy. He rued the fact that his temper had gotten the best of him again. Prancing gallants like Guy Lemontaine brought out the worst in him. Sighing, he vowed to avoid the courtier whenever possible.

As he walked back to his chamber, Leonardo's thoughts quickly returned to his patron and his irritation grew. Henry had no feeling for art. He simply wanted his wall covered. Next he would want the colors to match the cushions in his chair. The artist fumed in silent frustration. Why had he chosen such a thankless profession? Was his talent a curse? Or was it merely wasted? That he should be constantly at the mercy of tasteless fools like Henry seemed an abomination too great to bear. *God's bones,* he cursed under his breath.

Sara considered ignoring Leonardo's imperious commands, but thought better of it. After all, he was the only person she knew here and she needed his help. He was the only hope she had of returning to Todd Mission. Though deflated by his sudden attitude change, she resolved to play along until she accomplished her goal.

The early morning chill took her breath away, but she quickly forgot the cold when forced to relieve herself in a chamber pot. After filling the bowl, then rinsing off with freezing water, Sara vowed never again to take central heating and plumbing for granted. Though life might be simpler here, it was neither easy nor convenient.

Throwing on cloak and shoes, she set about gathering up

Leonardo's utensils. Once more, she was fascinated by his drawing pencil, brushes, and paint pots. Uncorking one vial, she inhaled a whiff and decided it was probably linseed oil. Various pots contained finely ground pigments—Terra Verte, umber, lapis, vermilion, chalk, Egyptian blue, and ochre. On a wall shelf, she found other colors—ultramarine blue, sienna, and another, darker red. Rolls of unstretched canvas stood next to the vials.

Searching around the easel for his drawings, she finally found them behind the stretched canvases. Curious, she unrolled the parchments and spread them out on the table. After all, she reasoned, she was his assistant and had a perfect right to view them. Again she was awed by Leonardo's talent. He had made detailed mathematical calculations to determine a vanishing point in the center of the mural. On another page, he had roughly sketched the figures. There were two central figures: one kneeling and one hovering above, throwing something. Other figures to the right and left appeared to have wings, like angels. Only the kneeling figure had been sketched in any detail. The rest were unfinished.

Sara studied the face of the kneeling figure, astounded at the wealth of expression displayed on his face. The combination of surprise and disdain on his haughty features was almost comical. He seemed to be saying, "this can't be happening to me." Sara laughed aloud. No one painted this way in the twentieth century.

While she was rolling up the parchments, Leonardo stomped in, a scowl on his face. "That fat pig should be skewered and stuffed with applesauce," he said.

"Who?"

"The King."

Sara could not suppress a smile at Leonardo's deadly serious expression. "What did he say?"

"He wants me to start on the mural right away, whether I'm ready or not."

"But you are ready," Sara said.

"How do you know?"

"I looked over your sketches. All you have to do is complete the figures."

Aghast, Leonardo just looked at her. "Is that so?"

She nodded.

"Well, it might interest you to know that I have only found a face for one figure. I cannot complete the mural until I find the other faces. It takes time to select just the right features, and they must all be convincing."

"At least you have the main figure completed. Who is he anyway?"

He sighed, exasperated. "The Pope, of course."

"And what is happening to him? It looks like an angel is throwing something at him."

"He's being stoned by Satan," Leonardo grinned, mischievously.

Sara's eyes widened. It was a fairly controversial subject even by twentieth century standards. "Aren't you the least bit worried how people will react to the Pope being stoned?"

"No, I don't really care what people think. The King is paying me and he is enthralled by the idea. Henry doesn't like the Pope and the Pope doesn't like Henry. It will be interesting to see who finally wins the argument."

Sara smiled. "I don't know if you'll count it a victory, but England will have an entirely new religion."

His mouth dropped open. "A new religion?"

She nodded. "The Anglican Church will become the Church of England. Four hundred years later, they've still got problems," she said, thinking of northern Ireland.

Leonardo shook his head. "Do you mean the world hasn't improved in all this time?"

"I'm afraid not. It may have gotten worse."

"Holy Mother." Sara was a constant source of amazement to Leonardo. But at the moment, he couldn't assimilate what she'd told him. He had other things on his mind.

"Well, the King wants his wall decorated so we must begin painting."

"Right now?"

"Yes, now." Snatching up his sketches, he handed the satchel and stool to Sara. "Mind that you pull that cap over your head," he ordered before they left.

With her long hair tucked under a beret, Sara thought she looked the part of an artist's assistant. She also felt the full burden of her new role. Following behind him, she carried all his supplies and stool. Obviously, he expected her to fulfill all the obligations of the job. Though she struggled under the weight, he didn't seem to notice. Breathing deeply, she told herself she must endure the situation for the present. *But not for long,* she vowed.

Even though he treated her like a slave, Leonardo was a Renaissance artist. Reminding herself of this fact, Sara grew excited. She would actually get to see him work. It would be like watching history in the making and something to tell her grandchildren when she got back. *If* she got back.

A great gust of wind chilled her to the bone as they walked across the open courtyard. When they passed the guard, she pulled her cloak tightly around her and ducked her head. No one noticed her. Relieved and a tiny bit elated, she fell into step with Leonardo as they entered the Great Hall.

As usual, workmen were everywhere. Variously occupied, they stood high above the room on flimsy scaffolds plastering or carving wood. At tables scattered throughout the room, they cut and sanded wooden planks or delivered materials. They were like a swarm of worker bees. Sara counted over fifty men, and the noise was deafening.

The artist stalked through the debris and Sara followed closely, trying not to call attention to herself. Leonardo's presence did not bother the laborers at all. They accorded him no special consideration. If anything, they considered him another crew member.

Disgruntled, Leonardo had to clear out a work space. He kicked boards and debris aside to gain access to the wall. A man stood plastering the wall on a make-shift scaffold a short distance away from them. Sara knew Leonardo would lose his temper when a huge glob of plaster fell near his foot.

"Take care, you fool!" Leonardo shouted.

The workman only shrugged and went on with his work without even looking down.

Snatching his stool away from Sara, Leonardo sat and stared morosely at the dim outline on the wall.

"So much dust has accumulated that I cannot see my outline," he lamented.

Taking a rag from his satchel, Sara quickly dusted the wall, but the outline was still very faint. Chewing her lip, she studied the wall, thoughtfully. Finally, she had an idea. "Would it help if you could trace your outline in black?"

Arching a brow, he glanced at her. "With a brush? It would take days."

"No. I have two felt-tipped pens. They're brand new and should show up pretty well even on plaster."

She retrieved the two pens from her purse and handed him one. He simply stared at it, then attempted to draw without success. "It doesn't work."

"You have to remove the cap," she told him. She removed the cap of the one she held, then with deft precision, she traced the outline of one angel.

Leonardo watched her, fascinated. "What is that tool?"

"A pen."

"A pin?"

"It has a supply of ink inside," she explained.

Mimicking her actions, he took the cap off his pen and made a few tentative lines. Soon, he was totally absorbed. Hours later, he was still working and the outlines of the mural were clearly visible. A few workmen stopped to admire the black and white drawing. Oblivious, Leonardo worked on.

Midday, a commotion arose when the King and a few of his courtiers dropped by.

King Henry the VIII! Sara couldn't believe it.

Following Leonardo's lead, she bowed low, risking a furtive glance at the notorious monarch. In person, he was small—not much taller than Sara. With layers of clothing, he looked barrel-chested and top-heavy, almost teetering on short, spindly legs. He was, however, something to behold. Today he dressed in red velvet trimmed in gold braid with a fur-lined cassock. Sara's gaze was drawn to the enormous codpiece protruding from his tights. On a trip to London, she had marveled at King Henry the VIII's armor displayed in the Tower of London. Worked into the metal was a giant housing for his private parts, so large they almost merited a horse of their own, Sara had thought.

Leonardo introduced Sara. "My assistant, Cassio, Your Majesty."

Henry nodded acknowledgement.

"Well, Leonardo. I see you are hard at work. I am very pleased," the King said.

"Sire, there is nothing more than an outline here," the high-pitched voice of Guy Lemontaine intruded.

"That's true," Henry agreed. "But it looks as if things are progressing. I can see the figures now."

"Beg pardon, Your Majesty, but I fear you are wasting too much time with this man. It has taken him too long to get this far."

Henry nodded. "It has taken a long time."

"I heard news of another artist newly arrived from Flanders. I can summon him if you wish." Guy's irritating voice grated on Sara's nerves.

"Now, Guy. Let us not be hasty," Henry temporized.

"Sire, you told him to begin painting today. I see no color at all."

"It is so. What of that, Leonardo?" the King demanded.

Turning, Leonardo stared into the cold blue eyes of Guy Lemontaine. Sara, who had averted her eyes to avoid detection, now followed his gaze and was momentarily startled. She knew those eyes and the impertinent set of the jaw. *Who was this man and where had she seen him before?*

Leonardo bowed his head to Henry. "I have my paints here and we begin right away, Sire."

"Excellent." Henry rubbed fat hands together. "I will come back to see your progress tomorrow." He stepped away to inspect the rest of the hall.

Guy remained, gazing at the mural critically. "You have an ambitious undertaking here."

"That is true," Leonardo agreed.

"I am not sure you are equal to it. It will go ill with you if you fail."

A muscle worked in Leonardo's jaw and he clenched his hands. Sara saw him struggle to suppress his emotions. Then, with an abrupt change of attitude, he moved close to Guy. He walked around the courtier, studying his face. Picking up his tablet, he made notes with a pencil. Uncomfortable under the artist's scrutiny, the courtier shifted from one foot to another.

Leonardo put a finger to his lip. "I beg you, Sir Guy, to allow me to sketch your face."

"My face?"

Sara's eyes widened, but Leonardo's expression was an inscrutable mask.

"Yes, if you would please," the artist affirmed. "You have the exact features I've been searching for. I would like to include them in my mural with your permission."

Sara was aghast. Obviously, Guy Lemontaine had no love for Leonardo and would like nothing better than to disenfranchise him. Why then, would Leonardo want to include him in the mural? Possibly to regain the courtier's favor and impress the King, she reasoned.

Flattered, Guy sat on the artist's stool, preening like a peacock.

Again, Sara was struck by his features and the calculating look in his ice-blue eyes. His gaze flitted to her, ringing a distant bell in her memory. Instantly she bowed her head, fearing recognition.

Totally engrossed in his work, Leonardo rapidly sketched Guy, now and then stopping to comment. "Perfect. Exactly right."

How, Sara wondered, handing him piece after piece of parchment, *could Guy Lemontaine be exactly right or perfect?* But she found no clue in Leonardo's expression, for he was raptly absorbed in his work.

An hour later he had completed several sketches, one of which was an amazing likeness. Guy, himself, was suitably impressed.

"I might like to purchase one of your sketches when you are finished," Guy said, patronizingly.

"But, of course," Leonardo effused.

"I haven't had the time to sit for a portrait," Guy continued, "and my mother constantly chides me. I would like to give her this sketch. It might satisfy her for a time."

What gall! Sara choked back a gasp. Leonardo merely smiled, but she thought his teeth were clenched. "As you wish, but first I will use it to complete the mural."

"Well, I shall take more interest in the proceedings now," Guy commented, rising.

"I do hope so," Leonardo said. "I am obliged to you for providing me with such excellent material. You will be immortalized in King Henry's Great Hall."

"I like the sound of that. Actually, I've been at court for some time so it is fitting," Guy said. Straightening his collar and sleeves, he bowed curtly to Leonardo, then strutted away.

Sara looked at Leonardo and smiled. "I had no idea you were such a diplomat."

"Diplomat?" he laughed. "Hardly."

"But you spent two hours flattering that pompous ass."

"Indeed, the fawning little fop actually thinks someone besides his own mother can bear his simpering looks."

Sara shook her head, relieved. "Then you don't really intend to include him in the mural."

Leonardo favored her with a full, dazzling smile. "Of course I do."

"Please don't tell me his will be the face of an angel."

"That face? Oh, no, Sara. I would hope you think I'm a better judge of character. I have a far more impressive part for Sir Guy Lemontaine."

"What is that?"

"Next to the Pope, he has the most important position in the mural. I have finally found the devil incarnate. Do you think he'll recognize himself?"

Oh no, Sara thought, gazing at the retreating form of Guy Lemontaine.

She had a terrible premonition that neither she nor Leonardo were long for this world.

Six

True to his word, Henry supplied an extra bed, stool, and two woolen blankets. Though she was more comfortable, Sara missed the cozy feeling of that first morning and often thought of Leonardo's lingering kiss. Obviously the brief episode had been a mistake since the artist hardly noticed her now, except when he needed something done. She followed his imperious commands without complaint, hoping that with her help, he would complete the mural quickly.

Roger had probably called the police by now and turned the Renaissance Festival upside down looking for her. She glanced at her watch and noticed only an hour had passed. *Could time be that different here?* she wondered. Everything was different here, and the thought that she might be stuck indefinitely in this time filled her with remorse. Though she had Leonardo, she was not totally sure he was dependable. There were moments when she saw that his existence here was just as tenuous as hers.

During the next few days, Sara saw the King several times. She wondered about his Queen, Anne Boleyn. Leonardo explained that the Queen had just given birth to her first child, Elizabeth.

"Oh, yes, I'd forgotten. Poor Anne."

Leonardo nodded sympathetically. "Henry wanted a boy, they say."

Sara shook her head. "That's not what I mean. She only has three years to live."

Awestruck as usual, Leonardo simply stared at her. "Does she take an illness?"

"No, she will lose her head."

Leonardo's hand flew to his throat and he had difficulty finding his voice. "Is that true?"

Sara nodded, grimly. "I'd advise you to watch yourself around your employer. He has a mercurial temper and is easily swayed. Before he dies, Henry will have six wives. He is fond of beheading those who fall out of favor."

"God's bones!" Leonardo exclaimed, hoarsely. "We must hurry and complete the mural."

At present, Henry seemed pleased with their progress, especially now that he could see some color. Leonardo had completed the figure of the Pope and was working on the angels. He was saving Satan for last, Sara thought.

She had tried to talk him out of using Guy Lemontaine's face as a model for Satan, but Leonardo would not be dissuaded.

"He probably won't even notice, the insufferable prig."

But Sara thought someone would see the resemblance and continued in vain to argue against it. They were debating the issue as they walked toward the Great Hall for another day of work. Suddenly, the Queen and her ladies appeared in the courtyard. Leonardo and Sara stopped to bow, respectfully.

Sara was surprised at how petite Anne Boleyn was. Barely five feet tall with an unremarkable face and figure, she looked incapable of attracting a man like Henry. Once she must have had some spirit. However, now that energy waned. Thin as a wraith, Anne barely acknowledged their presence, looking past them at some unknown object. Sara thought she might be looking into the future and shuddered.

Leonardo also studied the Queen closely as if for some clue that would indicate Sara was telling the truth. The ladies moved on and the artists continued to the Great Hall.

"The Queen doesn't look well," Leonardo affirmed.

"She's probably as well now as she ever will be again," Sara told him with a shrug.

Leonardo narrowed his gaze at her. "I find it most uncomfortable having you constantly predict the future like a sorcerer."

"Well, if you would listen once in a while, it might keep you out of trouble."

"Perhaps," he said, "but that remains to be seen."

Turning away, he busied himself taking paints out of the satchel and laying them in orderly fashion on a nearby table. Then he sat down on his stool to survey his recent work. Touching the saffron-colored robe of the Pope, he noticed the color remained on his finger. "It is not dry yet and with all the construction, I fear dust will corrode it."

"Just a minute," Sara said, withdrawing a bottle of quick-dry nail sealer from her purse. "Try a coat of this. It will dry fast and creates a diamond finish."

Leonardo held the bottle up to the light, then opened it. Inhaling the contents made him cough. "I've never smelled anything like this substance. What is it?"

"I have no idea. I only know it works."

Very cautiously, Leonardo applied a little to the Pope's robe, then sat back to view the results. Sara stepped up and blew on it. Grinning, he shook his head at her actions.

"Touch it now," she challenged.

He touched the robe, tentatively, then withdrew his finger. "It's dry!" He touched it again to make sure. "This is a miracle."

Sara shrugged. In her mind, well-manicured nails were not miraculous. However in 1533, such a phenomena would certainly cause a sensation. Looking at her pale, chipped polish, she thought it best to remove the rest. People in this age would not understand. While Leonardo painted, she withdrew the bottle of remover from her purse. The smell drew his attention.

"What is that?"

"Remover."

"You have something that will remove paint?"

"Oh yes. It will remove anything—fingernail polish, spots, paint. Once I even removed bubble gum from my shoe with this stuff."

He had that vacant look that told her she had lost him again. So she simply handed him the bottle.

"I can remove paint with this?"

"Try it."

He did and was as happy as a child with a new toy. "This is a wonderful creation."

Green eyes stared at her in rapture. Sara couldn't help but wonder what Leonardo would think of the twentieth century. He would be like a kid in a candy store.

With each passing day, Leonardo grew more enthralled with Sara. For the first time in his life, he could actually communicate with another human being.

As a boy growing up in Florence, he'd been ridiculed for his creativity. His artistic talent was obvious to everyone, but his other ideas were too far-fetched for even his teachers to understand. His sketches of motorized vehicles and complicated mathematical calculations only confounded those around him. They accused him of being a dreamer, a visionary. His own father feared his youngest son was going mad and sent him away to school.

After being ostracized by his peers, Leonardo learned to keep his own counsel. He furtively guarded sketches of various devices, contraptions, and spacecraft for fear he would be deemed mad and locked up. In fact, even he did not know the origin of his inventions. Often, he would dream something and upon awakening execute a complicated drawing. Or he might simply look at a thing and know how it worked. Immediately, his mind would set about improving it until he had devised a completely different concept. Frequently, the end product bore no resemblance to the original. He had long since given up on trying to halt the process, for it spun far out of his control. Sometimes he wondered if he were, indeed, mad. Until now.

Little by little he'd begun to talk to Sara about his ideas. She always listened intently and often confirmed his theories. She told him that his inventions were not the ravings of a madman. In her time, they actually had powered devices called motors. She said he was so brilliant that no one could understand him and that was the problem. Never before had another person accepted him nonjudgmentally. He could hardly contain his joy.

"I believe that one day the world will be completely run by these "motors" as you call them. Man will no longer use the horse."

"That's right," Sara affirmed. "It has already happened. Of course, the mechanization of the universe has created more problems than it has solved."

"How so?"

"Because we have now depleted our natural resources to such a degree that we may be unable to power our machines."

Leonardo was thirsty for any knowledge she would impart. "Tell me about the machines."

"We have machines for everything. We ride to work in cars, cook our food on electric stoves, do our work on computers, which incidentally have a memory capacity not unlike the human brain. We come home at night to watch television or speak to friends on the telephone. We set our alarm clocks before going to sleep to awaken us the next morning. But I'm not even scratching the surface here."

He was enthralled. "What of the men who invent these machines? How do your people treat them?"

She smiled. "In the twentieth century, all creative people are respected, at least. Some become very wealthy and famous."

"But mustn't they watch what they say?" He searched her face for answers.

"They can say almost anything they want in my country. We have complete freedom of speech. They might not be popular if what they say displeases a vast majority, but usually it is the odd viewpoint that garners public sentiment."

"You must have a benevolent ruler," he remarked.

"The people run the government, not very efficiently, I'm afraid. But we elect a president and if he doesn't do a good job or if the people don't like him, he will not be reelected."

"Like the Romans?"

"Yes, it is a little like the Roman government was. We have a Senate and a House of Representatives, all elected by the people."

"Then there is freedom to choose who will rule."

"We call it 'rule by the people.' "

Leonardo's green eyes held a dreamy, far-away look. *What would it be like,* he wondered, *to live in a time when artists, writers, and inventors were respected? Was it true that a man could express any idea without censure?* He couldn't imagine living in a place where a mercurial sovereign had no real control over his subjects.

Lost in reverie, he returned to his painting, stopping occasionally to ask another question. Sara patiently answered every question, fueling his imagination further. Her expressions changed as she spoke. Color flooded her cheeks and her amber eyes sparkled. Long after he looked away, her face remained in his mind.

Automatically and without any conscious effort, he began to incorporate her features into those of the angel in the mural who reached out to the Pope. The beatific spirit floated just above the Catholic patriarch, but the Pope, much too low, could not grasp her hand. When Leonardo realized what he'd done, he turned quickly to Sara to see if she had noticed. But she stared off into the distance wishing, he supposed, that she were somewhere else.

Sara was thinking of Leonardo and how lost he must feel in this restrictive world. The more she learned about him, the more intrigued she was. Leonardo's vision and perception was astonishing, even by twentieth century standards. He was far beyond his own time, even far beyond her time, and much more advanced than any man she'd ever met. She was beginning to believe he possessed a genius similar to that of da Vinci. Yet for all his creativity, he was surprisingly innocent. He said exactly what he thought, and while his forthrightness was refreshing, it was also a little alarming. In this day, such candor was dangerous.

When Leonardo prodded, Sara told him about her life in Houston. While she unburdened her feelings about her father and his subsequent stroke, he listened sympathetically. Now and then he took her hand when he saw tears welling in her eyes. For the first time in months, she felt comforted.

His rapt attention was flattering, but she realized that she had assumed the role of teacher to an eager pupil. By his own admission, he'd never been able to share his ideas with anyone. The information she gave him about life in the future had validated his far-reaching thoughts. Yet, for some reason, he wanted to know everything about her specifically. It struck Sara that no one ever had been that interested. Not even Roger.

She told him about her job at the university and her family but avoided telling him about Roger. Her diamond engagement ring was still in the pocket of her purse and there it remained. Leonardo didn't really need to know she was engaged. She wasn't even entirely sure she wasn't imagining this experience anyway. She had the feeling that one day soon she would be back home, explaining this whole fantastic episode to a psychiatrist.

* * *

Each day, they worked until dark. Cursing the fading light, Leonardo reluctantly packed up his paints. It seemed they had only gotten started when they had to stop.

Sara had her own crude system for measuring the days. She tied a knot in the laces of her jerkin. As they left the Great Hall, she tied another knot and counted them. Seven. She had been at Hampton Court a week already.

On their way to the King's kitchen for a bit of supper, they rounded a corner and Leonardo almost collided with the Commandant of the Guard. Sara took in her breath sharply and immediately lowered her eyes. Her heart pounded against her ribs and she could scarcely breathe.

"You there, artist," the Commandant said, gruffly. "Have you seen anything of the wench who fled into the courtyard a few days ago? I fear she must be hiding somewhere."

Leonardo looked puzzled. Then he suddenly remembered. "Oh, that girl. No, I never saw her again."

He tried to push past the soldier, but the Commandant caught his arm. "Who is that with you?"

"My assistant, Cassio. Now, if you please, we must be on our way. We've been working all day and I fear the cook will have nothing left."

The Commandant released Leonardo and the two of them hurried down the hall, but Sara could feel his gaze boring into their backs. Fear filled her with cold dread. What if he investigated and uncovered her disguise? They would both be killed.

Leonardo was thinking the same thing. "We will have to go back to work tonight. If necessary, we will work by candlelight. We must finish the mural as soon as possible."

They ate the remains of a greasy venison stew that wasn't nearly as savory as Sophie's had been. Had she not been so hungry, Sara would have stayed with bread and cheese. But she ate the stew and washed it down with wine.

The wine drove the fear away, replacing it with a warm, relaxed feeling. "You don't have to worry about the candlelight," she told Leonardo. "I have a flashlight."

Fishing in her purse, she produced her car keys, which had a tiny flashlight on the ring. She switched it on. Though it was only a penlight beam, it was very bright.

"Let me see that," Leonardo said, snatching it away from her.

He played with it for several minutes before handing it back.

"You see, we can work every night if you wish," she told him.

He looked at her and smiled. "I don't know how I managed without an assistant like you."

She returned his smile. He did need her. She almost hated to leave him. She felt a little twinge of regret creep into her thoughts and realized that she would miss him. He was so bright, so creative, and so very interesting. But pushing all thoughts of Leonardo to the back of her mind, she forced herself to concentrate on her goal.

Torches lighted the dark hallway as they made their way back an hour later. Some workmen still floundered around the Great Hall in the dark, with only the uncertain light of a few, sputtering candles. Leonardo and Sara sat side by side in front of the mural and worked with the aid of the small flashlight. When they heard the workmen bump into one another or curse when they dropped a tool, they exchanged a smug smile. Leonardo's smile lingered as he looked at Sara's alabaster skin. She was more beautiful than any angel he could imagine. He wasn't even sure he had truly captured her beauty.

That night they completed two more of the angels and part of the background. Upon close inspection, Leonardo was proud of the effect he'd achieved. He was most pleased with the lead angel. With Sara's features and raiment seem-

ingly composed of pure light, she floated above the landscape like a vestal virgin. He sighed, completely enraptured.

"What do you think?" he asked, handing the flashlight
to Sara.

"It is magnificent. Every detail is absolutely perfect."

"Yes," he agreed. "Especially the angels."

Even the workmen had left by the time they made their
way back to Leonardo's chamber. The palace was so quiet,
their footfalls echoed along the stone floor. Shivering, Sara
felt the cold through her shoes.

The room was even colder, forcing Sara into bed. Bur-
rowing into the straw mattress, she wrapped her cloak and
blanket firmly around her. But she was still cold.

Leonardo sat at the table sketching by candlelight. The
coppery highlights of his hair gleamed in the dim light as
he bent over his work. Through half-closed lids, Sara
watched him. Was it her imagination or was he animated
by a dazzling energy when he drew? Strong arms cradled
the parchment while nimble fingers worked the pencil,
softly, then more intensely. She could almost sense the light
and dark in his movements. Blinking, she thought she saw
more light around him than could possibly be emitted by
the one candle. Was he drawing it to him?

She drew in a quick breath. In that moment, she knew
she was in the presence of true genius. Her throat went dry
and she simply stared at him. It was as if she'd been accorded a rare privilege.

"Hah!" he shouted, pushing back his stool.

Shaken out of her reverie, Sara chided herself. Leonardo
was just a man. But she knew that wasn't true. He was an
extraordinary human being. Pulling the covers tightly around
her, she sighed. Absolutely extraordinary.

Leonardo carefully rolled up the parchment and placed
it alongside the other rolls near the easel. He had drawn
another sketch of Sara from memory. Soon he would paint
her portrait on canvas. Would she notice? he wondered. He

glanced at her small form, cocooned by the blanket. He had never tried to get the attention of a woman before. He had bedded many, painted many more, but he had always remained detached. This woman, however, touched his very soul.

She had the effect of making him feel vulnerable and powerful at the same time. He felt drawn into an emotional abyss with no exit. Soon she would leave and travel back to her own time. He had promised to help her do this. The selfish thought occurred that he didn't have to help her at all. By omission, he could force her to stay with him. But she would not be happy. Nor could he live with himself if he didn't at least try to honor his commitment. Either way, she would not be entirely his.

A moan drew him to the bed. "Sara, are you cold?" he asked.

"Yes."

The affirmation was all Leonardo needed to crawl into bed beside her. Wrapping his arms around her, he drew her into his warm embrace. She nestled comfortably in his arms as if she belonged there.

"Sara," he whispered into her hair.

"What?"

"You are beautiful. So very beautiful."

His words cut through the centuries to touch the innermost part of Sara's being and felt like little drops of rain on a soul left too long untended. She turned toward him. "Do you really think so?"

"I do."

She gave a little laugh. "No one has ever said that to me before."

Through the slatted window, a shaft of moonlight illuminated his face. His expression was incredulous. "No one?"

She shook her head.

"If you were mine, I would tell you every single day. I

would paint you a thousand different ways and capture your smiles and frowns forever."

"You would grow tired of that," she chided.

"No. You grow tired of some things. For years I have painted one hill outside Florence. I painted it in every season, each year since my boyhood. It remains the same, yet to me it is always new. Each time I paint it, I discover a new aspect of it—a rock, a tree, or even a flower that I have never noticed before. Your face is like that. I could never grow tired of painting you."

Nestled close to him, Sara felt the truth of his statement and understood him completely. In so short a time, she felt an intimacy with this man that she'd never dreamed possible.

Leonardo's arms encircled her tightly. His desire was obvious and pressed intensely against her stomach. She felt his hands range beneath her blouse to caress her breasts and with a delicate touch he toyed with her nipples. Spirals of feeling whirled madly through her body, igniting her passion like wind through dry leaves. Beneath the artist's hands, she went pliant, molding her flesh to his.

They fit together like two separate pieces of the same sculpture; his body was her counterpart. Soft skin and hard muscle blended together along with the differing shades of their red hair. *How alike, yet how dissimilar they were,* she thought.

When at last his lips claimed hers, she was again overwhelmed by Leonardo's magic. He was a sorcerer weaving his spell, drawing her further into his web. His tongue enticed, dueling with hers as his fingers explored the crevices of her body. Little fires here and there were ignited in the wake of his touch. Finally, engulfed by the heat, she could no longer tolerate her clothes. Divested of fabric separating them, they flung themselves together with a hunger almost frightening in its intensity.

Sara's hands savored the muscles of his shoulders and back. His skin was firm and smooth—not a bump or imperfection anywhere that she could feel. Fine hair covered a broad chest and tapered down to the mound of tight curls between his legs. Her fingers automatically closed around the hard shaft of his penis, wanting him inside her, willing him to take her then. Again he kissed her and moved to enter her.

"Leonardo don't, please!" she begged him, with the last of her resolve quickly disintegrating. She didn't want him to stop.

"But I know you want me," he whispered in her ear.

"Oh, yes," she affirmed, "but I am afraid."

He pulled away from her with his face full of concern. "You are afraid that I will hurt you?"

"No, not that." Her voice was a soft whisper. If he pressed her, she would give in and be lost forever.

He moved back, kissing her again and she melted into his arms. "What then? Let me love you. I can promise that you will be satisfied."

A small moan escaped her lips. "That's exactly what I'm afraid of."

"That I will satisfy you?"

"Yes," she breathed, kissing the hair on his chest. "I'm afraid if you make love to me, I will never want to leave."

Seven

Turning away, Leonardo stared at the ceiling. Since early manhood, women had never been a problem. He catered to them, treated them well, and they fell at his feet like beautiful flowers. It never occurred to him that he might have crushed a few along the way, for he genuinely felt that he had given and received in turn. Now he'd come across a woman he truly desired but could not have. The confounding part was that her reasoning was sound, given the circumstances. In truth, had he been in her place, he would have said the same thing. So he could not argue with her, nor was he angry. Yet his need for her had not diminished. If anything, her resistance fanned the flames burning inside him, and the heat was suffocating.

"Leonardo?"

The touch of her hand sensitized his shoulder, sending a burning arrow of passion down his arm. He turned away, folding his arms protectively across his chest.

"How do I know that tomorrow I won't awaken back in Houston? I'm not entirely sure you're real. You might be a dream."

Frustration made him irritable. Unable to stifle his emotions, he turned back to face her. "Reality is what you believe it is. Even if you are a dream, I perceive you as being here right now. And so, I have made you a part of my reality for the present. You speak of what might happen tomorrow.

But we don't have tomorrow. All we have is today. No, we don't even have today. We only have this moment."

Sara was lost in thought. "I believe what you say may be true. The simple fact that I've traveled through time tells me that I've been wrong about many things. But the one thing I do know is that I can't stay here."

"You mean you won't."

She stared into his eyes and her lip quivered. "That's not fair."

He saw her struggling with her emotions and felt a stab of guilt. "No, it isn't fair and I apologize." He smoothed the hair back from her temples, gently kissing her forehead.

She melted easily into his embrace while he rained soft kisses down her cheek, finally claiming her lips. Over and over he kissed her until, with a soft moan, she pressed herself against him. Full, perfect breasts tapered to a narrow waist. His hands moved over the rosy peaks, toying and teasing each into tight buds. Then he caressed the gentle swell of her hips, following the curve down the long legs entwining his. *She has the face of an angel and the body of a wanton temptress,* he thought.

"There is one thing that would make you stay," he whispered into her hair.

"I don't want to leave my family . . . my father." Her voice was barely audible and he could tell her resistance wore thin.

"None of that would really matter if you were in love."

"Love?" She repeated the word and it resounded in his head.

"If you loved someone, you would want to be with him wherever he was. Don't you think that is true, Sara?"

"Yes."

He kissed her again and felt her go pliant in his arms. She was his for the taking, but the word still echoed through his mind. He had used it often, whenever necessary. But for the first time, it had meaning. The realization was stunning and left him teetering on a precipice. Now he knew the same fear that Sara felt.

"Oh, God," he said aloud.

"What?" she murmured. Her arms drew him back to her.

"We must sleep," he said, dismissively. "We have much work to do tomorrow."

"I thought you said there was no tomorrow," she giggled, kissing him.

He pushed her away from him as he would a plate of tempting fruit. "Sara, it is very late and I am tired."

Rolling to the side, he moved to his own cot. There he wound the blanket around him and stewed in silent frustration. She was right. She was not meant for him or this world. He would take her back to Todd's Mission and that would be the end of it.

Having made his decision, he expected to be relieved. Instead, he felt a vast emptiness growing in the pit of his stomach. In his mind, he saw his ribs and soft organs turning to stone. The place where his heart had been was a yawning black abyss. He tried unsuccessfully to block out the image, but there it remained.

Sara. What cruel twist of fate brought her here? Had she only come to leave him with a bitter taste of what might have been? Or, perhaps she was punishment sent from all the women he had loved and left. And punishment it was, for he knew he would find a way to send her home. He would be left with nothing but the image of her, stamped on his mind for all eternity.

Across the room Sara shivered. The abruptness of Leonardo's departure chilled her more than the cold air. *What had she done to make him leave?* she wondered. Bereft and lonely, she lay awake for hours.

For the next ten days, they worked feverishly on the mural. Now the wall was ablaze with color. Consumed by his painting, Leonardo ignored Sara, only stopping periodically to bark out orders.

"Bring me the vermilion," he demanded.

She handed him the wrong pot.

"No, that's cinnabar. The other one."

"Well, excuse me, Your Highness," she retorted hotly. "Red is red."

"Cinnabar is darker," he told her. "I should have explained."

His changing attitude perplexed Sara. One moment, he treated her as part of the furniture. At another, he looked at her in a way that sent hot flames racing through her body. She told herself she was unused to an artist's mercurial temperament. But there was more to it than that. He seemed to be wrestling with his feelings, and she would have given anything to know just exactly what those feelings were.

The angels were completed and Leonardo began to work on the last figure in the mural—Satan. Bare-chested with only a vermilion cloth swathing his loins, the devil reached out to the Pope with long, muscular arms, and Sara was relieved. Guy Lemontaine did not possess such a perfect body. She imagined his physique to be as unremarkable as his face.

Leonardo was totally absorbed, and by the end of the day, the body of Satan was complete.

"I'm glad you decided against using Guy Lemontaine for the face of Satan."

Having returned to Leonardo's chamber, they feasted on cheese and crusty bread. By now, Sara was used to their meager diet. Except for the absence of green vegetables, she thought it very healthy.

"I haven't given up the idea. Tomorrow, Satan will have a face and you can decide who it is. Perhaps it will be Henry. The fat pig would enjoy that, no doubt."

His comment made Sara uneasy. "I don't think the King would be amused."

Leonardo shrugged. "I just want to finish it. Someone won't like it. That's always a certainty."

"I must get to Todd Mission, Leonardo. You promised you would help me."

He gave her a strange look. "That's all you think about, isn't it?"

"No. It isn't all I think about. But right now, it's a priority."

"And if we don't discover the mechanism that got you here? What then?"

"Well, I won't continue being your assistant, if that's what you mean."

"Is it so terrible working with me?" He arched a brow over vivid green eyes.

"I rather like it, but I can't imagine being a lackey for the rest of my life. Surely you can appreciate that."

He laughed and poured them each another mug of wine. "What could you do? Can you sew?"

"Of course not. I'm a professional."

"A professional what?"

"Teacher. I'm a professor, remember?"

He nodded. "Unfortunately, only men teach here and they do not receive much money."

Dejected, Sara sat on the stool and shook her head. A rap on the door interrupted their conversation. It was a page with a message from the King.

Leonardo conferred with the lad a few minutes before sending him away. He returned to the table.

"Come," Leonardo urged her, "we'll have to continue working tonight. Henry is having visitors and wants to show the mural tomorrow. If I can get it almost finished, he'll give me a bonus."

Quickly, he shouldered his satchel. Downing her wine, Sara followed him out the door. She was filled with uncertainty. Now that they were about to return to Todd Mission, she wondered if it would make any difference. What if she were stuck here and could never get back? What would she do? These questions had plagued her all along, but she had counted on Leonardo's help. He was a genius, far ahead of his peers. If he couldn't help her, who could? Pushing doubts to the back of her mind, she tried to keep pace with Leonardo's rapid stride. For now, she must concentrate on finishing the mural.

They worked until three in the morning. Sara was dozing on her stool when Leonardo nudged her. "We can go now. It's near enough to completion."

Blinking, she was unable to see in the dark. She tried to focus on the mural, but she was too tired. She only saw that all the faces were completed. Now they could sleep.

They made their way down the cold, empty hallway, meeting only a guard or two. Finally, they reached the artist's chamber. Sara quickly undressed. After rinsing out her underwear and blouse, she tumbled into bed.

When she awakened the following morning, Leonardo was gone. Lingering in bed, she thought of home and wondered about her family's reaction to her disappearance. She glanced at her watch. Only four hours had passed. *How was that possible?* she wondered.

Suddenly Leonardo burst into the room.

"Wake up, Sara," he said, coming over to sit on her bed.

"You're in fine spirits." She stretched and turned on her side.

"Look!" he exclaimed, pouring out the contents of two leather pouches. The gold coins pooled on the blanket. "We're rich!"

"Henry finally paid you. That's wonderful."

"And I've already hired a horse and cart for tomorrow."

"Oh, good," she said, both relieved and sad at the same time.

"Now you must get up and dress. Henry is taking the entire court to view the mural and we must be there."

Sara scrambled out of bed and hurriedly washed, then

retrieved her blouse and panties. Each night, Leonardo watched in amusement while she painstakingly rinsed out her underwear and blouse, hanging them in front of the open window to dry. She slept in the long woolen jerkin.

Now, while the artist poured himself a mug of wine, she dressed in her clean clothes and pushed her reddish-brown hair under the black beret. "I'm ready," she announced, accepting a sip of wine.

Leonardo smiled. "You look beautiful," he remarked. "Anyone with half a wit would look at you and forget the mural. Fortunately, these men are idiots."

He took her hand and led her out into the hallway, then dropped her hand and stepped in front of her. An assistant must walk behind his master. Sara sighed, wondering if a wife also walked a step behind her husband. But she already knew the answer to that question. In this time, women were a step behind and one down.

When they arrived in the Great Hall, Sara was immediately struck by the beauty of the mural. Although the background was more reminiscent of Italy's rolling hills than England, the figures were stunning. Each face was unique, both in the lifelike quality of the features and the individual expression. The characters could be identified by the way they looked. The angels had a celestial quality. However, the Pope's conflicted attitude was well described by a tug-of-war between his banal nature and his desire for divine inspiration. Satan both tempted and repelled him.

Sara's gaze rested on Satan and she stifled a little gasp just as the King and his courtiers entered the room.

"Ah, my mural," the King boomed.

Henry was accompanied by the Queen and several unknown dignitaries. His courtiers followed behind, echoing the monarch's enthusiasm. "Beautiful. Magnificent."

"Sire, Your Majesty." Leonardo bowed low to the King and Queen.

"Leonardo, you have done well. I am very pleased," Henry effused.

"Thank you, Sire."

"The Pope's face is wonderful," the Queen remarked with a smile.

"And look at Satan," the King said.

They all stepped closer to study the mural.

"The face of Satan resembles someone we know. Why, it's you, Guy!" one of the courtiers blurted out.

"What!" Guy peered at Satan's face, then whirled around to Leonardo. "You! You will pay for this!"

"I say, Guy," Henry laughed, "it is a good likeness."

Guy's face flamed bright red as he glared at Leonardo.

Leonardo only smiled. "I mentioned I wanted to use your features in the mural, Sir Guy. I asked you to sit for me, if you recall."

"You never said you would make me Satan."

Leonardo chuckled. "You've done a good job of that on your own."

Guy gripped his sword, but his fellows restrained him.

"Now, Guy," Henry admonished. "I'm sure Leonardo can alter Satan's face if it bothers you so."

Leonardo did not comment and continued to smile while Guy smoldered with rage.

With mounting agitation, Sara watched the interaction. At any time, the two would come to blows. Guy's blue eyes blazed into Leonardo's, reminding her of someone. All of a sudden, she realized who it was. Roger! Roger? Surely she imagined the resemblance, but Guy Lemontaine had Roger's self-righteous frown and his blue eyes were cold and brittle like Roger's often were.

Soon the King and his entourage left the Great Hall. As soon as they were out of sight, Leonardo collapsed, laughing.

"Did you see the look on Lemontaine's face? The silly

fop—what vanity! I expect he thought I would put his features on God himself."

"He is very angry, Leonardo. The first chance he gets,
he will put a sword through your back."

"Not likely. Did I mention that I'm very good with a
sword? Let him challenge me to a duel. I welcome it and
it would relieve the world of a very boring personality."

Sara gasped. "I can't believe you. Surely you wouldn't
take pleasure in killing someone."

Leonardo grinned, mischievously. "I've not tried it, but
I think I might."

Sara dropped the subject, convinced that the whole thing
would blow over if Leonardo forgot about it. He'd achieved
his revenge on the courtier. Tomorrow, they would be on
their way to Todd Mission and all would be forgotten.

That afternoon, they allowed themselves a small celebra-
tion. They took meat, bread, and cheese out by the river
and had a picnic of sorts. Leonardo spread a blanket on the
river bank, and the two of them feasted while watching
ducks bob for pieces of bread in the water nearby.

"Tomorrow you will be back at Todd Mission," Leonardo
said, taking a drink of wine. "If you return, will you miss
all this?"

"Yes," Sara had to admit. "I'll miss you most of all."

He lowered his eyes, smiling, and for the first time, Sara
noticed a small dimple to the right of his mouth. It was
both endearing and a little sad. Each day she noticed new
things about him that she adored. Now it irked her that she
might never see that dimple again.

"Have you a lover back home?" He asked the question
casually as he threw the ducks more bread.

They watched the birds swim furiously toward the
crumbs, then fight each other for them. Sara took her time
answering.

"I'm engaged to be married," she said at last.

His head snapped around and he regarded her with a cool

green gaze. "Oh? You've never mentioned him. In fact, you've acted rather fancy-free. Is that because he isn't here?"

Sara winced. "No. I mean, I don't know why I've acted as I have here. I'm not sure I understand."

A wry grin turned down the corners of his mouth. "It's because you think this is all a dream. In a dream, you can act as you please."

His words stung and Sara looked away. He was right, of course.

"Who is this man you are going to marry?"

"His name is Roger. Roger Latham," she replied, unable to meet his gaze.

"Well, no wonder you've been so anxious to return. I would hope you haven't missed your own wedding."

"Leonardo, you don't understand. I'm not sure how I feel anymore."

"I see," he said, coolly.

She wondered what he was thinking, but their conversation was interrupted by the arrival of a boy who came running from the palace. When he spotted them, he hurried over to them.

"Excuse me sir, but the King commands your presence immediately."

"I must go," Leonardo said to Sara. "Please gather our things. I'll meet you in our chamber."

While Leonardo followed the boy to the palace, Sara packed the remains of their meal in the blanket and carried it back inside. The chilly autumn air sliced through her and she shivered. But Leonardo's confrontation had chilled her more. She didn't want to leave him this way.

She didn't want to leave him at all.

After learning of Roger, Leonardo was in no mood to face the king. The interview was short. Furious, Henry pointed a beefy red finger at the artist.

"Someone has defaced your mural. It is now an abomination."

"What! I just finished it. It is perfect."

"No longer," the King said.

"Who would do such a thing, Sire?"

"Who, indeed? You are the only one who paints."

"I? I would not profit from vandalism."

"Nevertheless, you shan't profit from this at all, the way it stands."

"Give me time to sort this out, Your Majesty. I beg you."

"I'll be lenient." Henry's small blue eyes were cold. "But only for a short time, I assure you."

A short time later, Leonardo stormed back into the chamber, red-faced and furious.

"Someone has defaced the mural! Horrible black streaks are everywhere. And the face of Satan has been blackened completely."

"Oh, no. Can it be fixed?"

"Henry actually accused me of doing it myself. Someone put that idea in his head and I know just who might have done it."

"You think Guy Lemontaine did it?"

"Who else?"

Suddenly fearful, Sara grabbed his arm. "What are you going to do?"

"Just what I said," Leonardo replied. "I'm going to kill the man."

Searching around the room, Leonardo found his sword and strapped it on. Although it was in good condition, it looked ungainly on the artist.

"That's your sword?"

"It was my father's."

"And you know how to use it?"

"Of course I do. Every boy must learn how to defend himself."

Ornate and cumbersome, the sword looked more like a

mantel piece than a weapon. When he walked, it almost dragged on the ground.

"Leonardo, please don't do this. It is madness," Sara pleaded.

"Yes, it is madness, perhaps. But it is something I have to do." He strode toward the door, then paused. He fished in his doublet and tossed her a bag of coins. "If I don't return, go to the stable. The man there will give you the horse and cart. He'll ask for two coins, but give him only one."

Then he was gone.

Sara sat on the bed, not knowing what to do. If she went after him, he would only send her away. She would have to wait. And pray.

An hour passed, and thoughts flew through Sara's mind. Was this the way their love would end—at swordpoint? Was this actually another life? Would she die of grief, then be reborn in the twentieth century? None of it made any sense. The more she pondered Leonardo's fate, the more depressed she became.

He couldn't die. Not this way. And not without knowing she loved him. Tears welled in her eyes. She should have told him. She should have explained how she felt.

She twisted the leather strings of the purse in her hand and felt the heat of the gold coins within. If wishing could make it so then she would give everything she owned to keep him safe.

It seemed as though hours had passed and Sara occupied herself by perusing some sketches Leonardo had secreted under the bed. Carefully, she unrolled parchment after parchment. Awed, she now saw the full extent of his genius.

He was an inventor and an artist. He had drawn sketches for the operation of a motor, pulleys, and various other devices. Like da Vinci, he was fascinated with how things worked. He'd conceived of a better, more efficient way to mill grain. One parchment revealed a crude assembly line, including the moving parts and how each would operate. Sketch after sketch delineated different types of machines. Some were complicated, while others were simply powered by a hand crank. Still others were motorized by a crude use of solar power. Sara was truly amazed. His mind was so far-reaching. No wonder he felt out of place in this time.

Systematically, she rolled each parchment and placed them back under the bed, but she was still in shock a few minutes later when the door burst open.

Leonardo stood, framed in the darkness, like a conquering hero. Springing from the bed, Sara rushed into his arms.

"Thank God!" She threw her arms around him, then drew away at the sight of blood on his shoulder.

"His, not mine," Leonardo grinned.

"What happened?"

"The bastard admitted to the deed. He said he would do it again if he had the chance. He also promised to have me beheaded and that's the last thing he said."

"Did you . . . did you kill him?"

"Fairly, but yes. He is quite dead, I assure you."

"Oh, no." Sara passed her hand over her eyes. "I knew you shouldn't have gone."

"Yes, I should have. But never mind now. We must leave immediately before the King finds out."

"The King?"

"Henry will not be happy, I fear."

"But it was a fair fight you said. He should understand that. Especially if you tell him that the man admitted to defacing your mural."

Leonardo shook his head. "I doubt that will make a difference. Guy Lemontaine was the King's favorite and a distant cousin, I am told."

"Oh God! What will he do? Put us in prison?"

Leonardo was throwing things into his satchel, then into a blanket. He stopped and laughed.

"Oh, Sara. You are so naive. Henry wouldn't waste his time by throwing us in prison."

A sense of impending doom crept up Sara's spine. "What then?"

"I imagine he'll want our heads for this."

Eight

After hurriedly packing their belongings, Leonardo and Sara left the palace. Leonardo brought his sword, his satchel of paints, and the few parchments he could stuff into the leather pouch. Sara thought it strange that all her worldly goods were bundled into a kerchief and tied to her belt. Life here was certainly more simple.

The stable was a half-mile walk from Hampton Court. When they arrived, the stabler was sitting on a bench outside enjoying the warmth of the late afternoon sun. He gave Leonardo a toothless grin.

"Ole Brownie's been waiting for ye. I'll hitch him to the cart," he said, hoisting his large frame from the bench.

Leonardo kept looking over his shoulder as if he expected to see soldiers any minute. "Hurry it up," he called after the man. "I'm anxious to get on my way before dark."

A short time later, the stabler returned leading a broken-down horse tethered to a rickety cart.

"That's Brownie?" Leonardo exclaimed.

"Aye, he's the best I have and in demand of late. I've had to turn away two who came by after you yesterday," he replied.

Leonardo exchanged a look with Sara. "I don't expect they'd seen him, though."

The stabler held out his hand, palm up. With a sigh, Leonardo dropped a coin into it.

"How far be ye going?" the man queried.

"Todd Mission."

"Ah well, the roads are good and ye've a good day for it."

They climbed into the cart and soon they were on their way. When the palace was far behind them, Sara felt relieved.

"Doesn't look like they're coming after us," she said, smiling at Leonardo.

He shrugged. "They probably haven't found Guy Lemontaine's body yet."

Sara wondered what the soldiers would do to them. Then she inwardly recoiled at the thought of facing the Commandant of the King's Guard. Leonardo was right. They would surely lose their heads.

While Brownie plodded along at a respectable pace, Sara noted familiar landmarks on the way to Todd Mission—an inn and several small farms. The late afternoon sun turned the fields to gold. Now and then she saw a shepherd returning home with his sheep.

She thought of Sophie ladling out the evening meal in the Black Boar Tavern and wondered what she would say when they arrived. It had been three weeks since Sara had been abducted. No doubt the older woman had given up hope by now.

They passed by a small stream and Leonardo allowed Brownie to drink. Preoccupied, he stared off into the distance.

"Where will you go now?" she asked.

"Back to Florence, I expect."

He turned toward her and his fingers grazed her cheek, sending tiny flames of heat throughout her body.

"I will miss you," she said.

"You could go with me. I think you would like it."

Sara smiled. "I've never been to Italy, but I know I would love it. Especially if you were there."

"Then you will come with me?"

"No, I can't." At his crestfallen look, she took his hand. "Leonardo, I've told you before, this isn't the right time for me."

"Well, I suppose you could say it isn't the right time for me either," he argued.

"That's true. But life here is especially hard on a woman. I wouldn't be able to survive long."

He had to agree that she wouldn't last long. At first, he'd thought her too fragile. Now he thought her too headstrong. She'd most likely lose her head before her health.

"How are women treated in your time?" he asked.

"In the twentieth century, a woman can be as successful as any man. She can do what she wants, say what she will. I am used to having that kind of freedom."

He frowned. "There is no freedom here for men or women."

"See, that's what I mean. Your genius is wasted on this age."

"Genius, ha! No one would agree with you."

"Because they don't understand. While you were gone, I looked at some of your inventions."

For a moment his face clouded. "I asked you not to pry. It could be very dangerous."

"Your secrets are safe with me. I'm sorry I pried, but you left me alone too long. Your work is phenomenal. The inventions and the diagrams you've produced are very advanced."

"It warms my heart that you think so, but if others saw them, I would be burned as a heretic."

She shook her head. "You're far ahead of your time."

He brought her fingers to his lips and kissed them, "I am flattered, but I do not delude myself. It seems I am fated to be here now and must suffer the consequences, whatever they may be."

The horse had finished drinking and Leonardo flicked the reins. A deep sense of sadness enveloped Sara. Leonardo was so lost here, so unappreciated, and now she would have to leave him. The closer they came to Todd's Mission, the more dejected she felt.

By the time they arrived at the outskirts of the village, the sun had disappeared, and threatening clouds gathered overhead. When they reached the Black Boar Tavern, Sara scrambled down from the wagon and ran inside while Leonardo tethered the horse.

As usual, Sophie was busy, but she stopped serving to stare at the young lad who approached her. When Sara flung off her beret, the older woman gasped.

"God's bones, Sara. You had me worried half to death. After so long a time, I feared the worst."

Sophie enveloped Sara in an enormous hug while her patrons looked on, smiling. "I would have sent you a message, but I was in hiding," Sara explained.

"So I see. I might have mistaken you for a lad. Come sit and tell me how you escaped the guard."

At that moment, Leonardo strolled in and stood behind Sara.

"Leonardo helped me," Sara said and introduced him.

Sophie was quite taken with Leonardo. She fluttered her eyelashes and lowered her bodice as if she'd never seen a man before. Irked by her friend's behavior, Sara was about to say something when Sophie hurried off to get two flagons of ale.

Leonardo didn't seem to notice Sophie's flirtatious behavior, and Sara realized that he was probably used to having women fawn over him. This realization bothered her immensely. *What would happen when she went back to Houston?* she wondered. The thought of leaving Leonardo to the mercy of other women was suddenly more abhorrent to Sara than leaving him with the King's Guard.

Sophie returned with the ale. "So you never got word to your father?" she asked. Sara shook her head. "And you never ran into Roger?"

The mention of Roger's name drew a sharp reaction from Leonardo. "Roger? Is he here, too?"

Sara placed her hand on his arm. "No, but at first I thought he might be."

Leonardo pursed his lips in thought while Sara explained what had happened since she'd left Todd Mission. Sophie listened intently, casting frequent glances at Leonardo. Sara found herself becoming exasperated and a little jealous.

After a while, Sophie jumped up to care for her customers, leaving Leonardo and Sara alone at a table near the back.

"She's a comely woman, your friend Sophie," Leonardo remarked.

"Yes, but she's too old for you," Sara blurted out before thinking.

Leonardo fixed her with a level gaze. "Well, I guess if you return to your own time, I'll have to look for someone else."

His words hit her like a blow. He *would* find someone else when she left and had a perfect right to do so. It dawned on Sara that she couldn't bear the thought of Leonardo loving another woman. Yet, at the same time, she didn't know how to prevent it.

Sophie's return cut off further conversation. She set down hollowed bread full of hot soup and two more flagons of ale. While they ate, Leonardo studied Sara.

"Tell me again what happened before you woke up here," he said.

Now that he's met Sophie, he's eager to be rid of me, Sara thought, morosely.

Again she recounted the scene at the Renaissance Festival, drinking the mead and searching for the bathroom.

"Was there anything unusual about that night?"

Sara thought for a moment. "Well, there was a lot of lightning."

"Lightning?"

"Yes, the clouds were very dark and there was lightning in the distance. It looked like it might storm soon."

He withdrew some parchment and a pencil from his satchel, then wrote something down. "What else? What were you wearing?"

"The red skirt and white blouse, exactly as you first saw me."

He smiled, obviously remembering his first glimpse of her. "Nothing else unusual?"

"There is one thing. I was wearing a pair of amethyst earrings." Reaching in her purse she withdrew the one she had left. "When I woke up, one of them was gone."

Leonardo laid his pencil down and took the earring from her. He examined it very carefully, holding it before the candlelight. "Some stones are very powerful. I am told that amethysts recall the past. I wonder—"

"That's what she said!" Sara exclaimed, excitedly.

"Who?"

"The woman who sold me the earrings. She said, 'Amethysts recall the past.' "

"Then the earrings must be the key," Leonardo said.

Sara's shoulders sagged. "But I only have one. I lost the other."

Leonardo continued to study the earring, holding it to the light, turning it this way and that. "It's wonderful. Have you noticed how it catches the light just so?"

Sara was beside herself. If the amethysts were the mechanism by which she traveled, she would need them both to return. "It is beautiful, I know. But I don't have the other one. It won't work unless I have both, will it?"

He thought for a moment, then shook his head. "Let's look for the other."

Sara led the way outside to the oak tree where she awakened three weeks earlier. Glancing at her watch, she noticed that it was only five-ten and the date still indicated it was the first of October.

"Do you think time could be different here? It sounds crazy, but my watch says that only six hours have passed since I walked outside at the Renaissance Festival."

Leonardo was searching around the base of the tree. "I have always thought that time might be relative—that two or more events might be occurring simultaneously, but our perception places them in the past, present, or future. Your presence here is proof that time is not necessarily linear as some presume."

They searched around the ground and all along the pathway back into the Black Boar, but they found nothing. Though it grew dark, they stayed to make sure they had not overlooked the amethyst earring. Reluctantly, they trudged back into the tavern when they could no longer see.

Dejected, Sara sat at the table they had vacated earlier. Leonardo sat beside her and took her hand. "Would it be so terrible if you had to stay here with me?"

Tears welled in her eyes. "No, that's the worst part about it all. I really don't want to leave you."

"Of course, there's Roger back in Houston."

"My whole life is back in Houston,"

Sophie's patrons had slowly drifted out and she came back over to their table. "I expect you'll be staying the night," she said. "Sara, you can stay with me. I've a vacant room down the hall for you, Leonardo."

"Sara and I will stay together," Leonardo declared to Sara's astonishment. "We've been sleeping together every night for several weeks. I don't know why that should change now."

Sophie's mouth dropped open. "I beg pardon, sir. I didn't know."

Sara was embarrassed and couldn't imagine what her friend must think. However, at the same time, she secretly gloated. Leonardo had unmistakably laid claim to her. Warmth spread through her, settling in the pit of her stomach.

With a lighted candle, Sophie led the way upstairs to a

room down the hall from her own. When Leonardo dropped a gold coin in her palm, she gave a knowing smile. "You'll have your privacy here," she said. "There's no one else about tonight." Then she set down the candle and left them alone.

Sara unpacked the contents of her kerchief and wondered why she'd brought the red skirt along. It had caused no end of trouble. Yet, had it not been for the red skirt, she would never have met Leonardo. She smiled, thinking how her life had changed so dramatically.

The skirt was wrinkled. When she shook it, something dropped onto the floor.

"My earring! It must have caught in the hem of my skirt!" she exclaimed.

Then her gaze locked with Leonardo's. The certain knowledge of what must be hung in the air like a veil that had dropped between them. She'd found the other earring and now she would have to return. Filled with an indefinable sadness, she sank onto the bed.

Leonardo picked up the earring where it lay on the floor and held it up to the light of the flickering candle. Purple lights danced in the stone. He could feel the energy of the amethyst in his palm and, instinctively, he knew they had found the mechanism that brought Sara here.

Contemplating life without her, he felt a hollow, nagging loneliness. The amber light of her eyes had filled his vision over the last few weeks, obscuring all else. Without her, the future looked bleak and dismal. She would take away the sun.

A war of sorts went on within him. He could tell her he had been wrong, that he had no idea how she came here or how to get her back. But he would not keep her here against her will. Nor would he make love to her until she gave herself freely. Sadly, he realized it would not be in this life.

Oh, Sara. How can I let you go? And how can I go on without you?

He looked at her sitting on the bed. She had the forlorn, dejected look of a lost child. Deep love filled his heart and he knew he had to let her go. He loved her far too much to make her stay.

The sound of distant thunder drew him to the window. A storm was brewing. Lightning flashed in the distance. Instinctively, he knew that all the elements had to be right for the mechanism to work. Tonight might be the night. Still, he hesitated.

One moment more with her would have to last him a lifetime.

Sara heard the distant thunder and also knew. Soon she would have to leave. Moonlight poured through the window slit, haloing around Leonardo's reddish-gold hair. It glanced off his fair skin and the even planes of his face. She found herself memorizing each line, every detail of his face and body as if she would never see it again.

"Kiss me," she asked.

He came to her, enfolding her in his arms. His lips claimed hers in a gentle, insistent kiss. Willingly she melted against him as he deepened the kiss. More than anything, she wanted him to make love to her. Now. Tonight.

His fingers threaded in her hair, tightening as if he meant to possess her long, red-brown tresses. If he could bind her to him, perhaps she would stay.

She wound her arms around his neck, savoring the masculine scent of linseed oil that still clung to him. Her eyes fluttered closed.

"I want you, Sara." His voice was a rasp that echoed through her head. "But we won't make love unless you want it as much as I."

Sara kissed his cheek, his eyelids, the crisp hairs on the sides of his face. The desire she felt for Leonardo was unlike anything she'd ever known or dreamed.

"Say it," he demanded.

"I want it as much as you do," she whispered.

She reached for the laces of his jerkin when a loud clamor below froze her hand inches away from his chest. Leonardo broke away from her and moved to the window.

Moments later, Sophie rapped softly on the door. "It's the King's Guard," she choked out. "Hurry out the back door. I'll waylay them as long as I can. I vow this time they won't be lenient."

Leonardo grabbed Sara by the hand and they raced down the stairs, tiptoeing through the darkened inn to the back door. Loud pounding goaded them on until they were safely outside.

Thunder growled threateningly and lightning flashed through the distant trees. Sara looked up, remembering that day not long ago. "That's strange," she said.

"Strange, indeed. Where is your earring?" Leonardo asked.

"Here," she answered, withdrawing it from her purse.

"Put them on," he ordered, handing her the mate.

Quickly she put both earrings on and looked at him, quizzically. "I don't feel anything," she said. "It's not working."

Loud shouting emanated from the inn. Sophie had let the soldiers inside. They had very little time left.

"If I am right, this is where we say good-bye, Sara," Leonardo said, his green eyes filled with tears.

Good-bye is so final, she thought, moved by the emotion she saw in his face.

"I realize now that I've dreamed about you all my life," he told her. "Yours is the face I did not believe existed. Every time I look at you, my heart bleeds. Now that I've found you, I cannot have you."

Sara shook her head, tears welling in her eyes. "Please, don't . . ."

"Give me one kiss, my darling. It will have to last forever."

Inside the Black Boar, Sophie screamed when someone hit her. Sara winced, torn between the desire to help her friend and that of going home. "I don't think I can leave you," she said.

"Sara, sweet sweet Sara," he whispered. Beneath the oak tree, he gathered her into his arms for one last kiss.

His mouth closed over hers and she clung to him tightly. Thunder like a cannon shot exploded behind them, lightning cracked over their heads, and the oak tree swayed, showering them with leaves, but neither noticed. A light rain fell all around and the mist of a cloud enveloped them. Against Sara's cheek the amethysts shimmered, emitting a strange, comforting warmth that radiated to Leonardo. Energy spiraled around and through them in a dizzying dance.

Locked in a magical embrace, they were only vaguely aware of subtle changes—the waning moon, the distant movement of the tide, the last glow of a dying star. The faraway sound of a church bell mingled with a choir, colors intertwined like the ribbons of a maypole, children laughed, babies cried, seasons changed.

Leonardo pulled away from her, a little dazed. The intensity of the feelings he'd just experienced was overwhelming. It was as if he'd just returned home after a long absence. Sara was still here and no doubt the parting kiss had impeded her progress. Moving even a step away from her wrenched his heart, but now he could put off the inevitable no longer. It was time for her to leave and he couldn't bear to see her go.

Drawing his sword, he prepared to reenter the inn. "Sara, stay by the tree. At any minute, you will be returned to your own time and you will be out of this."

"What are you going to do?" she demanded to know.

"I will end this thing, once and for all," he said, striding to the door.

"No, Leonardo! You'll be killed! I won't let you," she cried. She hurried after him and clutched his sleeve.

"Stay!" he ordered. "You won't be safe with me."

Tears streamed down her face as she threw her arms around him. He was about to forcibly return her to the oak when he noticed the tree was different somehow. The sky above was devoid of clouds and stars sparkled overhead. Strange.

Loud laughter drew his attention to the Black Boar and he rushed through the door. Immediately overcome by the smoke, he staggered back against the wall.

"Whoa, buddy," a man said. "Better put that thing away. Might hurt somebody."

"Where's the Commandant?" Leonardo shouted. "Tell him I'm here. He need look no further."

"This place is a gas," the man commented to the girl sitting next to him.

"Maybe there'll be a sword fight," the girl giggled.

Leonardo started to charge through the room, but Sara was right behind him and caught his arm.

"They're not here. We're not there," she said.

"What? Where's Sophie?"

"Leonardo, we're in Texas. I came back and you came back with me."

Leonardo dropped his sword, his face white with shock. A passing waitress bent down, picked it up, and handed it to Leonardo. "I hope you've had a tetanus shot. This thing looks like it's seen better days."

Sara blinked and noticed the waitress was right. The sword was rusty and slightly bent. It looked like something Don Quixote would have worn. But she couldn't dwell on that. Right now she was concerned with getting them out of this place before something else happened.

Still in shock, Leonardo sheathed his sword and allowed Sara to lead him up to the bar. The bartender looked nothing like Sophie. Her brown hair was short and curly.

Leonardo had recovered his composure somewhat and was staring at the electric lights overhead.

"Did anyone leave a message for me? My name is Sara Carlyle—"

"Holy shit! You're Sara Carlyle? We've had the police and everyone in here looking for you. Your boyfriend left here about an hour ago, hopping mad. Said he's going to file a lawsuit. The boss is down at the office talking to the King right now."

"The King?" Leonardo repeated.

"Not that king," Sara told him.

"Where were you all that time?" the bartender asked.

"You don't want to know," Sara told her. "But tell your boss everything will be all right."

The bartender, whose name was Jodie, offered them a free glass of mead, but Sara politely declined. If she never drank another glass of mead in her life, she wouldn't miss it.

Sara could think of nothing but leaving. However, they made slow progress to the gate. Leonardo was distracted by the lights, the food, and the minstrels. He stopped to admire a woman painting designs on a little girl's face.

"Why are you doing that?" he asked the artist.

"Because it looks pretty," she replied.

Sara had to drag him away. "We have to catch a bus or something back to Houston. The Festival is about to close," she said.

"This is a wonderful place," he rhapsodized. "I love Houston."

Like a child, his eyes glowed bright green with wonder. Frustrated, Sara was forced to take a deep breath and go slowly. They passed the booths she and Roger had visited. Though it had been only a few hours, it felt like ages had passed since then. Oddly, they passed the place where they'd bought the amethyst earrings, but she couldn't find the shop.

"There was a jewelry shop right there. What happened to it?" she asked an artisan sitting outside his booth.

"There wasn't a jewelry shop here. Just me and the candle maker," he replied.

"But I bought some earrings there," she protested.

The man only shrugged. Leonardo tugged her arm and they were off in another direction, before she could question him further.

"I can't believe it," Leonardo shouted, twirling around, his arms upraised. "Everywhere I look, there is something new."

Sara couldn't believe it either. By now she was completely lost and had to consult a program to find the exit. She studied it intently until a blood-curdling whoop rent the air, causing her to drop the booklet.

Leonardo! Where is he? Glancing around, she saw a number of people standing anxiously around the merry-go-round. Sara elbowed her way through the crowd.

"What's that guy doing?" a woman asked her husband.

"Who knows? Maybe he's drunk."

Sara gasped. Leonardo was on his back beneath the carousel, probably trying to determine how it worked, she assumed. There was just enough space for his slender form, but his presence obviously made all the parents anxious.

"Leonardo, get out from under there. It could be dangerous!" she cautioned.

"Sara, come have a look! It's marvelous. I can crawl all the way over to the motor!"

"No, don't do that! Please! Look at all these people!"

He seemed to notice the crowd for the first time and he waved.

"Is he drunk or just plain crazy?" a woman asked Sara.

Shrugging, Sara gave a feeble smile. He was like a loose cannon that might explode at any minute. Then the full force of what had happened suddenly hit her. She had brought Leonardo into this life with her and he was not at all prepared. But then, neither was she.

Oh, my God! she thought. *What have I done!*

Nine

After much talking, Sara bribed a tour bus driver to drop them at FM 1960 and the Tomball Parkway. Then, before they boarded, she hastily placed a call to her brother Sam.

"Sara, where've you been? Roger came home without you. He called the police and—"

"Sam, I was lost. I'll explain everything when I see you, okay? Just pick me up at Willowbrook Mall."

Though Sam agreed to pick her up, Sara knew he'd demand some answers. She hadn't mentioned Leonardo, nor did she have any idea how she would explain where she'd been. Who would believe she'd just spent three weeks in the Renaissance at the court of King Henry the VIII? Or that she'd met a Florentine artist at Hampton Court and brought him with her? Everyone would think her insane.

As they boarded the bus along with others who had attended the festival, people smiled indulgently at them. They were in costume. No one seemed to mind that Leonardo's sword hit them in the knee, but the novelty would eventually wear off. The Renaissance Festival would soon be over. And what would they do then?

Never in her imagination had Sara considered this turn of events. She assumed that since she went back in time, she would eventually come forward, then resume her life as before. It did not occur to her that Leonardo would or could come with her. But here he was, and she was totally unprepared. It was still Saturday, October 1, 1996, but in the space of five hours, everything had changed.

Since she had brought Leonardo with her, she felt responsible for him. After all, he offered help when she needed it. The difference between their situations was immediately apparent. Leonardo loved it here and had no intention of going back. Ever.

Naturally, he was enthralled with the bus. To the irritation of the two women behind them, he pulled down the window and stuck his head out. A blast of chilly wind blew through the compartment.

"My hair!" one woman cried at the sudden rush of air.

"Oh, sorry," he said. "Your hair looks lovely."

The woman dimpled coquettishly and patted her well-coiffed graying head. "Well, thank you."

To Sara's embarrassment, Leonardo crawled under the seats, examined the overhead compartments, and made several trips to the front of the bus.

"He acts like he's never ridden a bus before. Is he a foreigner?" one lady asked.

"Very," Sara nodded.

On orders from the driver, Leonardo finally settled back in his seat. "You really can't do that sort of thing," Sara cautioned him.

"I can't? Why not?"

"People don't understand. They'll think you're strange."

"But I *am* strange. I don't know that I can hide that."

"Well, you'll have to do better than this, Leonardo. Why don't you just let me direct you, and I'll try to explain things as we go along."

He seemed to accept that idea and Sara relaxed a little. Leonardo was like a rambunctious child. Everything was new and different. Sara couldn't really blame him for being intrigued by this new world, but she was afraid his curiosity would get him into trouble. He had so much to learn.

Overwhelmed, Sara stared bleakly out the window. Of

course, she would be his teacher and this new role might change their relationship. The task ahead seemed formidable. She would have to set limits on a brilliant, inquiring genius. But it was for his own good. He could be dangerous.

For the remainder of the trip, Leonardo entertained the two ladies behind them by sketching their pictures then giving them each a drawing. They were completely smitten.

Not everyone would be so easily won over, Sara thought— her brother, for instance.

Sam was waiting for them when they arrived at the mall and cast a questioning glance at his sister and her oddly-dressed companion.

His mouth curved into a wry smile. He was a tall, masculine version of Sara with the same reddish hair and hazel eyes. "I thought you said you were lost. Were you lost by yourself or did you have company?"

"I can explain, Sam," she assured him.

Explain? There was no way.

"Are you from the Renaissance Festival?" Sam asked Leonardo.

Leonardo frowned, thinking. "In a manner of speaking. But we don't call it the Renaissance."

"Really? What *do* you call it?" Sam thought he was kidding and probably expected a smart reply.

"We don't call it anything."

"Sam, this is Leonardo Brazzi," Sara quickly interjected. "He's from Florence, Italy."

"Oh." Now Sam understood. "They must have imported him."

"Yes, they imported him," Sara agreed. "He's a very fine artist."

"Great! How long will you be here?"

Leonardo glanced at Sara and shrugged. "It's difficult to say. I don't even know for certain how I got here."

Sara laughed, self-consciously. "He means it's been a

whirlwind of activity. They really have kept him busy out there."

Sam led the way to the car and cast a sidelong glance at Sara. "You certainly know a lot about him. You know Sara, I don't like to interfere in your business, but I think Roger ought to know you're safe."

"I'll have to call him," she said with a weak smile.

Sara sat in the front seat opposite her brother. Leonardo leaned up against the seat, intently observing Sam insert the key in the ignition and start the motor. When the motor roared into life, the artist clapped.

"Wonderful," he said. "Absolutely wonderful. Tell me, where is the thing that makes it go?"

Backing up, Sam looked at Leonardo warily. "Do you mean the motor?"

"Yes, the motor. Where is it?"

"It's under the hood. Where did you think it would be?"

Again Sara jumped to the rescue. "It could be in the trunk, Sam. He's from a small village. They only have Volkswagens there."

Sara was so nervous, she chewed her nails—something she hadn't done in years. Would she have to field answers indefinitely? If so, she would soon lose her mind.

Though he gave Leonardo a cautious glance, Sam accepted his sister's explanation and shrugged.

"You speak English well."

"I had no choice. I spent two years at Hampton court."

"It's a beautiful place. What were you doing there?"

"Restoration," Sara said. "He was working on a mural there."

They drove for a while in silence. Then at a stop sign, Sam once again addressed Leonardo. "Where can I drop you? Do you have a hotel or something?"

Sara had developed a headache over the last few blocks. Now it pounded at her temples. "He's going to stay at my place tonight."

"Your place?" Sam stopped the car in the middle of the street.

Someone honked at them and he continued on.

"For tonight. Then tomorrow we'll make other arrangements. He doesn't know anyone in town. I just feel sorry for him." She held out her palms as if she were taking in a lost puppy.

"Uh huh," Sam said, pursing his lips. "Right."

They drove to the Memorial area of town where Sara had a townhouse overlooking the bayou. Sara got out and walked around to kiss her brother. Sam sat staring straight ahead.

"Thanks, Sam."

"You know how this looks," he said.

"It's not what you think."

"Yeah? What do you think I think? What would anybody think?"

"I'm just helping him out, okay?"

"Okay. You're a big girl, Sara. I've already told Mom and Roger that you're all right. You might give them both a call when you can."

Sara nodded and waved as Sam pulled away. Her brother hadn't believed a word of what she said. Deflated, she felt as if she'd just run a marathon. At least she was home.

Leonardo stood looking up at the street light, fascinated. She motioned him over. Opening the door to the townhouse, she switched on the lights. A simple act that she had taken for granted for years plunged him into a delighted frenzy. While Sara followed helplessly behind him, he went through every room switching on the lights, turning them off then on again.

"This is wonderful," he exclaimed. "Dark, light. Light, dark. You know, when you told me what life was like, I really didn't believe you. But it's all true. It's all true!"

Yes, it's all true. Sara passed her hand over her eyes. Her head was throbbing now. Maybe if she could take a warm shower and get some sleep, she could face tomorrow. Maybe.

Leonardo could not contain his joy. Not only had he eluded certain death, but he was now in a time that had heretofore existed only in his mind. Powered vehicles, lights that worked by a magical flick of the wrist, water that came from a spout! It was all too marvelous for words. For a while, he was lost in the wonder of it all, but then he realized Sara was unhappy.

She followed him nervously as she would a small child, with a continual frown on her face.

"It's all right Sara," he told her. "I must see how things work."

She shook her head. "You don't understand your surroundings. I'm afraid you will get hurt."

Her deep sigh told him there was more than that. It was as if she were sorry he'd come with her.

Soon he realized how much he did not know and Sara couldn't hide her displeasure. She'd showed him her bedroom. When she left to make some tea, he'd relieved himself in a vase that to him looked like a chamber pot. Of course she'd laughed about that. It was an old vase anyway, she said. Later she'd demonstrated the use of a device she called a toilet. Next, he'd opened a window, only to find that the air was already cooled for him.

She'd shown him how to operate a shower and he thought he understood. But, unable to stop the water, he'd flooded the room. He could tell she didn't like that.

What bothered him most was the change in her attitude. She treated him like a guest, like a stranger who had unexpectedly dropped in for a visit. This he did not understand. For weeks, they'd shared a room, eaten all meals together, and worked side by side. Now she expected him to sleep alone in a strange world all by himself.

"I think you'll be comfortable here," she said, showing him her guest bedroom.

"I'd rather sleep with you. We've been sleeping together for weeks now and I've gotten used to it."

"We have not been sleeping together!" she protested a little too stridently. "We've been in the same room, that's all."

"That's all?"

"Well, I mean—it's different here."

"Why different? Because of Roger?"

"Yes and no."

"Yes and no? What does that mean? In Italian, we say yes or we say no. We don't have something that means both."

"It's hard to explain, Leonardo. I'm tired. Let's talk about it in the morning. Good night," she said and kissed him on the cheek.

After Sara left Leonardo lay alone in the dark room with cold, refrigerated air blowing on him from a little grate in the ceiling. His mind imagined the cool air going through little tunnels into hundreds of homes like Sara's. *What type of power supply could accomplish such a feat?* he wondered. The mere thought of a giant power source mitigating air to people made him claustrophobic. When he could stand it no longer, he tiptoed to the window. Opening it, he drew in a deep breath of fresh air. The night sounds soothed his spirit. It wasn't such a strange world after all, he decided. Perhaps he would even learn to like it here.

Sara took a long, cleansing shower, washing off the grime of the last three weeks. Over and over again she soaped, reveling in the warmth of the water, the smell of shower gel, and real shampoo. The soap she'd been forced to use at Hampton Court had taken the oil from her hair, but she'd never felt clean.

Wrapped in a warm terrycloth robe, she tiptoed by the guest room and climbed into bed. Tired as she was, she couldn't sleep. She kept thinking of Leonardo, wondering if he was all right. Finally, she drifted off into a troubled sleep and awakened early. Drawing on her robe and slippers, she wandered into the kitchen. She was not in a good mood.

While making coffee and toasting English muffins, she thought again of Leonardo. What was she going to do with him? He couldn't live with her. Her family would be appalled. Not to mention Roger. Suddenly, she remembered that she'd forgotten to call Roger last night. "Oh, no!" she said aloud.

She realized this was the first time she'd thought about her fiancé in weeks, and that troubled her. While she made coffee, she imagined what she would say to him. Leonardo's presence in her townhouse would be difficult to explain. She popped two English muffins into the oven and was still pondering her dilemma when Leonardo walked into the small kitchen.

He had stripped to the waist and wore only his form-fitting tights. She couldn't help noticing how well they hugged his lean hips and buttocks. He caught her staring at his chest and she turned away, embarrassed.

"Would you like some coffee?"

"Coffee? Henry served coffee at court, but I never had a cup. It smells good."

In an instant he was at her side, inspecting the coffee-maker, poking his finger in the grounds, peering in the water reservoir to see what made the device work.

Sara sighed and shook her head. She reminded herself he'd only been here one day. She couldn't expect him to adjust overnight—everything was still new and wonderful. It was fun to watch his green eyes light up with pleasure at each discovery he made.

He followed her to the oven and rapturously inspected the heating coils. Sticking his hand inside, he burned his finger, but didn't seem to mind.

"Everything is run by electricity," Sara explained.

"Everything? Why? Is there no fuel left?"

"Not much, I'm afraid."

"No wood?"

"We don't use wood for fuel at all now. Anyway, electricity is more efficient and clean."

She did her best to explain how electricity worked. Leonardo took in every word. Lost in thought, he accepted the English muffin and lathered it with a low-calorie spread. "The butter tastes rancid," he commented, "but I like the coffee."

"That's not butter," Sara corrected, picking up the plastic tub.

"If it's not butter, what is it?"

"It's called margarine. It's supposed to be better for you, but I must confess that I don't know what's in it. I agree it doesn't taste as good as butter."

Sara showed him all the kitchen gadgets and demonstrated how they worked. Fascinated, they had to open several cans of fruit before Leonardo was satisfied. She put another English muffin in the toaster and he was thoroughly amused when, seconds later, it popped up, completely browned. Sara laughed and hugged him affectionately. Just knowing him was an adventure in itself.

They enjoyed a leisurely Sunday morning, drinking coffee and looking at the paper. Leonardo wanted to know all about the government.

"Is this a picture of your president?" He pointed to a political cartoon.

"Yes. It's funny, isn't it?"

"Won't the artist lose his head for that?"

"Oh, no. I told you we have complete freedom here. Anyone can say or draw whatever they want."

Leonardo rolled his eyes. "Complete freedom. How wonderful!" He propped his feet up on an ottoman and sighed deeply. "You know what Sara? I think I'm going to like it here," he said.

Sara smiled and was about to respond when the doorbell

rang. Pulling her robe around her, she hurried over to the tiled entryway.

Roger, dressed in starched gray chinos and a blue oxford shirt, stood waiting outside the door, hands on hips. His blue eyes flashed. "I expected you to call me last night," he said. "Sam was a little foggy—said you were lost or something. At least you could have called me to let me know you got home safely."

Though she felt a little guilty, she looked up at him and shrugged. "I'm sorry, Roger. Honestly, I was too tired last night. I was going to call you this morning. I just hadn't had a chance," Sara offered.

The truth sounded like a lame excuse and Roger obviously didn't like it. He pushed past her into the small kitchen where Leonardo sat.

"What's he doing here?" Roger asked Sara.

"I can explain, Roger. The Renaissance Festival was about to close and we—"

"Now I understand why you didn't call." Roger's voice was cool and disdainful.

"No, you don't understand. He had no place to go, so I said he could stay with me."

"How nice of you. Who the hell are you?" Roger demanded. Roger's gaze took in Leonardo's bare chest and form-fitting tights. "Are you some kind of a dancer or what?"

Leonardo rose and leveled a green look at his rival. "I am Leonardo Brazzi, an artist. And I know who you are."

The instant animosity between the two men charged the very air with electricity. It was as if they hated one another on sight.

"Oh, really?" Roger's voice was brittle. "Then you know I am Sara's fiancé."

"I know you *were* Sara's fiancé. But that may have changed."

"What?" Roger barked out the question like an angry dog and circled the table.

Fear knotted Sara's stomach. "Stop it!" She tried to interpose herself between them, but Roger moved in front of her.

"Roger, Leonardo is my friend. He is new in town and he is staying with me until he can find his own place."

Roger's frosty gaze was riveted on Sara. "We're engaged. How am I supposed to react to that?"

She gave a deep sigh. "I don't know, but that's just the way it is."

"Sara, you're behaving strangely. First, you just disappear at the Renaissance Festival. Then you suddenly have a roommate. Next you'll be taking stray dogs off the street, and I'm just supposed to accept that?"

"Stray dogs?" Leonardo thumped Roger on the chest. "Perhaps you'd better watch your language. I am told that women are free to do what they want here."

"Get your hands off me!" Roger slapped Leonardo's hand away. "I want you out of here right now!"

"Roger!" Sara shouted.

"You get out!" Leonardo returned. "I was here first!"

Roger lunged at Leonardo and the two of them rolled over the table and onto the floor, locked in a desperate struggle. Panicked, Sara tried to wrench them apart, to no avail. They rolled into the living room and Roger dragged Leonardo to his feet, his hands clamping around the artist's neck. Then Leonardo broke his hold and drove his fist into Roger's eye. Grunting furiously, Roger lunged at Leonardo and again they tumbled over the couch, narrowly missing the flagstone fireplace. When Roger reached for a poker, Sara screamed. Leonardo seized the opportunity to knock it out of his rival's grasp.

They're going to kill each other, Sara thought, her heart in her throat. She ran to call the police.

They were still at it when she returned. Quickly she filled

a pitcher full of cold water and poured it over them. The water startled them for a moment, and Leonardo laughed in surprise. After the brief pause, Roger lunged at him again.

"Bring me my sword, Sara," Leonardo ordered.

"I will not. You must both stop. Right now!"

They were beyond hearing. When the police came a few minutes later, Leonardo had Roger by the throat and his eyes were bulging out.

The officers broke them apart.

"Arrest this man!" Roger demanded, hoarsely. "He tried to kill me."

While one officer guarded the combatants, the other filled out a report. "We'll have to take you both down to the station."

"No, please," Sara protested. "This has all been a terrible misunderstanding. I don't want to file charges."

"All right, ma'am. We'll write this up as a domestic dispute. Next time, we'll have to arrest them."

After the policemen left, Roger sat on the couch, fuming. Finally, he rose to leave.

"I want him out of here tomorrow, Sara!" Roger said, holding an ice pack to the black eye Leonardo had given him.

Leonardo folded his arms across his chest. "Next time, I may have to kill you," the artist informed him.

"I take that as a threat. Sara, you're my witness. If this man even so much as comes near me again, I'll have him thrown in jail."

Something in Roger's furious gaze reminded Sara of Guy Lemontaine. *Yet how could that be?* she wondered. *Guy was dead.*

Sara walked Roger to the door. He turned and narrowed his gaze at her. "Do you have anything to say?"

"No, Roger, I don't," she answered.

"I see," he said. "Well, if you should come to your senses, you know where to find me."

He stalked out and Sara closed the door with a deep sigh. Walking back into her living room, she had second thoughts. She was engaged to marry the man and owed him an explanation. But he had acted abominably—like some animal. Of course, Leonardo had too.

She picked up pillows, replaced the fireplace poker, and as she cleaned up the remains of their breakfast in the kitchen, she grew angry. *The nerve! Both of them!*

She found Leonardo out on the terrace, his arms still folded across his chest.

"Well? Are you going to say anything?" she asked.

"Yes," he replied. "Roger is certainly not the right man for you."

Sara shook her head in astonishment. "That is an interesting comment, considering the fact that you behaved no better than he just now."

He waved away her comment as if it meant nothing. "That was bound to happen."

She moved in front of him and placed her hands on his shoulders. "We don't settle disagreements in this way, Leonardo."

"Oh, really? You didn't see me fighting alone, did you? Some things cannot change, even with the passage of time."

"You provoked that fight," she accused.

"You have two suitors, Sara. There was bound to be a fight of some sort. And if he returns, I am sure it will be worse for him."

Sara held up her hands. "No, no. You'll go to jail for that, don't you see?"

"I see no other solution."

Sara's hands began to shake and her lip trembled. She had brought a mad, impulsive genius into this life and she couldn't control him.

Leonardo had no idea of how things worked in this age,

and suddenly she wasn't sure she'd have the energy to instruct him. It would take too long and too much. Also, she wasn't entirely sure he would even listen. Now, because she felt sorry for him, she had probably ruined her whole life. Could she salvage her relationship with Roger after this? She didn't know, but she felt it the only sane move she could make under the circumstances. "Leonardo, I'm going to marry Roger."

The artist gave her an innocent smile. "Not if he's dead."

Ten

Though compelled to help Leonardo, Sara still felt an obligation to Roger. After all, they were engaged. But since the Renaissance Festival, everything had changed and her feelings fluctuated. One moment she thought she should marry Roger, then she looked in Leonardo's eyes and was lost. Bewildered, she did not know what to do. Was Leonardo a figment of her imagination? Could they have a relationship? She was terribly afraid to fall in love, afraid that he might not be here tomorrow. Her worst fear was that she might suddenly awaken to find she had only been dreaming.

If it was a dream, however, the dream was convincingly real. Leonardo and Roger instantly hated each other and must be kept a safe distance apart. If the two were to meet again, one of them would be killed and it would be her fault.

She kept wondering why her world had been turned upside down. Had she come back alone, her life would have gone on as before. She would be planning her wedding with Roger. Leonardo's presence here forced her down a new path. She could no longer see her way clearly. Each step was a complete surprise.

At noon, Sara's mother called to invite her to Sunday dinner.

"Please bring your friend along," her mother said tactfully.

"All right," Sara agreed, realizing Sam had already told her mother about Leonardo.

She wondered what her mother would think of him, then realized he had nothing to wear but a pair of tights and his jerkin. He might as well have pierced ears and a tattoo.

"We have to go shopping," she told him.

They dressed hurriedly and were soon on their way to the nearest mall. Leonardo was fascinated with all the buttons on the dashboard of Sara's car. Punching them one by one, he opened the sun roof, activated the windshield wipers, and turned on the CD player.

"You could live in your car," he announced gleefully.

"I suppose I could." She smiled at him, thinking how original and fresh his observations were. Being with him was like looking at the world through new eyes. She loved to see his eyes light up when he discovered something new. His low, gritty laugh was infectious.

In his Renaissance costume, Leonardo immediately attracted attention in the department store. Sara had worked out a speech explaining that Leonardo worked at the Renaissance Festival. Since his bags had been lost on the flight from Italy, he needed a few clothes. The salesmen easily accepted her explanation, but she didn't really like to lie. Inwardly, she questioned how long she could keep up the facade.

Sara quickly selected chinos, jeans, and slacks and matched them with plaid and denim shirts. Underwear, socks and shoes, and a wool blazer completed a wardrobe sufficient for almost any event in Houston. While Leonardo changed in the dressing room, she charged the purchases on her credit card.

Moments later, when he emerged in a blue work shirt and jeans, Sara simply stared at Leonardo. He looked like a model who had stepped off a magazine page. With chiseled features, broad shoulders, and trim waist and hips, he was truly handsome.

"How do I look?" he asked.

Sara couldn't reply for a moment. "Great. You look great," she had to admit.

She continued casting furtive glances at him, not believing what she saw. *God, he's good-looking,* she thought. *The clothes look like they were made for him. Could stepping into another century be as easy as changing clothes?* she wondered. Again, she felt a twinge of fear. What if he were suddenly drawn back to his own age? But she wouldn't allow herself to think about that possibility. He was here and so was she. All anyone really had, she reminded herself, was this moment.

They just had time to drop their purchases at the townhouse. Before leaving again for her parents' house, Sara showed Leonardo how to put his hair into a pony tail.

"All the guys wear their hair like this," she said, pulling the freshly washed reddish-blond hair into an elastic band. The feel of his hair, thick and wavy in her hand, excited her. Running her fingers through it, she marveled at the weight of it and smoothed it neatly back.

"I like it," he said. "It stays out of my eyes."

Sara changed into a pair of black slacks and light jacket. Quickly she ran a brush through her hair and applied lipstick, then they hurried back out to the car.

As they drove out of the parking lot, Leonardo touched her hand. "What will your parents think of me?" he asked.

"I don't know," she replied, honestly. "I told you my father hasn't been well so I'm not sure how he will react. My mother is a different story. We'll have to wait and see."

The house was less than a mile away. Soon they pulled into the tree-lined circular drive of the Carlyle house and Leonardo gave a low chuckle. "Your family lives in a castle! Why don't you live here with them?"

"When I was younger I lived here, but now I like having my own place. I enjoy the freedom of living alone."

Leonardo looked at her strangely, then shrugged.

The sprawling red brick house was fronted by a broad

porch in the style of an old plantation house. Huge potted mums in yellow and gold were on either side of the white double doors. Sara rang the bell.

Sam answered. "C'mon in," he said, nodding curtly to Leonardo.

Leonardo was awestruck. Stepping into the entry hall, he gazed up at a sweeping staircase leading to the upper floor and the huge cut-glass chandelier above. Sara watched his green eyes take in the details of the crown molding and the floor-to-ceiling windows. With his swift, assessing gaze, he missed nothing. He ran his fingers along the textured wallpaper and stopped to admire a painting on one wall.

"Mom and Dad are in the study," Sam said.

Sara took Leonardo's arm, gently urging him ahead of her into the cozy paneled study. Bookshelves filled with books and mementos were on every wall except one where a cheery fire burned in a huge fireplace. In front of it were a couch and two wing-back chairs.

"Hi, Mom." Sara went over to a wing-back chair and gave her mother a kiss. "I'd like you to meet my friend, Leonardo Brazzi."

A small, sprightly woman in her early sixties, Sara's mother wore her graying hair atop her head in a little bun. Dressed in white slacks and a white silk blouse, she looked perfect, as always. Reading glasses, her only concession to age besides her hair, hung neatly on a gold chain around her neck.

"I'm so glad you could come," Kathryn Carlyle said. "Sam tells me you have just come over from Italy."

"I am from Florence. But I've been living in England for two years."

"Oh, really? How interesting."

Sara's father sat at his desk across the room. Once tall and robust with a full shock of white hair, Ben Carlyle had shrunk over the past year. The pale flesh hung on his slender frame, and his bright blue eyes had dulled. From time to time, Sara had noticed a flicker of light. Right now, he studied them intently.

"Dad? How are you feeling, Dad?" Sara asked.

He made some unintelligible reply.

As they made their way over to him, Sara frowned, trying to understand. Leonardo frowned too.

"Dad, I've brought a friend to dinner. This is Leonardo Brazzi from Italy."

Leonardo leaned closer, straining to hear when her father said something else. Then the artist smiled warmly and stretched out his hand. Ben Carlyle took it, pumping it up and down.

"I am pleased to meet you," Leonardo said.

The older man beamed and nodded.

Sara was a little surprised at her father's response to Leonardo. He seemed to like him immediately. Ben continued to hold the artist's hand and uttered several more garbled phrases.

Sara shook her head. "Dad has lost the ability to communicate," she explained to Leonardo. "The doctors can't explain it. He acts like he's talking, but we don't understand a single thing he says."

Leonardo seemed not to hear her, concentrating instead on her father. He bent over and said something in Italian. At that, Ben Carlyle smiled and patted Leonardo's hand.

"I think he likes you," Sara said. "What did you say just then?"

"I told him not to worry."

"Why did you speak in Italian?"

"You told me once he spoke Italian. I don't know if he understood or not."

The maid stepped in to announce that dinner was served. They all gathered in the dining room and Sam escorted Ben Carlyle to his place at the head of the table. Sara sat next to her father with Leonardo on her left. Kathryn Carlyle sat by her husband on one side and her son on the other.

The maid passed huge platters of turkey and ham around the table, followed by bowls of vegetables, potatoes, and a basket of bread.

From the corner of her eye, Sara saw Leonardo try to spear two potatoes with his knife. Finding it dull, he produced his own knife from his pocket. Sara watched her mother and brother gawk in amazement as the artist skewered pieces of meat with his knife and herded them onto his plate. But her face went beet red when he ignored his fork and began eating with his fingers.

"That's the way everyone eats at the Renaissance Festival," Sara said, discarding her own fork and picking up a piece of turkey with her fingers. "It's so much easier. You don't have to waste all that time cutting and dicing."

Sara's father suddenly got into the spirit of things and threw his fork over his shoulder. "Aha!" he said, grabbing a turkey leg from the platter and biting into it with gusto.

Ben held up the turkey leg in challenging fashion to Leonardo who correspondingly held up a piece of turkey dripping with gravy. Both men made simultaneous growls as they tore off the flesh and chewed. Then Leonardo wiped his grease-smeared mouth on his sleeve. Ben followed suit.

"Oh, my God," Kathryn said.

Sara laughed self-consciously. "They're just having fun, Mother."

"I'd hate to see his cleaning bill," she remarked.

Sara had not seen her father so animated since his stroke. On some level, he responded to Leonardo, and that couldn't be all bad, she decided. Actually, the meal was sort of fun, not to mention comical at times. When Ben threw his turkey bone back onto the platter when he finished, his wife jumped as if he were aiming for her.

At that moment, Sara realized how stilted and rigid her family life had been. Everything always had to be just so. Napkins belonged in the lap and elbows off the table. Her mother had decreed that no more than two bites should be cut at any one time and the knife must rest on the edge of the plate. There had been rules for everything. Now, in the space of a few moments, those rules were out the window. She wondered if Ben Carlyle would ever use a fork again. Probably not, she thought, suppressing a smile.

"We're having raspberry brûleé for dessert," her mother said cautiously, as if wondering what Leonardo would do with that.

In fact, when the maid delivered his bowl, he drank it, scooping the raspberries into his mouth with his first two fingers.

"Excellent," he said, belching loudly.

Ben Carlyle laughed heartily and followed suit, with the red juice dripping down his cheeks. He flicked it off and a drop fell on the white sleeve of Kathryn's blouse. She just looked at it and blinked. Then the older man managed a small belch in response.

"Well, I'm glad everyone is enjoying this, but frankly, I'm not hungry anymore," Sam said, pushing back his chair. "Besides, I've got to go into the office. Roger has something he wants to go over with me."

He aimed that last comment at his sister, but Sara looked away.

At Roger's name, Ben Carlyle frowned then spewed a few raspberry seeds out with an unintelligible expletive.

Sam shook his head. "I wish I knew what you were trying to say, Dad, but I don't."

Ben smacked the table with his fist and said something else. Leonardo cocked his head, as if trying to make out the words.

Sighing, Sam leaned over and kissed his mother on the cheek. "Sara, see you later. Nice to see you again," he said halfheartedly to Leonardo. Then he left.

Sara's mother sat silently for a few minutes, then suddenly smiled brightly as if she'd just awakened from a bad dream. "Why don't we all go back into the study and we'll have Irma bring coffee in."

Leonardo followed Ben Carlyle over to his desk while Sara and her mother sat by the fire. The two men were huddled together, and frequently Ben burst out laughing. Leonardo laughed too.

"What are they doing over there?" Kathryn wanted to know.

"I don't know. I think Leonardo is drawing. Apparently Dad likes him."

"Apparently," her mother said with a deep sigh.

"Mom, I'm sorry if the meal was a little chaotic. But actually, I've not seen Dad this animated in a long time."

Pursing her lips, Kathryn nodded, conceding the fact. "I used to love to hear him laugh." Her eyes misted with tears. "Perhaps you could bring Leonardo back again, if he likes him so much. We'll have sandwiches or something," she tittered.

Suddenly they were both laughing hysterically. "Mom, you should have seen your face when Dad threw that turkey leg."

"The whole thing was ridiculous, wasn't it?" her mother agreed, tears running down her cheeks.

"Absolutely," Sara giggled.

Kathryn wiped the tears from her eyes with a handkerchief she always kept in her sleeve. "But seriously, how is Roger taking all this?" She nodded her head in Leonardo's direction.

"Not well, I'm afraid. He's pretty mad."

"Can you blame him?"

"Not really, but right now I can't do anything about it."

"Who is this man? Someone you just ran into at the Renaissance Festival? Sara, you know that's not like you."

"I know, Mom. But sometimes things happen that you aren't prepared for and you have to kind of go with the flow. You know?"

"Yes. Well," Kathryn smoothed her hair back into the bun atop her head, "Going with the flow is all right. Just be careful you aren't swept downstream."

Her mother's words still rang in Sara's head hours later when they drove away. *Be careful you aren't swept downstream.* She glanced over at Leonardo who had settled back into the seat with a satisfied look on his face.

"Well, how do you like my family?" she asked.

"I like your father."

"What were you two doing all afternoon?"

"Drawing."

"My father can't draw."

"Yes, he can. He's very creative."

"Well, of course he always was creative. I just never thought of him as artistic."

Leonardo shrugged. "It's all the same thing."

They drove in silence for a while. "I don't think your mother and brother like me."

"They do," Sara countered defensively.

"They don't. They wonder where you found me. Have you told them the truth?"

"Good Lord no!"

"Then they'll never understand, will they?"

By the time they arrived back at Sara's townhouse, she was tired.

"I have some reading to do for my eight o'clock class tomorrow, so why don't you watch television?"

"What?"

She opened the doors of the entertainment center and flicked on the TV with the remote control. She handed him the remote.

"This changes the channel and this adjusts the sound," she pointed out, indicating the different buttons.

Raptly absorbed by the changing images on the screen, Leonardo absently accepted it.

Oh, well, she thought. *He'll figure it out.* She left him alone and sought refuge in her bedroom. Taking out her books, she sat down on her bed to read. But she couldn't concentrate on anything. Her mother's words kept echoing through her mind. *Too late, Mom,* she thought. *It's already happened.* She'd been swept downstream and the scenery had changed. The future she envisioned had been completely reconfigured in the space of a few hours. Now she saw everything differently—Roger, her family—and she couldn't deal with any of it. What she really wanted to do was run away. Then, climbing into bed, she realized that she'd done that and everything had gotten worse. Pulling the covers up over her head, she willed herself to sleep.

When Leonardo awakened, Sara was gone. She'd explained she would have to leave early for her eight o'clock class at the university. Whatever that meant.

Traces of her were everywhere. Her nightgown hung over the towel rack in the bathroom. He gently fingered the silky material, then touched it to his cheek. It still bore the scent she wore and evoked her image in his mind. He saw her sherry-colored eyes and full mouth. He wanted to kiss her, but she wasn't there.

Small house slippers by the door brought a smile to his lips, and he thought how he'd like to put his own slippers beside hers. If he had slippers.

Sighing, he followed her trail into the kitchen. Instead of coffee, she'd made herself some sort of milk drink. Taking a sniff, he decided against that. He'd make coffee himself.

After searching, he found a can of coffee and a dipper. He poured several heaping dippers into the coffee maker and filled it with water. Proud of himself he watched it brew. The brown liquid dripped down onto the hot burner making a sizzling sound.

A mug! Where were the mugs? Frantically he searched the cabinets, found a mug, and placed it under the steady stream. The mug quickly filled and he retrieved another, then another. He filled six mugs and still the liquid continued to drip down from the reservoir and onto the cabinet. Finally, he jerked the plug from the wall. The device was uncontrollable, he thought. Mopping up the cabinet, he thought of how troublesome all these inventions were. Opening a bottle of wine every morning was much simpler. He wasn't even sure he liked coffee, but he had enough to last him all day.

He showered, this time making sure he put the shower curtain inside the tub as Sara had demonstrated. He was fascinated by the shower massage. While he washed, he aimed it this way and that, rotating the showerhead until it spewed out in a fine mist. Then he changed it to a knife thin stream that left a red mark on his chest. When he finally remembered how to turn off the water, he was relieved. He wondered if he would ever get used to life here.

Dressed in his new clothes, he decided to watch television while he drank his coffee. He aimed the black remote at the television as he had seen Sara do. Nothing happened. Again and again, he aimed it. When he pounded it against the coffee table, it fell apart. The battery dangled by several small wires. Curious, Leonardo detached the battery and untwisted the wires. One thing led to another until he had the entire remote control dissected on the coffee table. Now that he had it apart, he couldn't remember exactly how it had gone together. Each time he tried to reconnect it, he ended up with extra parts.

Finally, in frustration, he swept the extra bolts back into the casing and jammed it together. Then he tossed it on the table.

Next, he explored Sara's townhouse. He inspected her bedroom, taking careful note of the pictures on her dresser. Roger's wasn't there, he was happy to see. He opened a door to another room, only to discover it held nothing but clothes. *How could one person have so many clothes?* he wondered. They were all hers, he concluded, judging by the size. At the bottom of the room were hundreds of shoes neatly arranged in rows. Leonardo was overwhelmed. Was something wrong with Sara that she needed so much outer apparel? This puzzled him for some time until he found other, smaller rooms also filled with clothes.

Bored, he sat down at her desk near the kitchen. Pushing the antique roll-top back, he examined the slots filled with papers. *Paper must be plentiful because Sara has so much of it,* he thought.

Many papers contained math problems that he quickly ciphered and laid aside. One or two were letters from friends. Not wishing to intrude, he returned these to their slots. Then he came across some printed sheets, folded lengthwise and stuffed beneath a crevice.

The first page contained a lengthy poem that Sara had written. Though he still couldn't read English well, he managed to read this. The poem was simply written and straight from the heart. As he read, he was struck by the beauty of the words. It was about a butterfly that had stayed too long in its cocoon, dreaming of the day when it would soar high into the sky. Now it was afraid that the time had past, that the moment for flight had been lost somehow. Yet, it could not be contained any longer. Searing light as the cocoon opened terrified it more. Then, as the protection gradually fell away, it stood naked and wet, vulnerable now to the outside world. At that moment, it stood poised and ready, not knowing if or when it would ever fly.

Leonardo read the poem over several times. Each time he was touched by the images she'd evoked. *Sara. Each day I see another side of you and, like a stone, you have many facets, many colors.*

There were other poems in the stack of papers and all were good, though none as moving as the first. He wondered how many people had read Sara's poems or even knew she wrote. Carefully he replaced the papers exactly as he had found them, then closed the desk.

At one o'clock, he realized he was hungry and decided to cook lunch. In Sara's refrigerator, he found a paper carton of ravioli. The smell reminded him of home and suddenly he was ravenous.

Remembering how to turn on the oven, he set the temperature for three hundred fifty and popped the carton in. Then he waited. Drinking more coffee, he read the morning paper. Fifteen minutes later, a strange smell began to emanate from the oven.

Peering in, he panicked when he saw the carton was on fire. The enveloping smoke immediately set off the smoke alarm and Leonardo grabbed a wet towel. Frantically, he lashed at the fire. The burning carton fell out onto the floor and he stomped on it.

In her office at the University of Houston, Sara received a call from the security guard at her townhouse development.

"Miss Carlyle? Can you come home right away?"

"What's happened?"

"The smoke alarm went off. The fire department is on the way. I believe there's a fire in your townhouse."

Eleven

The contrite look on Leonardo's face as he pleaded forgiveness touched her heart. Glancing around her kitchen, Sara saw coffee leaking from the coffeemaker. The remains of ravioli and red sauce had splattered all over the stove and floor. Over it all, fire extinguisher foam dripped from cabinets like dirty shaving lotion. It was a surrealistic nightmare. The orderly life she knew before had completely disappeared.

"Look at this place!" she blurted out.

"I'm sorry, Sara. I'll clean it up. When I'm finished, you'll never know anything happened."

She studied him warily. "We'll do it together. But not now. Right now, I just want to sit down."

Gingerly stepping around the foam, she retrieved a bottled drink from the refrigerator, then sat on the couch. Picking up the remote control, she aimed it at the television. Nothing happened. She pressed the buttons, impatiently. Suddenly the casing popped open. The inside contents were ejected along with the extra wires and screws. It fell onto the table like a jack-in-the box toy suspended by a few coiled wires.

"It is broken," Leonardo announced after the fact.

"I can see that."

"It wouldn't work and I tried to fix it," he further explained.

This explanation finally pushed Sara over the edge. Tears

cascaded down her cheeks and she sobbed uncontrollably as if her heart would break.

Scooping up the remote, Leonardo hurriedly tried to repair it, hoping to assuage her. She waved him away. "Forget it. I don't care about it."

She put her hands over her face and her shoulders shook with the sobs. He sat beside her in helpless dejection. He couldn't apologize. He'd already done that. Everything he said or did only made things worse.

He realized that his presence here had disrupted Sara's life—made her miserable. He was a nuisance. Like some small child, he had wreaked havoc in her home and ruined her remote control. The only thing to do was to leave her in peace.

Slipping into the guest bedroom, he recovered his satchel and walked back into the living room. He bent and kissed Sara on the cheek. "I am leaving now."

She looked up, her sherry eyes swimming with tears. "What? You can't do that!"

"I can and will," he retorted.

"You don't know your way around. You'll get lost or thrown in jail."

"I'm not a child, Sara. I have traveled in other countries where I was unfamiliar with the customs and language. I need time to think. So do you."

"Will you come back?" She followed him to the door, blowing her nose on a tissue.

"If I am welcome."

"Of course you are welcome, Leonardo. You rescued me from the Captain of the Guard, I—"

"You owe me nothing, Sara. You saved my life by bringing me here with you. Any obligation you may have felt has been repaid in full."

He turned and stalked out her door, having no idea where he was going. "Leonardo?" She ran after him.

"Yes?"

She pressed her card into his hand. "Here's my address and phone number." She squeezed his fingers. "Please, be careful."

He gave her a confident salute and set out full of purpose. An hour and a half later, he was still in the townhouse parking lot unable to find the exit. Finally, the security guard came to his rescue.

"Are you lost?"

"A little. I'm trying to find the main road."

"You mean Memorial Drive?"

"That will do."

"If you'll go down this street, turn left at the corner, you'll be right on Memorial. There's a bus stop."

"Oh, a bus. Thank you very much." Sara had told him about public transportation and pointed out a bus when they went shopping.

"I'll open the gate for you." The guard returned to his post, then like magic two gates opened. Walking through, Leonardo waved to the guard. *There was so much to learn,* he thought.

A short time later, he arrived at the bus stop. A black woman holding a strange contraption that looked like a giant hat smiled at him.

"Excuse me," he said. "But what is that you are holding?"

She looked at him strangely. "An umbrella. Keeps the sun off."

He nodded.

"Where you from?" she asked.

"Italy. I'm staying with a friend."

"Oh," she nodded. "You goin' downtown?"

He thought for a moment. "Yes," he replied. He had no idea what she meant, however, he was going wherever the bus would take him. His thoughts turned to Sara. The vision of her tearful, dejected face wrenched his heart, and he wondered if he should return at all. But where else would he go?

"Well, the bus comes at three-forty," the woman said. "It'll take you right to Main."

That settled it. He would go to Main. Wherever that was.

Soon the bus approached and they boarded. The woman gave the driver some coins. Leonardo took a gold coin from his pouch and handed it to the man.

"What is this?" the driver asked holding the coin up to the light.

"It's all I have," Leonardo said simply.

The driver turned it this way and that. "Is this gold?"

"Yes."

"It looks old."

The artist shrugged. "It's from the sixteenth century."

"I can't take this. I don't have any change and this here is worth more than the bus ride, I can tell you that."

"But I want to go to Main."

The black woman turned and retraced her steps, then dropped some more coins in the container. "You be here tomorrow and pay me back, you hear?" She smiled and winked, then made her way to the back of the bus.

Leonardo sat in the front seat near the driver. "If that coin is all you got, you ain't goin' to get very far," the driver commented. "You need cash, compadre?"

Leonardo frowned, trying to understand the man's words. "Cash?"

"Money, you know. Dollars."

"That's right, I don't have money. I haven't been here very long. I'm from Italy."

"Well, you can't go around trying to pay for things with this here gold coin. You'll want to trade it in."

Leonardo and the bus driver had a lengthy conversation about antiques and old coins. He explained he'd gotten the coins in payment for a painting. The bus driver nodded, but expressed concern that the artist was carrying around such a treasure.

"You have to be careful these days. There's a lot of crime in Houston nowadays. You might run into gangs of kids with knives and guns.

"Kids?"

"Young boys with nothin' better to do than go around killin' people."

Frowning, Leonardo nodded. Obviously, he knew very little about life here.

Eventually the bus driver directed Leonardo to a coin collector's shop on Caroline Street.

"You have been much help," Leonardo thanked him, alighting from the bus. He waved at the black woman as the bus drove away.

The collector was overjoyed with the coin Leonardo gave him to appraise. "Where did you get this?"

The artist told him the same story. The dealer was astonished. "I've never heard of this kind of payment."

Thinking of Henry, Leonardo smiled. "My employer was very eccentric."

"I can't believe it. The condition is excellent. I would say it was a good forgery, but the gold content is consistent. This coin is worth quite a bit of money. I can only offer you twenty-five hundred dollars."

Leonardo shrugged. He was unable to judge value here. Paper money seemed worthless compared to his gold coins, but the bus driver was right. He needed cash.

The collector ran his tongue over dry lips. Leonardo's indecision made him nervous. "Five thousand and that's my last offer."

"All right," Leonardo said. "I need cash."

"It will take me a while to round up that much money," the man said.

"I can wait," Leonardo smiled.

The process took two hours. Eventually, the dealer's

brother-in-law appeared with the money and apologized for the fact that they didn't have any large bills.

Leonardo thought if the paper got any larger, he wouldn't know where to put it. As it was, the money bulged from the various pockets of clothing. He turned to leave, but the collector waved him back. "I'd be interested in buying them if you come across any more coins like that."

"That's good to know," he smiled and left the shop after getting directions to Main.

Downtown Houston was a short walk away. Suddenly, he was in the midst of mountains—mountains made of steel and glass. Walking down the sidewalk with his head up, he tried to see the tops of the buildings. Dazzled by the reflected light, he bumped into several people.

Finally, he stopped to stare. There were buildings of glass, buildings made of mirrors, and fountains of water running down the glass. Could this be true or was he dreaming? It was like a fantasy land. This must be where the government of Houston was, he thought. The kings lived in these glass palaces. Then he remembered Sara had said they had presidents instead of kings. The presidents must be very wealthy men.

All around him, people rushed across streets crowded with automobiles, trucks, and buses. *Where are the people going in such a hurry?* he wondered. Perhaps to see the presidents. He was completely awestruck. However, he was the only one on the sidewalk standing still. Business men carrying rolled up papers or brief cases maneuvered around him as if he were a statue.

A little dizzy and tired of walking, he stopped at a restaurant to order a sandwich and a cappuccino. Then he settled back to observe five o'clock traffic outside.

"You're smart to wait it out," the waiter said, indicating the line of honking cars outside. "Are you going to take in a show?"

"A show?"

"Many people wait for the traffic to die down and take in a show. I've heard there are still seats available for the one at Jones Hall."

After paying for his meal, Leonardo followed the waiter's instructions and walked around the corner to Jones Hall. There he watched a musical production about a doctor named Jekyll who invented a potion that transformed him into a monster. At night, he was a completely different person named Mr. Hyde. The music and scenery were unlike anything he'd imagined.

Completely enchanted, Leonardo wished Sara could have been with him. Then he realized she'd probably seen many productions like this one. Dejected, he wondered if he could introduce Sara to anything she hadn't already seen or experienced. At the same time, he wondered if he'd ever get used to this new life. There was so much to learn. This world was completely different from the one he knew.

After the show, Leonardo asked about buses. The usher informed him he would have to take a taxi. By now, he had learned to play along even when he didn't understand.

"I am from Italy. I don't know where to find this taxi."

Usually, after he explained he was from a different country, people were eager to help. In fact, the usher personally escorted him out to the cab when it arrived.

He showed the driver Sara's card. "That'll be at least twenty dollars, maybe more," the driver estimated.

"That's good," Leonardo smiled. His pockets bulged with paper money. He could take many taxi rides. However, while he relaxed in the back seat, he calculated how many dollars he would have if he traded in all his gold coins. Fifty thousand paper dollars or more if he found a collector who would pay dearly for the coins. From what he could tell, that amount of paper would go a long way. But it was all he had in this world. Once it was gone, he could easily starve to death.

Obviously, he had to find a way of obtaining more paper.

He was still considering this new problem when they arrived at Sara's townhouse twenty-five minutes later.

He paid the taxi driver thirty dollars and the man seemed happy. He gave Leonardo his card. More paper. He thanked the man and put it in his pocket with the rest. Soon, he thought, he would need an extra bag for all the paper he needed to carry.

When she opened the door, he could tell Sara was distraught again. She greeted him with a wild-eyed look. "Where have you been? I've been worried sick. I was about to phone the police!"

"Again? What have I done now?" he asked.

"You could have called. You had the number."

"Called? How?"

Her shoulders sagged as she realized he didn't know how to use a pay telephone or any telephone for that matter. "It's all right, Leonardo. I just had no idea where you were."

"I was downtown."

"Downtown?"

"Yes," he smiled, proudly. "I ate dinner and saw a show."

"But . . . but you didn't have any money."

"I didn't have cash. But now I have a lot." He emptied his pockets on the table. Even he marveled at the amount of paper he had stuffed in his clothes. It seemed to have multiplied.

"Where did you get that?" Sara demanded.

Leonardo was offended by her tone. "I didn't steal it. I sold one of my coins. A man gave me five thousand dollars."

Her mouth dropped open. "You're kidding! You sold one of the coins Henry gave you?"

He nodded.

How ingenious he is, she marveled. *I would never have thought of that.* "But you can't carry all that around with you. It might be dangerous."

"I know," he agreed. "There is much crime and kids with knives and guns."

Her mouth quirked up in a smile. "That's right."

"What's a gun?" he asked.

She drew him a picture and he was horrified. "They give these things to children?"

"Anyone can go out and buy one," she explained. "The government can't control the situation."

His eyes widened. "Children buy weapons and kill people and the government can't do anything about it?"

She shook her head.

"Even a fool like Henry could control that."

They talked until one o'clock, then Sara announced she had to go to bed. They walked to their rooms, but he stopped her with a light touch on her arm. "I am sorry I caused a fire. But I am not sorry you worried about me. I like that."

On impulse, he bent down and kissed her. His lips on hers were feather light and soft. Desire swiftly rekindled the smoldering coals that lay deep in the pit of her stomach, and she pressed her breasts into the hard muscles of his chest. Just as her arms reached to draw him near, he restrained her, gently pushing her away.

"I know you are tired," he whispered. "Sleep now, beautiful Sara. I will see you on the morrow."

She stood in her doorway, looking after him with a wistful smile on her face. Quickly disrobing, she pulled on a nightgown and slipped into bed. Confused thoughts tumbled through her mind. She was engaged to one man and living with another—a situation that could not continue. Yet she would not force Leonardo to leave. He was not ready. Or was she not ready? Having him near was like a dash of spring in the middle of winter. The occasional thunderstorm was nothing compared to the blindingly bright sunlight that followed. The clear green of his eyes renewed her, restored her soul in some essential way. But what, she wondered, did she truly feel for him? Love? Pity? Admiration? She did not know. And until she did, things would have to continue as they were.

Leonardo was aware of Sara's conflicted feelings. He was a nuisance. But this nuisance was a man all the same, and she was a passionate woman. Though his need for her had never diminished, he knew he would have to proceed carefully. He had a formidable rival who would, at any minute, reappear to claim Sara's hand. Clearly, Roger had laid firm groundwork to win Sara's heart. He had become a part of the family already by working in the family business. Sara had indicated that she had a very nice income and money of her own. This only complicated matters because Leonardo could never allow himself to rely on her money. He had to make his own way and lay his groundwork carefully so that his contest with Roger would be equal. However, at the moment, he did not know how to accomplish this task.

On the following day, Sara left early and said she had meetings at the university until late afternoon. Leonardo left the townhouse at approximately the same time as he had the day before. Walking by the security guard, he waved and the gates opened. In two days, he had learned many things. When he arrived at the bus stop, the woman waited with her umbrella.

"I knew you would show up today," she said, smiling.

Leonardo handed her a five-dollar bill. "Here is the money I borrowed," he said.

"That's too much," she said.

"You were kind enough to help a complete stranger. Allow me to show my gratitude," he bowed.

"Well, I swear. You are a gentleman," she said, holding out her hand. "My name is Marie Hall."

He took her hand and shook it firmly. "Leonardo Brazzi."

The bus driver was glad to see him again. When he learned Leonardo was an artist, he directed him to Texas Art Supply on Montrose Street. As Leonardo walked the short distance to the store, his mind filled with ideas. Perhaps if he began painting again, he could accumulate more paper. In this way, he could support himself and Sara, too.

Of all the miracles he had seen thus far, Leonardo was by far the most impressed with Texas Art Supply. Standing in the middle of the store, surrounded by paints, brushes, canvases already stretched, and hundreds of other supplies, he was completely overwhelmed. He wanted to cry, laugh, dance for joy. He longed to buy everything in the store, pile his basket high with supplies, but he had no idea where to begin.

"May I help you?" A young man in his twenties with long brown hair and an earring stood behind him.

"Yes, I need help," Leonardo answered honestly. "I need everything, and I do not know where to begin."

"You work in oil, acrylic, or water color?"

"I thought there was nothing else but oil and tempera."

"Ah, a purist."

Leonardo shrugged; again he did not understand. "I use oil and—"

"That's great. All the old masters used oil, and some think it is the only medium for the serious artist. But I like acrylics, too."

Though Leonardo didn't exactly comprehend his words, the young man had a friendly smile, and he liked him at once.

"Are you an artist?" Leonardo asked.

The young man smiled acknowledgment. "I'm Dove Riddell. You probably haven't heard of me yet. But you will."

Leonardo introduced himself, explaining he was an artist from Italy. Opening his satchel, he allowed Dove to take stock of his supplies.

"Wow, you mix your own paints! I've heard some artists

are going back to that to get pure colors, but you have to be careful. Some pigments are poisonous. I use tubes myself."

Leonardo could hardly contain his astonishment as he followed Dove from counter to counter. The colors! Colors he had never imagined or seen were captured in little tubes for the artist to use. A rainbow awaited his brush. And the brushes! Every size and shape were there for the taking. Like a hungry man on his first trip to a food market, he stuffed his basket with everything he saw.

The whole process took almost two hours. Leonardo and Dove discussed many things in that time. Leonardo thought they had a lot in common.

"I'll need an easel, too," he said. "But I don't know where I'll put it."

"Do you have someone to paint with?" Dove asked.

"No."

"I have a studio. You could paint there if you like. I could use the company. If you chip in on the light bill, you've got a place to work."

It was the beginning of a friendship, Leonardo knew. When he showed Dove a few of his sketches, Dove was awed.

"Man, you are good. Have you ever been in a juried show?"

"No. I have done many commissions."

"This is great! If you can wait for a while, I'll take a break and show you the studio. It's not far from here."

Dove's old van had been hand-painted with bright colors and strange symbols. Inside, the smell of paint permeated the vehicle. He was a serious artist supporting himself while he learned his craft.

His studio was a converted garage on Waugh Street with plenty of light and storage space. It was perfect. They unloaded Leonardo's supplies and easel.

"You can paint any time you want. Just come by and pick up the key," Dove said.

Leonardo thanked him and asked to be dropped at the bus stop. They shook hands, and Dove was about to drive away when he stopped and rolled down the window.

"What kind of commissions did you do in Italy anyway?"

"Murals."

"Murals? God! That's great!" Dove waved and drove away.

Filled with a renewed sense of purpose, Leonardo checked the bus schedule, then walked down Montrose to a specialty store. There he purchased a bottle of Chianti, cheese, and bread. "Tonight we celebrate," he thought.

Roger Latham sat in the boardroom of Carlyle Chemical overlooking the bayou. Sitting with him at the polished wood table were the senior engineers—fuddy-duddies, old men who had worked under Ben Carlyle and still clung to the past.

"Gentlemen, I'm sure you know from my memos that we have to cut expenses drastically. Revenues have been falling off and we really have no choice."

Bert Weimer had been with the company since its conception and had been a constant thorn in Roger's side. "I really don't understand what the problem could be. Our sales are up—this should be our best year ever."

Roger frowned. "I have the figures right here, if you'd like to go over them. This will not be our best year ever. Not by a long shot."

"I don't see how we can cut back any more," another engineer said, "unless we start cutting personnel."

"It may come to that," Roger said, with a sad look on his face.

Bert Weimer narrowed his gaze. "Ben wouldn't like that.

He also had an entire team regulating the pollution controls. You've cut the team down to one man, I understand."

Roger shrugged. "Ben isn't here."

An hour later, Roger met with his second-flight supervisors who were an engineer and two chemists he had recently hired.

Seated around the same table, the men looked at him expectantly. Roger made a steeple of his fingers and thoughtfully studied them. "Men, I'm going to need your help and support. We're going to have to cut way back, and I'm afraid some of the old guard will be stepping down."

The engineer nodded as if he'd anticipated this.

"In order to make ends meet and make a profit, we'll all have to cinch in our belts. The others didn't feel they could go along with the plan. But I think you understand how important this is," Roger said, directing his gaze at the engineer.

The engineer nodded. "Yessir."

"Well, then," Roger said beaming. "We're going to have a new team and a new company. We'll all share in the profits."

Leonardo arrived at the townhouse before Sara and straightened the kitchen. After laying out a platter of cheeses, olives, and sliced fruit, he managed to cook pasta without burning anything. To this he added spices, tomatoes, and olive oil to make a savory sauce.

When he heard Sara's key turn in the lock, he quickly lighted candles and dimmed the light. *Tonight,* he thought. *Tonight I will make her mine.*

Sara never cooked and so was pleasantly surprised by the smell wafting through the door. Drawn into the room by the warmth of the candlelight, she stared at the table. An elegant repast waited with candles, platters of food, and a bottle of wine.

"This is wonderful," she said. "Did you cook this?"

Smiling, he took her jacket and escorted her to her chair. "Of course."

"I am very impressed."

"Tonight we celebrate," he said, pouring the wine.

He told her about his new friend and the fact that he would be painting in Dove's studio.

Sara was skeptical. "Who is this Dove character? You can't just meet someone on the street like that."

"I did not meet him on the street. I met him in Texas Art Supply. He works there."

"Still, you don't know anything about him."

Leonardo spread his hands. "I know all I need to know."

As he described his exploits, Sara felt a small twinge of something she could not understand. Green lights danced in his eyes, and his expression was eager. In the space of a few days, he'd met a friend and learned how to get around in a city of four million people. She was astonished. Gradually, he was moving away from her and she wasn't sure she liked that.

His hand closed over hers as if he knew what she was thinking. "It'll be all right, Sara. You'll see."

They feasted on the meal he prepared. Sara couldn't believe how wonderful it all was. There was nothing he couldn't do. The more she learned about Leonardo, the more he fascinated her.

He poured more wine and the warmth spread through Sara. She watched him as they talked. *How handsome he is,* she thought. The candlelight reflected in his eyes and cast his chiseled features into soft relief.

When they had finished eating, he led her into the living room. He placed two candles on the coffee table and sat beside her on the couch.

"Leonardo, you are full of surprises." She smiled.

Taking her hand, he brought it to his lips. "I would hope so," he said, kissing her fingers, one by one. He brought her index finger into his mouth and gently sucked on it, probing it with his tongue. Sara's breath caught in her throat. She stared into his eyes, eyes now as green as a spring meadow inviting her to him. His lips moved from her index finger and took her middle finger into his mouth. Startled, she felt wildly new emotions pulsing through her blood. It was as if she'd never been touched before. When he pulled her ring finger into his mouth, she thought she would cry out with longing. Desire flooded her body and she could feel it in every cell, in her fingernails, clear to the roots of her hair. She thought at any moment, she might explode with passion.

"Sara," he whispered, his gritty voice at once both hard and soft. "I love you."

"Oh God!" she said and fell into his arms.

She did not remember taking off her clothes. It was as if they fell away of their own accord. Suddenly, they were naked on the soft carpet with the candlelight above them. She felt his fingers touch her feet, inspecting each toe, then move up the curve of her leg. But she couldn't wait for his kiss and drew his face toward hers. Deliriously wet, drugging kisses left her breathless and longing for more. His mouth moved away from her lips, to her cheek, and down the column of her neck.

He murmured something in Italian, then groaned when his mouth closed over a taut nipple.

Never had Leonardo experienced such passion. It flowed from her body like a magical energy into his, then back again. With every kiss, it grew more intense. Her auburn hair lay inflamed around her face, infusing it with an ethereal glow. She was like some ancient goddess come to life. With every kiss, he partook of that hallowed light, drawing it in, breathing its essence. Desire was a living, breathing thing. And Sara embodied it completely. Even in his mouth, he felt each nipple harden more, filling him with deep longing. When at last he pressed against her, hard muscle to soft flesh, her breasts burned into his and he felt indelibly melded to her.

Sara's hands splayed in his hair, drawing him to her again and again. When he lay against her, she explored the contours of his back, running her fingers along sinewy muscles. Her fingers traced the skin as it stretched tautly across the broad expanse of his shoulders. She followed the muscles as they tapered down to firm buttocks.

She felt his fingers touch the curve of her knee, then move to the moist cavern between her legs. Arching into him, she opened herself to him as a butterfly to the sun. Then on cue, he ground his mouth down on hers. He drove his tongue to meet hers, blending his hard body with her softness. She was ready for him when he pushed deep inside her. With every thrust, the energy flowed between them, heating the blood as it passed through every cell. All the feelings and emotions Sara had kept hidden for so long erupted to the surface in tears of joy. Then suddenly, they were one. Linked by something timeless and divine, they were irrevocably connected.

A dizzying spiral of emotions churned around them, whirling faster and faster, sending them far away into the night. Thoughts like stars ignited the blue-black sky and once again they were beyond this life. Or any other.

A distant chime rang twelve times calling them home. Gradually, the stars faded. Still dazed, Sara blinked, trying to decipher what had happened. Moments later, she felt Leonardo's body against her and gazed into his eyes.

"Now I understand why I came with you."

"You do? Why?"

He smoothed back her hair and kissed her. "Isn't it obvious, Sara? We were meant to be together."

Meant to be together. Was it true? His words went deep inside her and found some confirmation there. Never had she felt so bonded to another person or so completely fulfilled. Yet her fears eddied around her and she couldn't push them back again. What if he just disappeared one day and went back to his own time?

"I don't know. I—"

"Yes, you do know," he nodded, very decidedly. "Tomorrow, you should call Roger and tell him."

Twelve

Furious, Roger paced his office. Sara had not called or given any indication that the situation had changed. *How dare she defy him like this!* Gazing at the bayou through his office window, he considered his options. He could have this Leonardo Brazzi arrested or deported as an illegal alien. He knew a lawyer who specialized in that sort of thing. But he imagined Sara's reaction. She would be compelled to defend the ingrate. No, he must be subtle; he must be smooth. He wanted Sara. She was essential to his long-range plans. According to the terms of the trust Ben had set up, she and Sam had to agree before anything could be done with the company.

With a great deal of effort, Roger composed himself, then invited Sam in for a little chat. It was time to call in his markers.

Not long after their little chat, Sam phoned Sara. "I think you owe Roger an explanation," he told her.

Still basking in the glow of the previous night, Sara gazed at Leonardo dozing beside her. *How could she explain this?* she wondered dreamily.

"Sara? Are you still in bed?" Sam's strident tone filled her with an odd sort of guilt.

"Yes."

"Don't you have class?"

"Not until eleven."

Leonardo flung his arm across her breast and snuggled close. Sara couldn't suppress a warm sigh of pleasure.

"Sara, I don't understand what's going on with you. But I do know that Roger has been a madman for days now. Quite frankly, I'm worried that eventually he'll blow up. And I can only guess what might happen then."

"What are you saying, Sam?"

"I'm telling you that Roger can ruin us. He saved the company from bankruptcy, but he could just as easily reverse it all."

"And that would be my fault?" Sara inquired.

"Yes, it would."

A momentary stab of guilt knotted Sara's stomach. Roger had been good to her and to her family. She hated the thought of being responsible for what happened to the family business, but now she no longer loved Roger. If she ever had. The relationship was over and she hoped they could part amicably.

Awake now, Leonardo toyed with her nipples and coaxed each into a tight bud. Sara moaned.

"Sara, I don't think you're taking this whole thing seriously."

Leonardo's hands ranged down her stomach to the soft mound of curls between her legs.

"I'm sorry, Sam. What did you say?"

"Never mind," he snapped. "At least call Roger, okay?"

"Okay," she said.

Tossing the phone to the floor, she melted into Leonardo's arms.

Later, after Leonardo left for the studio, she called Roger. Leonardo was right. She had to break off their relationship.

When Roger answered the phone, he was pleasant, but the hurt was evident in his voice. Immediately, she felt a twinge of guilt. Under the circumstances, he had every right to be furious with her. Instead, he was a perfect gentleman and agreed to meet her for lunch to talk things over.

For the next hour, she tried to think of what she would say to him. Earlier her motives had been clear—she was repaying Leonardo for his help. She would have told Roger that she was giving a homeless artist a place to stay until he could get his feet on the ground. Now, however, all that had changed, and Sara was truly confused. Her feelings for Leonardo had deepened. He was no longer just staying there. They were living together. How could she explain all this to Roger? If she told him she was in love with another man, that implied commitment on her part, and she was not ready yet. It would be easier to ask for space. Fervently, she hoped that Roger would let it go at that.

Confrontations made her nervous. By the time Sara arrived at the trendy Italian restaurant off Allen Parkway, she was very uptight. The smell of roast chicken permeated the room as the waiter led her to a secluded table where Roger waited impatiently.

He rose and kissed her lightly on the cheek. "I ordered for us," he said. "I don't have much time."

Roger never had time, Sara suddenly realized. For anything.

"Sara, I think I've been really patient," he launched into the conversation after sitting down. "But I think you can see my position in this whole thing."

Sara smiled and said nothing.

"This artist has got to go," he continued.

Watching his eyes, she imagined him in a board meeting, convincing those around him to pursue a given course of action. He was very persuasive.

"I'd like him out of your townhouse by this weekend."

Sara blinked. "I'm afraid that's impossible. He has nowhere to go."

"So? Let him go back where he came from."

She couldn't help smiling. "He can't do that."

"Why not?"

"He's more or less broken all ties with his past. He just

needs to start over." She felt her nerve dissipating under his penetrating gaze. Their relationship had to end, she knew that. But she felt so guilty for ending it this way.

Roger placed his hands on the table as if to steady them. "Sara, I don't understand your involvement with this man or why you feel compelled to help him."

She put her hand on his arm. "It's difficult to explain. He helped me when I was lost and now I'm returning the favor."

He sighed deeply. "At the Renaissance Festival? Is that where he helped you?"

She nodded.

The waiter delivered salads topped with slivers of hot roasted chicken. Roger began eating immediately, stabbing the chicken viciously with his fork. A bite told her it was delicious, but Sara lost her appetite. Instead, she watched Roger methodically shoving the salad into his mouth.

When he cleaned his plate, he paused to take a long drink of water. "It really isn't like you to do this sort of thing, taking in stray animals and so forth."

She frowned. "He's not an animal, Roger. He's a human being—a very talented artist."

"Still, I don't think you know much about his character. Who knows what he's really after?"

Sara was thinking she knew more about Leonardo than she did about Roger.

"I think he has ulterior motives," Roger stated.

"Ulterior motives?"

"That's right. I believe he intends to undermine us all."

"Oh, Roger. You're overreacting."

"Really? Did you know he's been over to see your father three times this week?"

This information startled Sara. Why would Leonardo visit her father without telling her?

Roger nodded. "You see? There may be a lot you don't know about this man."

Still pondering the information, Sara did not comment.
"Sara, do you want to break off the engagement?"

Sara felt herself waiver for a moment. Roger offered
safety and security. Leonardo offered her creativity and passion, but could she build a life on that? She didn't know
anything for sure, but she knew she couldn't go through
with the marriage. Not now. "Roger, I guess right now I
need a little space."

The expression on his face was one of abject astonishment.
He hadn't expected this, and obviously it rattled him.

She slid the engagement ring off her finger and handed
it to him with a small smile. He stared at it as if he'd never
seen it before.

"All right," he finally said. "I have no choice but to accept this. Are you going to marry that . . . that man?"

"I'm not going to marry anyone right now," she assured
him.

"But he's living with you, right?"

"I've tried to explain that he just needs a place to live
until he—"

"I've heard all that," he cut her off. "Sara, I want to
marry you, but the offer won't be open indefinitely. I can
only hope you come to your senses before it's too late."

Leonardo was sitting beside Ben Carlyle, studying a word
he transcribed. He felt sorry for Sara's father and resolved
to visit him every day if possible. He'd established a routine
of painting in Dove's studio, then taking the bus to the Carlyle house on Memorial Drive. After spending an hour or
so with Ben, he walked to Sara's condominium.

Though Kathryn Carlyle had not been overjoyed, Ben
seemed glad to see him again. Leonardo suspected the old
man would welcome any visitors. Ben always took him into
his office as if he were a client. Once there, Leonardo took
over. Usually, they drew or looked at pictures in a book.

Sometimes he had the distinct impression that Ben was trying to tell him something when he excitedly launched into a nonsensical monologue. Most of the older man's speech was unintelligible, but now and then, Leonardo thought he understood a sentence or a word. Oddly, the occasional words were in either Italian or Latin, but the dialect was archaic and difficult to interpret. He had to listen very carefully because Ben could not be persuaded to repeat himself. The old man's mind was soon off on another tangent.

Today, Leonardo studied the word he had just transcribed, unsure as to whether he had heard it correctly. He repeated the word. Ben parroted it back in his garbled speech. Translated into English, the word meant traitor.

Leonardo pressed him to explain. Ben narrowed his eyes as if he were contemplating something evil. Then the moment passed and he shrugged.

It was odd, Leonardo thought, how eager Ben was to communicate something, then like a child, he was onto something else.

After having spent some time with the man, Leonardo had come to believe that there must be a way to talk to Ben Carlyle. He vowed to discover it. Surrounded by degrees and awards, Ben seemed a shadow of the man he once was. He held fifteen patents on various chemical compounds and had devised a method of chemical detoxification to safeguard the nearby bayou. Where had that brilliant mind gone? Or had it gone?

Leonardo studied the word on his tablet. *Traitor.* What did Ben mean by that?

With a sigh, he withdrew his sketch pad from his satchel and the two of them drew. Ben worked industriously on his drawing. When he had finished, he proudly showed Leonardo.

It was a pencil drawing of a stream. Along the banks were various buildings or houses. One of the houses was larger than the others and Ben had drawn black wavy lines from it to the stream. Arching his eyebrows, he waited for Leonardo's response.

"Very good," Leonardo said.

Ben shook his head. Evidently, this was not the response he expected.

He thickened the black lines, making holes in the paper. Leonardo didn't know what to make of that.

"Do you mind if I keep this?" he asked.

Ben waved it away with a deep sigh.

Later, on his way to Sara's, Leonardo thought about the word *traitor* and the sketch Ben had drawn. The old man had something on his mind. If only he could figure out what it was.

Sara was waiting for him when he returned and kissed him when he walked in the door.

"I wondered where you were," she said.

"I was painting. Then I went to see your father."

"Why didn't you tell me? I would have come along."

"I wanted to see him alone. I had an idea that I could talk to him."

"And?"

"I'm not sure. At times, I think I understand a word or two, but I haven't made much progress overall."

"Really? You mean he's speaking another language?" No one had even suggested this. Her father's speech sounded like gibberish.

Leonardo nodded.

"What language? Italian? It certainly doesn't sound like Italian to me."

"I'm not sure yet. It could be some sort of combination. Sometimes I think it may be Latin."

Sara was astonished. "I can't believe it. That's wonderful."

"He drew a picture today," Leonardo said, handing her Ben's drawing. "See what you think of it."

Together they studied the drawing. It looked like a child's creation, but something about it caught Sara's attention.

"I wonder if this stream is the bayou," she mused, reflectively. "If so, then something is flowing out of this house into it." She paused, frowning. "Perhaps he learned of a company that is polluting the bayou. Or maybe it is Carlyle Chemical. That may be what he is trying to tell us."

Leonardo shrugged. "I must confess that never occurred to me."

"But that is ridiculous. My father went to great lengths to make sure the bayou was protected. Why would he be drawing pictures like this? Unless, as Roger says, he's forgotten all he knew." She shook her head. "I'll check this out with Sam."

"Sara, I think you were right all along. Your father just cannot speak the way he once could. That doesn't mean he's lost his mind."

She hugged him impulsively. "Thank you for giving me that hope. I know he likes you. Perhaps if you keep trying, one day he'll recover his speech."

"I think he might."

Then she told him she had broken off her engagement to Roger.

Sweeping her gallantly into his arms, he kissed her ardently. "We must go out and celebrate."

They dined at a little Greek restaurant near Woodway and San Felipe. There was only one other couple there and they sat on aluminum chairs at a table covered with plastic. *Roger wouldn't be caught dead in a place like this,* Sara thought. But it was divine and exactly right.

Over dinner they talked about Leonardo's painting. Dove had encouraged him to enter a piece in the art league's juried show. Sara watched him as he spoke about his work, noticing, for the first time since he'd been in Houston, the reappearance of his creative energy. She'd been afraid he was lost here, but she should have known that true creativity transcends time. That same glow suffused his face, radiating through vivid green eyes.

He communicated passionate energy through the touch of his hand on hers. He brought her fingers to his lips and desire raced through her entire body. At that moment, even with Greek music blaring in the background and neon lights flickering overhead, he was the most arrestingly attractive man she had ever seen.

"Dove says I paint like an old master," Leonardo chuckled. "Should I tell him when I was born?"

She shook her head. "I don't think he's ready for that. You're an old, old master."

He frowned, suddenly concerned. "You don't think I'm dead, do you?"

"Hardly," she laughed. "Most of the men I've met are really dead compared to you."

Leonardo's thoughts were back on his work. "Dove tells me I must accumulate enough pieces for a show. So, I will be very busy."

"I can hardly wait to see what you've been doing," she said. "I hope you'll invite me to the studio."

"Perhaps I'll take you there myself. Dove wants me to buy his car." He smiled.

Sara shot him a worried glance. "But you don't know how to drive a car!"

"I can learn. It can't be more difficult than a microwave oven."

She had to agree he had a point. Leonardo had learned a great deal in a short time. Now he knew how to get around, how to operate a microwave oven, and soon he would buy a car. He had a whole new life of which she had no real part. Though proud of his progress, she wondered if he would soon leave her behind. All he talked about was Dove this, Dove that, and she felt a little left out.

She wanted to talk about them and the future of their relationship. But it wasn't the right time. He was determined to make his own way in this new and strange environment. She would have to be patient.

That night they made love once again with such joyful abandon that her fears were swept away. He found each sensitive crevice and, with his touch, funneled into her body all the passionate force of his creative energy. Every newly awakened cell echoed his name, resounded with his power. Driving deep within her, he more than claimed her. He made inroads into her secret soul that both surprised and frightened Sara.

Suffused in Leonardo's golden glow, she took him into her, felt the seeds of his genius take root in her fertile mind. Rising up, exhilarated, she met him on a higher plane. Soulmates connecting once more in fiery, tumultuous reunion.

At some point later that night, Sara awakened. Lying there in the stillness with her lover beside her, she realized that something deep within her had moved.

Glancing over at Leonardo, she knew that she was wholly changed and would never again be the same.

Sara forgot about everything except Leonardo. He was in her thoughts all day and in her dreams at night. *Was it healthy to be so obsessed by her love?* she wondered.

He phoned one afternoon to announce he would pick her up after class in his new car. When he arrived, she couldn't believe her eyes. He proudly alighted from a hand-painted neon van complete with a tableau of the Beatles on one side and a huge peace symbol on the other.

"What is this?" she asked.

"My new car," he announced. "How do you like it? Dove did the artwork himself."

"I'm not surprised," she said.

"You don't like it?" he asked, crestfallen.

"Well, it's not that I don't like it. Most people don't paint their own cars."

His green eyes widened in astonishment. "They don't? Why not? Look at all he's done." He opened the door, inviting her inspection.

She had to admit the interior was elegant. Dove had upholstered the seats in a dazzling Moroccan print and gone to great pains carpeting the floor with Turkish Kilims. "It is lovely," she said, halfheartedly. She got in beside him, shouldering a seatbelt that looked like a cast-off guitar strap.

It was the type of art-car that would have been campy in college. But almost twenty-eight, Sara was no longer a student. Though she'd outgrown this sort of thing, Leonardo was just discovering it. They would have their differences, she reminded herself.

His driving needed some improvement. He drove haphazardly, weaving in and out of traffic as if he were in a movie chase scene. Having heard horror stories of Italian drivers, she wondered if it was genetic. "You don't have a driver's license, do you?" she asked.

He looked affronted. "I have one. Don't you know it's against the law to drive without a license? I bought one from Dove."

He flashed the license at her. The license had Dove's name on it and a picture that looked nothing like Leonardo.

Wondering what Dove was using, she patted her seatbelt and closed her eyes.

Dove's studio was a converted garage with good lighting. There was a small bath and sitting area, but the remainder of the huge room was lined with shelves and storage areas for canvases and boards. Paint had been mixed on the walls creating a crazy-quilt design resembling an abstract painting. Warm and cozy, it was redolent of turpentine and oils.

Dove greeted them in paint-spotted jeans and work-shirt. Though a bit mangy, he was a pleasant surprise. Sara guessed him to be about her age with dark hair and big brown eyes. He smiled a lot when he talked, and she liked him immediately.

Dove's father had been an artist so he knew about art and was very serious about his profession. He took her on a tour around the studio, pointing out his work, then let it slip that a well-known art dealer had recently bought one of his collages.

"I don't have enough pieces for a show, but I can get Leonardo into a gallery whenever he's ready," Dove assured her.

Looking around the room, Sara saw only two of Leonardo's paintings and these were half-finished. It wasn't that easy to break into the Houston art community. She only hoped Dove wasn't inflating Leonardo's ego. Still, he was obviously happy and doing what he loved. *Few people could say that in this century,* she thought.

After the tour, Leonardo dropped her back at the university. He kissed her good-bye in front of several students, but she didn't care. She watched him careen down the street, praying he would not be arrested.

On the following day, when Sara excitedly informed her brother that their father had been communicating with Leonardo, Sam was not impressed.

"I think you're grasping at straws, Sara. Why would he talk to a complete stranger rather than his own family?"

"I wondered that myself," she admitted, "but Leonardo believes he may be speaking a different language."

"Don't you think the doctors would have picked that up?"

Sara shrugged. "I do think that the drawing he made is very interesting." She handed him Ben's sketch.

"What is this? It looks like something a preschooler would draw. What deep meaning am I supposed to infer?"

"Well, look at that big building with all that dark stuff coming out of it. That could be Carlyle Chemical."

"Sara, you're out in left field. Who put that interpretation on it? Your artist friend? If so, I'm not sure he ought to keep visiting Dad."

"Dad likes Leonardo."

"Well, I don't like him putting weird ideas in his head."

"Isn't it worth checking out?"

"What are you talking about? I go to work every day at Carlyle Chemical and not much has changed in the year Dad's been gone. Dad was always worried about pollution. That's why he engineered all the safeguards."

"So you think it's all right?"

"Of course it is. If you want, I'll ask Roger if he's noticed anything, but personally, I think Dad has lost it. He's living in the past, Sara."

Deflated, Sara wondered if Sam was right. Ben Carlyle had always been concerned about protecting the environment. Carlyle Chemical was one of the first companies in the southwest to implement environmental controls. The EPA had applauded their initiative, and Ben had received a personal letter from the vice-president. But that had been five years ago. Why would her father be worried about something he effectively handled years ago? Perhaps he was, as Sam suggested, still living in the past.

Roger sat at his desk with Ben Carlyle's sketch in front of him. He drummed his fingers on the desk, thinking back over the events of the past three months. Ben had visited the plant several times, having taken the car when Kathryn was out playing bridge.

Roger hadn't known he was there until Ben furiously charged into his office. Shaking his fists and gesturing to the bayou, Ben jabbered excitedly. Temporarily unnerved by the old man's presence, Roger couldn't think what to do. Ben might ruin all his plans, and he had no intention of letting that happen. Fortunately, Sam intervened and took his father home. Embarrassed and apologetic, Sam promised it would not happen again.

They had all dismissed Ben's ravings as that of a senile old man until recently. This Leonardo character had stepped in and started "communicating" with Ben. Given time, more damaging information might surface and Roger couldn't allow that. The artist had to go.

Roger had never been a violent man, but he'd hated Leonardo on sight. Since their first meeting, he'd had dreams of strangling the artist, of his hands closing around the man's throat and watching with pleasure as his eyes bulged out. Now he had taken his woman and threatened to sabotage his business. He felt totally justified in getting rid of him. Still, he stopped short of hiring someone to kill him. He could always resort to that later if all else failed. It would be far better to lure him away to New York or Paris. Out of sight, out of mind.

Smiling, he dialed the art league. "I'd like to speak to the head of the committee. Yes," he said to the voice on the other end of the line, "I'm interested in making a sizable donation to the art league."

The days passed quickly and Sara looked forward to coming home each night. Leonardo always had something exciting to tell her.

He won first place in the art league's juried show. That night Dove threw a party for him at a wine bar on Montrose. Sara suddenly realized that Leonardo had many new friends. In fact, they hardly had a minute to themselves. He received congratulations from artists and businessmen, she noted. They all smiled politely at her, but she could have been part of the furniture. Still, she was glad Leonardo was adjusting. He was adjusting so well, she wondered if he needed her now. That thought made her uncomfortable. She'd given up a lot for him. Would he do the same for her?

Leonardo was thinking of Sara. Now that she'd given up Roger for him, he had to prove himself worthy of her love.

He could not continue living in her house and eating her food. It hurt his pride to think she was supporting him. He must be independent. Men in this age worked to earn money for their wives. He too would have to earn money, but he had no idea how to accomplish that.

Dove suggested he live in the studio where he could devote more time to painting.

"You spend too much time driving, man. And you have too many distractions."

It was true. Yet when he thought of moving out and leaving Sara, his heart constricted. How could he face a day without her? What if Roger reestablished his claim in his absence? Would she wait for him? Would she understand? A war erupted within him, and his two separate sides drew him first one way then the other. Days passed. Finally, he decided he must move out. For her sake.

Soon he would make enough money to get his own place and she would move in with him.

As Sara drove home on Friday night, she suddenly realized that the following day would mark three weeks. Leonardo had been in this time three weeks—exactly the amount of time she had spent in his time period. The thought filled her with a strange kind of foreboding. Would he suddenly fade back into his own time? Might he disappear without warning?

She pressed her foot down hard on the accelerator and as the car picked up speed, her heart pounded against her ribcage. *Oh, God,* she prayed. *Let him still be here.*

She breathed a sigh of relief when she saw the van parked out in front. Laughing to herself, she thought that a short time ago she would have been embarrassed to be seen in such a vehicle. But now she'd gotten used to it. Everything had changed. *She* had changed.

Exhilarated, she rushed in the door.

Leonardo sat in the midst of packing boxes, looking through some sketches. He looked up and smiled. "Oh, Sara, I'm glad you're home. You can help me decide if I am to keep these sketches or put them in the trash."

Suddenly terrified, Sara collapsed on the couch. "What are you doing?"

"Packing. Dove thinks I ought to move in with him so that I can devote more time to painting. He says I spend too much time traveling back and forth."

"So Dove makes all your life decisions now?"

"No, he only made the suggestion that I move in for a while. He says in a few months, I will have enough for the show. Otherwise, it might never happen." At her crestfallen look he joined her on the couch. "Sara, don't you understand that I must be independent? I must make my own way. I cannot allow you to support me. I do not wish to be a burden."

"You have not been a burden!" she cried. Angry tears filled her eyes. "You said you loved me. You told me to break off my engagement. Now you're leaving. What am I supposed to think?"

He pulled her gently to him and, with his thumb, brushed her tears away. "Sara, nothing changes between us. We will be together every minute when I'm not painting and you'll have your own place back again. As soon as I can I will get a place for the two of us. But I must be able to provide for you. This is important to me—to us. Don't you see?"

Her lip trembled, but she nodded. "I guess so. You need to think of your career."

"That's right, I do. You told me once that you were a professional, that you needed to have your work. Without it, you did not feel worthwhile. Remember?"

Choking back her tears, she nodded. He was right, of course. She had to allow him to have his own life. But the terrible fear that he would not need her any more robbed her of all joy. She tried to smile.

"Sara, will you help me sort through these sketches?"

"Yes," she said, halfheartedly. For the rest of the evening, they sorted and packed until Leonardo's meager possessions were all contained in an odd assortment of boxes.

Over a bottle of wine, they talked and toasted and watched the fire die in the fireplace. Later, they made love with a desperate intensity that left them both breathless, lingering in some faraway plane.

"I love you Sara," he said, kissing her nose. "I love you more now than yesterday."

"I love you, too." She said the words. And for the first time, she felt as if she were truly in love. Yet she wondered how he could leave her if he really cared.

A crisp, cold morning dawned and Leonardo was up early. By the time Sara awakened, he had loaded the van. With leaden feet, she trudged into the kitchen to make coffee.

Full of enthusiasm, Leonardo didn't seem as sad. "Dove says the time is just right for my style of painting. He says there's a real Renaissance going on right now. Can you believe it?"

Dove again. Sara almost felt jealous of Leonardo's new life, then she bit her lip. *He deserved to have friends. He deserved to be successful.* She just wanted to be a part of it all. And right now, she felt terribly insecure.

When they had finished their coffee, he jumped up. "I must go, my darling."

"So soon?" She hated herself for saying that. She felt like a carping wife.

"I'll be back," he promised with a kiss. "Let's have dinner on Sunday."

"Okay," she said, her voice a sad whisper.

A short time later, she watched him drive away. She waved bravely until he was out of sight, then broke down in tears. She was totally bereft. She chided herself for being possessive and overprotective, but none of it had any real impact.

He was gone and he had taken with him a vital part of her soul.

Thirteen

Lost in thought, Leonardo drove down Memorial Drive. On impulse, he swerved off onto the road leading to the Carlyle house. Pulling to a stop, he sat in the driveway, thinking about Sara.

He took out his sketch pad and pencil, then wrote the first two lines to a poem:

"Every time I see you, my heart bleeds.
Little by little you are taking my soul from me . . .

Sara. How could he live without her? Yet it was for her sake he left and for her sake he wanted so desperately to succeed.

This world into which he had come was both strange and wonderful. He loved all the devices, the contraptions, and the motors. But here business took precedence over all else. Courtship and romance were idealized abstractly in songs or moving pictures. From what Leonardo could tell, a man of this age felt he had wooed a lady when he had taken her out to a restaurant several times. He was then entitled to be her bed partner. Afterwards, they married. That was it. He suspected that some women were never even wooed.

In his time, a man had to win his lady. To do so, he had to turn inward to find the words to touch her heart and in the process, learned more about himself. Leonardo liked the old way best, but resolved to win Sara's love under the terms of this age. He would use all his talent and ability, for he wanted her completely. For all time.

Alighting from the van, he walked up to the Carlyle house. Sam answered the door. He looked at Leonardo critically, as if they'd never met. "I can't say I'm glad to see you again."

"Oh?" Leonardo cocked an eyebrow.

"There's been a family upheaval," Sam responded, irritation lacing his words. "Since you arrived, my sister has completely lost her senses, and my father is worse than ever."

Keeping his temper in check, Leonardo only shrugged. "I'm here to see Ben."

"I'm not sure my father wants to see you."

Leonardo's anger flared, and he pushed past Sara's brother. "Then he can tell me to leave. I'm here to visit him, not you."

He hadn't intended to be rude to Sara's brother, but he had things to attend to and was in no mood to be bullied. Ben smiled when he walked into the study.

"I brought you something," Leonardo said, withdrawing a new sketch pad and a set of pastels. "I saw these at Texas Art Supply and I thought you might like to play around with them."

Ben jabbered excitedly, but Leonardo couldn't catch a word. Then, like a child, he grabbed the pastels from Leonardo and began to draw.

Sam stood in the doorway like a sentry. "I don't think you ought to encourage my dad to make those drawings. It just gets him worked up."

Sam's words infuriated Leonardo, but for Sara's sake, he reigned his feelings. "This is the way he communicates."

"I don't really think you could call that communicating. The drawing you gave Sara looks like something a kid would do."

"I don't agree. He was trying to convey a message. Ben thinks someone is polluting the bayou."

Sam frowned. "Maybe. If so, he's living in the past. We've already handled the pollution problems. He put in the controls himself."

Ben's head snapped up and he let out a stream of unintelligible invective. When Sam didn't respond, Ben went back to his sketch pad.

Sighing, Sam left the room.

They drew for almost an hour and the exercise calmed them both. Leonardo's thoughts drifted to Sara and he was suddenly sad. He missed her already. He wondered if she would move in with him at Dove's studio, but he knew her answer. It would be uncomfortable and cramped. Still he worried that he had made a mistake in leaving her.

He forced himself to concentrate on what he had to do. Soon he would be a contender worthy of her full attention. Then he would ask her to marry him.

Ben nudged him and handed Leonardo his drawing. After studying the pastel, he decided Sam was right. Ben's artwork was childlike. This one depicted a family. The mother and father were large figures, resembling pastries he had recently seen in a bakery. What did the lady call them? Cookies. They looked like big cookies. The three children were smaller versions of their parents, except for one that was totally black. It stood, hands out, between the parents and the other two children and looked charred, almost as if it had been burned.

"Is this your family, Ben?" Leonardo asked, first in English, then in Italian.

When he asked the question in Latin, Ben smiled and said something Leonardo could not understand. He thought the old man might have replied affirmatively, but the word was unrecognizable.

"Who is this black person?"

The question sent Ben into a rage. His face turned bright

red and he balled up his fists ready to fight. Though he asked the question in three different languages, Leonardo couldn't get Ben to identify the black child.

On impulse, Leonardo tried a different approach. He pointed to each figure and gave it a name, gauging Ben's reaction. At Sara and Sam, Ben's expression was pleasant. Leonardo took this as confirmation. When he got to the black figure, he said Roger's name.

Ben's eyes narrowed and, picking up an ink pen, he stabbed at the figure, poking holes in it. It *was* Roger. With a kind of vindictive joy, Leonardo realized that Ben hated Roger. Now all he had to do was find out why.

The old man's attention waned. Leonardo collected the pastels and put them in the desk drawer. He kept the picture, however. Later he would use it for evidence.

Filled with new resolve, Leonardo backed the van out of the driveway. It was as if he were unraveling a mystery, piece by piece. If Ben hated Roger, that could only mean that Sara's father knew something about Roger that no one else knew. What?

Had Sara been an unwitting pawn in some larger drama? If so, she was well out of it. The one thing he knew was that Roger could not be trusted. There had to be a way to loosen the hold he had over the Carlyles. He just had to find it.

Leonardo was still lost in thought when he arrived at Dove's studio. In anticipation of his friend's arrival, Dove was cleaning.

"You've made a good decision," Dove said. "What did Sara say about your moving in here?"

"She understands I need to work, but she was hurt, I think."

"She'll get over it. Especially when you have your first gallery show. How's the van running?"

Leonardo frowned. "Not very well. Yesterday it stopped for no reason. A man came and said I was out of gas."

Dove shook his head, trying to suppress a smile. "You have to make sure it has enough gas."

"I didn't know that."

"Don't people drive cars in Italy?"

"Not where I'm from."

"How do they get around?"

"They walk."

Dove helped him move his belongings into the studio, then left for work. Walking around the empty room, Leonardo could hear his footfalls and was aware of the sound his breath made. For the first time in months, he felt completely alone. He didn't like the feeling. Soon, he told himself, I will make my mark in this world. Then I can provide for Sara and our children. She will come to me freely with no regrets.

Sara tried to imagine Leonardo's new life. After only a month in Houston, he had more friends than she did. She thought his world was a lot more interesting than hers. He wasn't working, he was painting, and painting was fun. She felt envious.

Intellectually, she understood his reasons for moving. He was the type of person who needed to be independent. Other men might have stayed, but Leonardo was not like other men. That was why she loved him.

The day dragged on. Once or twice she thought of calling him, then decided against it. He was painting and would not want to be interrupted. Her thoughts returned to the days when she had worked alongside him at Hampton Court. Looking back now, she almost wished they were still there. Life was much simpler.

At four o'clock, Roger called and invited her to dinner. "I'd like us to be friends, Sara. No strings attached. I just miss you."

He sounded so sincere and genuine. Why shouldn't they

be friends? She saw an opportunity to smooth things over and, since she had no other plans, she accepted.

She experienced a small pang of guilt when she wondered what Leonardo would think. He wouldn't like it. But he was busy and she was bored.

To her surprise, Roger took her to the Post Oak Grill, a popular restaurant near the Galleria where everyone in Houston went to see and be seen. Something about the evening reminded Sara of their first date, for he'd brought her to a place much like this.

All the trees along Post Oak Boulevard sparkled with seasonal lights. In front of the restaurant, Roger braked to a stop, and the valet sprinted up to his Porsche.

"Welcome back, Mr. Latham," he said.

Another valet hurried to help Sara out. "Good evening, madam."

The restaurant was crowded, but they were shown to Roger's favorite table near the piano bar. Sara gazed at the mural of a French cabaret on the wall and immediately thought of Leonardo. It was done in impressionistic style. Instinctively she thought he'd appreciate the bright colors and treatment.

Roger was a perfect gentleman, amiable and in a very good mood. It was as if they were good friends and all else that had passed between them had been swept away. Sara was a little amazed at his behavior. For a change, he was totally solicitous, making sure she had everything she wanted. He ordered her favorite wine while they snacked on crusty French bread.

"I'm glad you're not angry, Roger," she said, smiling.

"Well, I was hurt," he replied, honestly. "But I have tried to see things from your point of view. Marriage is a big commitment, and I want you to be sure."

She couldn't meet his gaze. Was anyone ever really sure when they married? Did he suspect she was sleeping with

Leonardo. Of course he did. Yet, he was being very mature about it all. Obviously, he cared about her.

A small commotion drew their attention to the back of the restaurant when former President Bush and his family filed in the rear entrance. They took up an entire section of the restaurant and the patrons turned to stare. When they were finally seated, everything returned to normal.

"I've always liked this restaurant," she remarked. "You never know who you're going to see."

"Oh yes," he affirmed. "Whenever I can get away, I have lunch here. You'd be surprised how many business transactions occur at these tables."

It had bothered her that Roger was tight with money. But tonight, she ordered an appetizer and the most expensive entree on the menu and he didn't flinch. Perhaps she had underestimated Roger, she thought, sipping her wine.

Roger studied her furtively, over the rim of his wineglass. Repeatedly he'd chastised himself for allowing Sara to slip through his fingers. But she wasn't gone yet. She hadn't married the bastard. So he had a little time to reconnoiter and launch a new offensive. He vowed to reclaim what he'd lost.

Tonight he prepared to make his first move. Life was like a chess game, he mused to himself. And he played chess very well.

"I heard your friend won first place in the Art League Show," Roger said.

"How did you know that?"

"It was in the paper," he smiled. "I'm sure he's very happy."

Sara's spirits plunged, and she felt empty inside. She missed him terribly, but tried not to show it. "He is happy. I'm sure it will enhance his career."

"Enhance? It will make his career. I understand the guy who won last year is in Paris now."

"Paris!" The shocked look on Sara's face almost brought

a smile to his lips, but Roger forced himself to nod innocently. From Sam, he'd learned that Leonardo had moved
into a studio to paint. He had taken the bait. "Yes, he got
on with some gallery and jets back and forth between Paris
and New York. Art is big business. Didn't you know that,
Sara?"

"Well, yes I did know that. But I thought . . . it took a
while."

"This is the day of the fax, my dear. Things happen overnight."

"But Paris, my God."

"It can be heady stuff. The roar of the grease paint, the
smell of the crowd."

Ignoring Roger's attempt at humor, Sara couldn't stop
thinking about what he'd said. Her gaze focused on the
colorful mural on the wall. It depicted Paris in the days of
the Impressionists with all its gaiety, laughter, and creativity.
She could envision Leonardo there, and sadness welled up
within her. She knew how talented he was. He was a genius.
She just hadn't thought that others would see it, too. At
least, not so soon. Dejected, she realized she didn't want to
share him with anyone. However unfair, she wanted him all
to herself.

"Sara," Roger took her hand, demanding her attention.
"That's the way art is. I knew a woman once who was
married to a very fine artist. They were both from the same
small town. She worked hard to support him through those
lean years. Then after his first gallery show, he left her and
moved to New York. Poor Wanda. All she has now are a
few of his early paintings." Shrugging his shoulders, he let
out a deep sigh.

"He . . . he just left her?"

"Well, she was a small-town girl. Not the type for New
York. I understand he's had many girlfriends since then.
And of course, there's the gallery groupies who follow him
around everywhere he goes."

His words sliced into her, hitting the mark. Leonardo was good enough to make it big. Then where would she be? He said he loved her. But was love enough? Would he leave her behind to pursue his career?

By the time their entrees arrived, Sara had completely lost her appetite. Assailed by doubts, she now felt she shouldn't have let Leonardo move out. *Where was he?* she wondered, *and what was he doing now?*

Inspired, Leonardo had gone right to work and painted feverishly. After leaving Texas Art Supply, Dove brought a gallery owner by, and he was interested in several of Leonardo's paintings.

"Bring them by when they're finished," he told Leonardo. "I think I might have a buyer."

"I told you," Dove said later. "You've got to get busy. Your stock may go up overnight, and you have to be prepared."

Dove was right. Living at the studio would enable him to produce more. Leonardo painted into the night and arose early the next morning. He worked largely from memory, completing several variations of the mural he'd painted for Henry. Without the Pope, of course. They were classical representations of angels and political figures locked in a struggle of the divine versus the mundane.

But he was not entirely satisfied with them. They lacked a certain element that would bring them up to date. Though confounded by this dilemma, Leonardo completed three paintings and sat back to survey them.

They were good, probably the best he could produce— then. But this was now. His paintings did not relate to the present age. Placing one back on the easel, he stared at it. A seminude Adam, sitting in paradise, was contemplating an apple. His internal struggle was portrayed by angels on the one side and the devil on the other. In the distance, Eve beckoned to him.

How boring, Leonardo thought. He began to sketch, first in charcoal, then with a brush. Chuckling to himself, he added color. When he had finished, Eve stood in front of a red sports car. Her nude body was draped in a fur. Diamonds encircled her neck and sparkled in her ears. *The* real *temptation of Adam,* Leonardo thought.

Midday, Dove walked in, coffee cup in hand. He passed by the painting once, backed up, and stopped. "I don't believe it," he said. "That's fantastic. Too wonderful."

Leonardo laughed. "I think I should make the apple gold, don't you?"

"Absolutely."

Leaning back, Leonardo folded his arms across his chest. Now he was satisfied. The question was whether or not it would sell.

Later that afternoon, Leonardo went to the library. He wanted to learn something about pollution. The librarian was very knowledgeable and referred him to several articles on the subject. Then she helped him locate specific information relating to Buffalo Bayou. Ben Carlyle and Carlyle Chemical Company appeared frequently in Houston newspapers and business journals. Long before it had been fashionable to do so, Ben had been concerned with preserving the environment and was at the forefront of a movement to clean up the bayou.

There were pictures of the intricate system he had designed and installed at Carlyle Chemical. Leonardo made a copy of the design. From the look of it, the installation had been very costly. Its efficient operation required a team of trained workers.

He took down the name of the local EPA office in Houston. On Monday, he would pay them a visit.

While Leonardo was reading about Buffalo Bayou, across town in Memorial, Timothy Blanton, age six, found his pet duck dead on the banks of that same bayou. Scooping up the bird, Timothy hurried inside his home to inform his parents.

Unschooled in the effects of chemical poisoning, the Blantons had no idea the duck had died a horrible death. They only knew it hardly resembled their longtime family pet. Unbeknownst to them, Timothy had also been exposed to the toxins so when he developed a mild fever a short time later, they were not too concerned.

But Timothy was very sick indeed.

Sara waited all day for Leonardo to call. When he did, she was irritated.

He described his new paintings, told her he had painted almost all night, and gotten up early this morning to finish. Filled with enthusiasm, he was stunned by her cool reaction.

"Sounds like you've been very busy," she remarked curtly.

"I thought you'd be happy, Sara. Are you angry with me?"

"No, I just have other things to do, rather than wait around for you to call."

"I am sorry I forgot the time." He could feel her anger and was at a loss to know what to do.

She did not respond, so he thought he should hang up.

"Well, then I'll pick you up at seven tonight. I will say good-bye and you can do your other things."

"Wait!" she demanded.

"Yes?"

"When did you learn how to use a telephone?"

"Yesterday. Dove showed me."

Sara was even more dejected when she hung up the receiver. He didn't need her at all. He was functioning very well on his own now. Soon he would be off to New York or Paris.

Then she realized how insecure she must have sounded. Her imagination had run wild, conjuring up all sorts of unpleasant scenarios when nothing had changed. Leonardo was working exactly as he had promised. She simply missed him.

Pushing doubts aside, she spent the day in happy anticipation. Two days without him and she couldn't wait to see him again, couldn't wait to kiss him once more. Then when he picked her up later that evening, Dove and his girlfriend, Stacy, were in the van. Sara didn't want to kiss him while others looked on so she only hugged him, reigning her churning emotions.

They went to a wine bar on Montrose Boulevard and the four of them squeezed into a tiny booth.

"I love this place," Stacy said. "It's so cool."

Stacy wore a T-shirt that said, "Art is Life" and she couldn't have been more than twenty, Sara decided. Big blue eyes doted on Dove as if he were a god.

Dove noticed that for the first time, local artwork graced the walls of the wine bar. "Leonardo, we need to introduce ourselves to the owner and get in a good word," Dove said.

The two of them left the booth.

"I love being around artists, don't you?" Stacy asked.

Forcing a smile, Sara nodded. "Yes," she said, honestly.

"It is so exciting. I wish I could paint. Dove has painted me several times. Leonardo said he wanted to paint me, too."

"He did?" Sara didn't like the sound of that.

"Yeah, I guess I have that kind of body that looks good on canvas. I'm too busty to be a regular model."

Sara stared at her. A heart-shaped face was framed by long, straight blond hair. Busty was the right word. Her white T-shirt stretched tautly across full breasts. She had the classic features of a nymph, she thought dispiritedly. Imagining Leonardo painting this girl in the nude plunged her into total despair.

"Leonardo is really good."

"I know."

"I mean, really good. His paintings could be in the Loo or something."

"The Louvre?"

"Yeah. He's that good."

For all we know his paintings may be there, Sara thought. "He is good," she agreed.

"Isn't it great to know somebody like that? Dove says there's no telling how far he'll go."

There's no telling how far he'll go. The words rang in her ears. When Leonardo returned, she couldn't help noticing that Stacy doted on him, too. Though she was not yet thirty, Sara felt suddenly old. Could she compete with twenty-year-old girls in tight T-shirts who were too busty to be regular models? Groupies, Roger called them. Then she remembered Wanda, left with only memories and a few early paintings.

Leonardo took her hand and brought it to his lips. The touch of his fingers filled her with the old familiar warmth, and she felt betrayed by her own body. She wanted him so much. But glancing over at Stacy, she saw that Stacy and probably all of her friends also wanted him. She withdrew her hand. She would not share him with anyone.

"What's wrong, Sara?"

"I don't feel well. I'd like to go home."

"But we haven't eaten yet."

"I'm not hungry."

"All right. I will take you."

With hurried excuses and good-byes, they left Dove and Stacy at the restaurant.

Lost in thought, Sara fell silent during the long drive to Memorial. Completely overwhelmed by her fears, she gazed miserably out the window.

Leonardo didn't know what to say or do. Sara was acting strangely. Perhaps she was really ill. Immediately he wondered whether he should take her to a doctor or perhaps a hospital. When he offered to stop, she snapped at him.

"No, I want to go home," she said.

He'd never seen Sara this way and he was concerned. She just stared out the window as if she didn't notice he was there. "I saw your father yesterday," he offered.

This caught her attention. "You did?"

"Yes. He drew another picture. This one had Roger in it."

"Roger?"

"Did you know that he hates Roger?"

"He doesn't even know Roger. How could he hate him?"

"He colored Roger black."

Frowning, Sara thought for a moment. "You think that means he hates Roger?"

Leonardo nodded.

"He only met Roger once or twice before his stroke. Dad gets so excited, then angry. Often for no reason."

"He has a reason. No one understands what he says."

"And you do?"

"Sometimes, I catch a word or two."

Sara gazed at him, astonished. "That's wonderful. Then Dad hasn't lost his mind after all?"

"I'm not sure, Sara. But I don't think so."

She let out a sigh of relief, and it seemed as if she felt better. Then she gazed out the window once more.

They arrived at Sara's townhouse and Leonardo hurried around to open the door for her. When he did, the handle came off in his hand. After helping Sara down, he threw the handle inside and closed the door.

For the first time, Sara glanced critically at the van. Girls like Stacy and her friends would love a hand-painted van like this one. But it was a piece of junk, and she thought she was too old to be riding around in an art car. The thought that she was too old depressed her. If she stepped out of the picture, there would be plenty of pretty young things waiting to take her place at Leonardo's side.

As they walked to her door, Leonardo took her hand. Immediately his energy flowed into her hand, up through her arm and straight to her heart. *Damn him,* she thought, trying to extricate her hand from his.

"You really don't feel well, do you?" he asked, full of concern.

His fingers smoothed back little tendrils of her hair, and she could feel the passion, clear to the roots. Weak and vulnerable, she hated herself for being so easily influenced. It was as if he'd cast a spell over her and she was powerless to resist him.

His lips grazed hers lightly. "Can I get you anything, Sara?" he asked, pulling away. "I am worried about you."

She seized the opportunity to fish her house keys out of her purse. Quickly she turned the key in the lock. "It's all right," she assured him. "I'll be fine."

"Are you sure?"

He reached for her, but she stepped back, knowing if he touched her again, she couldn't let him leave. She nodded. "Good night."

He stood for a long time silhouetted by the porch light. He wanted to follow her inside, turn down the cover, and tuck her into bed. But she'd made it clear that she didn't want that. In fact, she didn't seem to want him at all.

Walking back out to the van, Leonardo felt he'd made a mistake moving away from her. Had he remained, he would have known she was ill and attended to her. In only two days, she seemed a stranger to him. How could this be?

He had been so sure he was right. He would fight like men in this age fought and become financially successful. Then he would win her love. Instead of feeling victorious over his recent gains, he only felt confused and bewildered.

If this was the way to win her love, why did he now feel as if he were losing her?

Fourteen

It was the Monday before Thanksgiving. The crisp, clear air portended winter. Rising early, Leonardo painted for a few hours then called Sara to see how she felt.

"I was worried about you," he told her.

She assured him that she was well. But Leonardo sensed a new distance between them. She agreed to meet him for lunch, and he was relieved. Perhaps it was a passing mood.

At ten o'clock, he set out for the Houston EPA office. Pulling the van into a second story parking lot, Leonardo walked to the entrance, marveling at the building. He could not get used to buildings made of glass. They looked frozen, like fragmented pieces of ice that could melt at any moment. Inside the ice building, he located the EPA office on the register. It was on the third floor.

Though fascinated with pulleys, he did not like riding in elevators. He felt cramped in a little moving box so he preferred to walk up three flights.

After thirty minutes, a smartly dressed woman who identified herself as an agent ushered him into an office. "How may I help you?" she asked.

Leonardo stated his concerns about the bayou.

"We're always pleased to know our citizens are concerned—"

"I'm not a citizen," he corrected her.

"You're not? Are you just visiting?"

He thought for a moment. He wasn't sure. At any minute,

he might be pulled back to his own time. "I'm hoping to stay here," he replied honestly.

"I see. Then as a newcomer to Houston, I'm not sure you understand how busy this agency is. We keep close tabs on all companies that have already contaminated existing sites. At this time we have no reason to suspect there are any problems with Buffalo Bayou. We test the water regularly. As far as we know, the companies along the bayou have been complying with our standards all along. Was there a particular company you were worried about?"

"Carlyle Chemical."

She seemed surprised. "Carlyle Chemical was the first company in the Southwest to put in pollution controls."

"Yes, I know. I don't know if they are still working," he said.

"You're suggesting Carlyle Chemical is polluting the bayou? That company has been the model for many other companies across the country. I'm afraid you are mistaken."

"No. I think you must test the water."

"Please, Mr., uh . . ."

"Brazzi."

"We do test the water, frequently," she said, growing impatient.

"It's a big bayou," he said.

"Yes, it is."

"Is it possible that you test the water in one area and in another area there is pollution? Or perhaps, you might not be testing for the right chemicals."

The woman was exasperated now. "Mr . . ."

"Brazzi."

"Mr. Brazzi. We test for a variety of chemicals in several different sites. Of course, anything is possible, but what you've suggested is highly improbable. Because of their past record of compliance, we have no reason to suddenly suspect Carlyle Chemical has changed its policy."

"But I think—"

"I'm sorry, I have an appointment in a few minutes." She rose and escorted him out the door. "Thank you for coming by."

Leonardo left the EPA office bewildered and dejected. The woman had spoken about Carlyle Chemical as if the company could do no wrong. With Ben at the helm that was probably true. But Ben wasn't there any more. Roger was.

Even if he had proof of Roger's duplicity, Leonardo doubted he could convince anyone. At the moment, he had no proof. All he had was a sketch and his intuitive feeling that Ben knew something that no one else did. He wanted to think Roger was a blackguard, that he had been using Sara and her family for his own gain. Was it wishful thinking on his part or had Roger really pulled the wool over everyone's eyes? He had no way of knowing. Only Ben Carlyle knew.

For Sara's sake, he vowed to continue visiting her father. He was Leonardo's link, the one hope he had of winning over her family. If he could help Ben regain his ability to communicate, the balance would tip in his favor.

Timothy Blanton's fever had not abated by Monday morning and he developed a rash. His parents took him to the doctor. The doctor immediately noticed the boy displayed symptoms of toxic shock.

"We'd better check him into the hospital for observation," he told the Blantons.

After thoroughly questioning the family, doctors at Memorial City Hospital suspected that Timothy had been exposed to toxic chemicals. The fever and rash occurred as the result of an extreme allergic reaction. But no one could determine what chemicals had caused the reaction.

"It could be anything," one doctor concluded. "Paint stripper, chlorine shock used in the swimming pool or some household cleaners. If you read the labels on many of these products, you'd wonder why they sell them. Since his exposure was minimal, he should be back to normal in a short time."

Roger congratulated himself. Seated around the table were five investors suitably impressed with Carlyle's financial report for the past six months.

"I must say," one investor said, "I hadn't expected this big a jump. How do you account for this revenue increase, Latham?"

Roger smiled. "Of course, the market has improved. However, the main difference resulted from a change in management. Ben Carlyle had begun losing interest long before his stroke. He was a brilliant man once who went downhill. Fortunately, we managed to salvage the company before he took it down with him."

The men nodded agreement.

"On the basis of what you've seen today and the proposal I've outlined, I hope we're still in agreement to take the company public."

"We are," they all said enthusiastically.

"I have here a letter of intent for the purchase of Americana Petrochem."

"Hold on, Latham. Didn't I read an article about an EPA crackdown on that company? Something about polluting an entire subdivision," one investor inquired.

Roger held up his hands, placatingly. "It's perfect, Josh. With Carlyle Chemical's reputation, we'll waltz in like white knights. I've got a press release already written."

"What about penalties?"

"All covered. I've got an agreement with the EPA for a long-term cleanup. They'll suspend all penalties."

"That will cost millions of dollars, not to mention time and manpower."

Roger's blue eyes narrowed and a wary expression flitted across his features. "We'll do the very best we can, but remember gentlemen, once we take the company public, we'll be using the proceeds from both companies to raise stock prices. Then we will sell at what I expect to be a very large profit. So really, the responsibility for the cleanup will fall to the new owners, I suppose."

The investors all liked that. They agreed wholeheartedly and clapped Roger on the back. Money talked louder than anything, Roger thought, smiling triumphantly. He had no intention of cleaning up someone else's mess. Pollution was a crusader's cause, not his. He intended to buy an island and retire before he was forty.

To pull this whole thing off, however, he needed the co-operation of the Carlyle family. That Ben had always staunchly declared that the company should remain in the family did not bother Roger. Soon, Ben would be safely ensconced in a rest home where he would jabber out his days. He had already convinced Sam that Ben Carlyle had lost it and would need institutionalizing. Sam agreed that taking the company public was the modern way to quickly multiply their profits. Ben's stock had been placed in trust and could be sold with Sara and Sam's joint agreement. Roger had Sam in his pocket and until recently, he'd counted on having Sara's consent also.

Since the arrival of the artist, the situation had altered and not for the better. Now that she had broken the engagement, he was no longer sure she would go along with her brother. He had time, though, to reverse that.

When the investors left, Roger concentrated his attention on Sara. He'd already laid preliminary groundwork and planted seeds of doubt in her mind. He felt certain the artist would soon be gone. All he need do was throw a little money his way. Though Sara would be distraught for a while, he would be there to comfort her. The merger would be efficacious—personally and financially. He needed a

wife, and he wanted Sara's stock. He believed that the two
of them were well suited, at least for the present. Lining
up his assets, he set about removing all obstacles to his
goal and placed a call to a gallery owner he knew.

"Look, I've agreed to give him a show. I can't do more
at this point."

"Bryan, I want him to be popular."

"I think he will be. He certainly has the talent."

Roger paused for a moment, considering this last comment. He had not imagined the man had any talent at all
and was mildly surprised. He discarded the information as
it was of no real concern to him. "Why don't you find him
a buyer from New York?"

"I can't do that. It's too soon. He's an unknown."

"What if I buy a painting through a New York investor
just to get things moving a little faster?"

The gallery owner was aghast. "That would be—"

"I know what it would be and I don't care. I want his
head to swim. I want him seduced by his own brilliance. I
want him out of here."

The gallery owner finally agreed to find an investor.
Roger hung up the phone, secure in the knowledge that
Leonardo would soon be out of the picture.

Time for the second phase of his plan. He dialed a florist,
then a jeweler. He ordered a dozen roses sent to Sara every
single day. Over the phone, he bought a diamond necklace
to go with the tennis bracelet he had given her last year.

"Wouldn't you like to see them before they're delivered?" the jeweler asked.

"I'll see them often enough when she wears them," Roger
said.

With the stage set, he turned his attention to his work.

The following week, Sara attended a conference at Rice
University. It was a dry consortium of English professors

who met once a year to discuss curriculums and listen to lectures by boring experts. She passed the time thinking of Leonardo. They'd met for lunch, then had a quick dinner the night before, but it was never enough. It was like they were dating again after having been engaged or married. There was a certain awkwardness about their meetings now, and she wondered if their relationship could survive this separation.

Leonardo's life had changed so radically. He was fast becoming an important figure in the art world. Certainly, he belonged there, but did she? Among his friends, she felt a little odd as the only one wearing makeup, jewelry, and conservative clothes. Could she fit into his new world? Was that what she really wanted?

She needed time to sort out her feelings. But between now and Christmas her work schedule was crammed with finals, consultations, and meetings. She would be unable to see Leonardo or even think about their relationship.

She arrived home after the conference to find her townhouse filled with roses. It looked exactly like a funeral parlor, and the scent was overwhelming. *Who could have sent them?* she wondered. *Leonardo?*

Picking up a card, she read, "All my love, Roger." Then, "Thinking of you, Roger." And, "I miss you, Love Roger." Her spirits plummeted. She wanted Leonardo to say these things, not Roger. A single rose from Leonardo would have sent her heart soaring to the clouds. A room full of red roses from the wrong man was like a jarring, discordant note in a symphony. The wrongness of it reverberated through her.

Dropping the cards on her desk, she sighed and listened to messages on her answering machine. There were three calls from Leonardo wondering where she was. In the last message, his worried tone touched her heart.

"I miss you so much, Sara. I don't like living apart from you. Perhaps it was a mistake to move out."

He was at Dove's studio, and they agreed to meet for lunch at on outdoor restaurant on Montrose. Though it was cool, they sat outside and lunched on Caesar salads. Seeing him again after a three-day absence lifted her spirits. He focused his entire attention on her, and it was as if the sun had broken through the clouds warming her all over.

"I hate being apart so much," he said. "When I don't hear from you, I become worried."

"I'm sorry I haven't called. I have a lot of work to do right now. In fact, this weekend I have to prepare for finals."

"I won't see you?" he frowned,

"Not for a while. This is the worst time of the year for me. But I thought you would be working anyway."

"I plan to, but not all night."

His green eyes drew her magically into him, and Sara's resolve to concentrate on work evaporated. When he looked at her in that way, she forgot all else and felt terribly vulnerable. It was as if her heart were directing traffic in a crowded thoroughfare giving no thought to the body's safety. She gave a deep sigh. "I don't like being separated from you either."

He patted her hand. "Should I move back?" he asked.

She nodded. "After your show. That was the reason for the move in the first place."

They talked about his work, and she was genuinely pleased to know he was making progress. After they ate, he walked her out to her car.

"We must see each other more often," he admonished her. "At least twice a week. You don't wish me to lose my mind, do you?" he asked.

"No, I wouldn't wish that on you or me." She smiled.

He took her in his arms and she melted. All her doubts faded away when he was near. Sighing, she got in her car.

Leonardo kissed her good-bye and watched her drive down the street. Filled with a sense of loss, he trudged over to the van. They had been separated only a week and it felt like a lifetime. Now he understood why there were so many divorces in this century. So many things conspired to pull two people apart. He needed to work, but he needed to be with Sara. He had to have his own place to paint which meant he couldn't live with her. Now because of their work, they couldn't find time to be together. *Where did it end?* he wondered. It was like juggling hundreds of different balls at once and hoping they would all stay up there, at least for a while.

Dejected, he drove back to the studio, but inside he felt a growing emptiness.

Sara drove away with a heavy heart. The same emptiness gnawed away at her. After just seeing Leonardo, she missed him already. Returning home, she felt the loneliness close in on her. She wandered through every room, thinking of him. The kitchen reminded her of the day he'd set off the smoke alarm and alerted the fire department. Soon after though, he'd learned how to cook. Now he cooked much better than she did.

Collapsing on the couch, she remembered making love in front of the fire, feeling his sensitive fingers on her skin, his lips on hers. She closed her eyes and a knot formed in her throat.

The doorbell rang and she leaped to her feet. Was it Leonardo? Hastily, she wiped away the tears, then opened the door.

A pimply-faced youth handed her a box from a local jeweler.

She tipped him and, mildly deflated, returned to the couch. The box contained a beautiful diamond necklace and a note from Roger.

The stones caught the light and sparkled brilliantly. *Why was Roger doing this?* she wondered. He'd always been tight with money before. Now he seemed to have changed.

"You were meant for beautiful things, Sara," Roger said when she called.

"Thank you. But I can't accept this," she said.

"Why not? You liked the tennis bracelet I gave you last year."

"That was then. This is now."

"It's the artist, isn't it?"

"Yes," she said, finally.

"Has he asked you to marry him?"

"Well, I . . . Not yet, he—"

"Then if you're not engaged, there's still a chance for me. I don't give up easily, Sara. You should know that."

She did know that. Roger was like a terrier and would hang on until the end. They talked a while longer. When she hung up the phone, she felt more depressed than ever. Here was Roger, eager to marry her, at any time. But she didn't love him. She loved Leonardo who had to prove himself somehow. She and her loved one seemed at opposite ends of a tread mill, trying hard to get back together. *What is wrong with this picture?* she wondered.

Since Sara was busy, Leonardo drove over to the Carlyle house to see Ben the following day. Kathryn greeted him at the door. "I'm sorry, Leonardo," she said. "Sam believes you've upset Ben too much. He doesn't want you coming by any more. Ben has his nurse to keep him company now."

She seemed sincerely apologetic. *Roger is behind this,* Leonardo thought. He bowed politely and walked away.

He had no intention, however, of following Sam's orders. Sooner or later, Ben would have to come out. Perhaps his nurse would take him on an outing.

He resolved to wait and see. Parking the van down the street from the Carlyle house, Leonardo watched the house all day without seeing Ben once.

The day after, he returned and took up his post down the street. Discouraged, he realized that Ben was being held prisoner in his own home. He thought of scaling the brick wall surrounding the house, but if he were caught entering the house illegally, Sam might have him arrested. Then he would never see Ben again. Thoughts flew through his mind, and he discarded one plan after another.

He was about to drive away when Ben and his nurse finally left the house. His spirits leaped. They were going somewhere. It was three o'clock on Wednesday afternoon. Leonardo followed them in the van.

To his surprise, they went to Memorial Park. The Carlyles allowed Ben an outing, giving him some small measure of freedom. A heavyset woman, his nurse wore a starched uniform, sensible shoes, and her faded blond hair in a hairnet. She had pleasant features, Leonardo noted, and might once have been pretty.

Ben and the nurse walked for a while. Afterward, the two of them sat on a park bench and watched the joggers.

Leonardo planned his attack—a direct frontal approach. Walking casually by them, he noticed Ben and acted surprised.

"Ben! How are you! I haven't seen you for such a long time."

Ben grinned jovially and shook hands with Leonardo.

Leonardo explained to the nurse that he and Ben were old friends. "He's looking good, isn't he?" Leonardo asked the nurse.

"He certainly is. Personally, I don't think he needs a nurse. But I can't complain about the money."

After a lengthy conversation, the nurse, whose name was Smitty, was thoroughly enchanted by Leonardo. She preened like a girl when he sketched her portrait. "You have wonderful features," he told her.

"Why, thank you," she said, dimpling.

He turned his attention to Ben. The old man strung a few words together and this time Leonardo thought he was beginning to understand. Ben's inflection was strange and, at times, slurred. However, often Leonardo recognized a word in either Latin or Italian. He began to write them down.

Smitty was interested. "Do you understand what he's saying?"

"Sometimes I think I do. Often I catch words I recognize in either Latin or Italian."

"Really? You mean he's speaking another language?"

"Apparently so. At least part of the time."

"What does his family say?"

"They think I'm making it all up. His son asked me not to see Ben again."

"Oh, dear," Smitty lamented. "He seems to like you, so that seems a shame."

"Yes, it does. I think they're wrong, don't you?"

"Yes, but I can't go against their wishes."

"What about Ben's wishes? He likes to see me. I know he does."

She nodded in agreement. "I don't know."

"They're convinced he's lost his mind. I'm not. I just want to help."

She saw that he was sincere. "Perhaps it wouldn't hurt if he saw you once in a while when we come to the park. I'll be here to supervise."

"Thank you, Madam." Leonardo took her hand and kissed it.

Smitty tittered and held her hand out to inspect it as if she could visibly see his kiss imprinted there.

Leonardo was not invited to the Carlyles' Thanksgiving dinner. Roger had intimated that he had a wonderful announcement to make and the whole family needed to be present, so naturally he was included, to Sara's irritation.

"We'll just have family this year," Kathryn told Sara pointedly.

"But Roger is coming," Sara reminded her.

"Of course dear, but he's one of us."

Sara felt that the family was conspiring against her. They

liked Roger and disliked Leonardo. They were forcing her into an uncomfortable situation, and she told her mother so. Kathryn ignored her.

On Thanksgiving Day, she spent the morning helping her mother and the cook prepare dinner. As usual, everything had to be perfect.

"I hope Roger likes sweet potatoes," her mother fussed.

Sara shrugged. "If he doesn't, he won't eat them."

Kathryn sighed. "I want to have things he likes. I should think you'd know what he eats."

"Mother, you know I've broken the engagement with Roger. Throwing us together like this won't work."

"You need to keep an open mind, dear. Besides, this is really a business meeting, Sam says."

Sara ignored her mother. She wondered what Leonardo was doing. She'd tried to call him several times, but there was no answer at Dove's studio. Where was he?

Roger arrived bearing wine and some pastries he'd bought at a French bakery. Sara stood aside watching her mother and brother fawn over Roger. Their feelings were obvious. They loved Roger. As far as they were concerned, he was already part of the family. Sara wondered how she would stand this constant pressure. She felt smothered, overwhelmed.

Dinner was uneventful except for the fact that Ben Carlyle ate with his hands.

"My God! When did this start?" Roger was aghast.

"I'm afraid Leonardo taught him that," Kathryn acknowledged, embarrassed.

Ben emitted a loud belch apparently aimed at Roger. Then he laughed heartily.

Roger shook his head in disgust. "I can't believe it. He's really regressed, and I don't think your friend has helped the situation, either," he said to Sara.

Sara smiled to herself as Ben drank out of his bowl and tossed a turkey leg over his shoulder. She thought her father was much more animated than usual. Obviously, he took pleasure from Roger's discomfort.

Later they all gathered in the study for Roger's important announcement.

"All the investors are in agreement," Roger said. "We're going to take the company public soon."

Kathryn gasped. "What does that mean, Sam?"

"It means, Mrs. Carlyle," Roger answered for her son, "that you are shortly to become a very rich woman."

"Oh, I like that," Kathryn said, beaming.

Sara frowned. Her father had been adamant about keeping the company in the family. "Dad always said he wanted to keep the company private. I'm not sure he would be in favor of this."

"He'd be in favor of making money, Sara," Roger corrected. "Ben didn't understand this aspect of the business world. It takes a certain expertise because we'll be playing in a bigger league now."

Sara glanced over at her father. Ben jabbered a few sentences that she couldn't understand. No one else paid any attention to him. They talked about him as if he weren't there, she thought, sadly. "I don't know."

"Sara, you don't understand this. We'll be listed on the exchange," Sam interrupted. "We won't have to worry anymore."

Suddenly, Ben began to jabber again, pointing his index finger at Roger.

Roger looked uncomfortable. "Why don't you have the nurse take him out for a walk," he suggested to Sam.

"The nurse is off today."

Roger continued to try to explain, but Ben's voice rose above Roger's in a loud harangue. At a loss, they all looked at one another. "I'm sorry," said Kathryn. "I don't know what's wrong with him."

"He's overexcited again. Mother, I spoke to the director of Memorial Pines yesterday," Sam said.

"Memorial Pines. A rest home?" Kathryn exclaimed. "Oh, I don't think—"

"No!" Sara said. "Dad does not need to go to a rest home. Leonardo says he is trying to communicate."

"Leonardo doesn't know!" Sam said.

"I won't listen to this another minute. Mother, why don't I take Dad out for a walk," Sara volunteered. "I need some fresh air anyway."

"But Sara," Roger protested, "you need to hear this. I'm not finished explaining about the public offering."

"I don't care about the damn public offering. My presence here isn't needed any more than Dad's."

Walking over to her father, she kissed him on the cheek. "C'mon Dad," she coaxed. "Let's get a little fresh air."

Ben spewed out a few more unintelligible sentences, twirling his finger in the air, then finally allowed his daughter to draw him to his feet.

As they walked by Roger, Ben paused, looking Roger straight in the eye. He screamed a word, showering spittle all over Roger's tie. Disgusted, Roger turned away.

Sara led her father out the front door and away from the house. Ben continued to talk, looking back at the house. Drawing his arm through hers, she urged him on. "Oh, Dad," she said. "I don't think you like all this, but I don't know what to do. They won't listen to me. I wish I could understand you. Why can't I?"

She felt helpless—as if she and her father were marooned on two different worlds, unable to breech the large chasm in between. Roger was proposing they take the company public and reap the benefits. It sounded wonderful. They could all use the money. But now something new had been added. Sam thought their father should go to a rest home. It was almost as if he wanted Ben out of the way so that he and Roger could go on with their plans. A knot formed in the pit of her stomach. Following her father's gaze back at the house, she felt an eerie feeling creep up her spine.

Fifteen

Leonardo thought that if he couldn't see Sara, at least he could continue to see Ben. Two or three times a week, he met Sara's father in Memorial Park where they sat on a bench and watched joggers. An early freeze had forced the leaves from the trees and now they crunched under the runners' feet.

The nurse, Smitty, looked forward to seeing Leonardo as much as Ben did. When the two of them huddled together, she craned her neck to watch. Ben mumbled words and Leonardo tried to repeat them several different ways.

"They told me he couldn't talk," she said to Leonardo. "But you seem to understand him."

Leonardo nodded.

"The family will be pleased. What a wonderful Christmas present."

Leonardo shot her a wary glance. "They want to put him in a home."

"My goodness, no. He doesn't need to be in a home," she protested, outraged. "I'll vouch for that."

"Then you may lose your position," the artist informed her.

She spread her hands, dejectedly. "We can't just keep quiet about this. Surely his doctor should be told of his progress."

"Not yet. I'd like to be able to work out a system so that

everyone can talk with him. Then they can't very well do anything."

Smitty agreed and left the two alone.

Each day after meeting with Ben, Leonardo took his notes home and transcribed them. After much study, he concluded that Ben's language was a mixture of Latin and Tuscan Italian. Occasionally, when excited, the old man threw in a Greek phrase, which made the going difficult. Now Leonardo had developed a response pattern in which he repeated each word or phrase in Italian and asked Ben for confirmation. If that didn't work, he repeated the word in Latin. Eventually, they agreed. Sometimes, however, Ben's attention wandered and he forgot what he'd just said.

Persistence paid off. The word "traitor," which Leonardo had caught earlier, continued to resurface in Ben's conversation. Sara's father believed that someone in his company was a traitor, but until now, he had been unwilling to identify him. Leonardo concluded that Ben wasn't sure he could trust anyone. His family, it seemed, had all turned against him. Ben had lost hope. Unable to communicate, he'd had nowhere to turn until Leonardo suddenly appeared.

"You are not a businessman," Ben said, although the way he said this was comical. In his garbled mixture of languages, it came out, "You are not a man of commerce."

Leonardo agreed. "No, I am an artist."

"You will not understand," Ben sighed disconsolately.

Then the younger man put a hand on Ben's shoulder. "I do understand, and I should tell you that I am in love with your daughter."

This news took Ben by surprise, and he wasn't sure how to react.

"She has broken her engagement with Roger."

At the mention of Roger's name, Ben became agitated. Standing, he gestured wildly and his speech was unintelligible. Smitty jumped up, concerned.

"What happened? What did you say to excite him so?"
she demanded.

"I don't know. I'm not sure."

With some effort, Leonardo calmed Ben down.

"You mustn't let him get worked up like that," the nurse
cautioned. "He could have another stroke. And then I don't
know what we'd do."

So Leonardo took a different track. They talked of other
things—trees, flowers, and birds. But the question of Roger
was always in the back of Leonardo's mind. If Roger had
saved the family business from ruin, why did Ben hate him
so? Perhaps the old man just resented handing over the reins
to someone younger. Still, Leonardo suspected it ran deeper
than that, and he vowed to get to the bottom of it before it
was too late.

Whenever possible, Sara's mother and brother applied
pressure on her to give up her relationship with Leonardo
and reconsider her plan to marry Roger. Since Leonardo
had moved out, they increased their efforts.

"You're not getting any younger," her mother reminded.

"What's that supposed to mean?" she snapped. But she
knew her mother thought it was time she settled down. Sara
was almost twenty-eight. All her college friends were married and many had children. She truly believed she loved
Leonardo, however the weeks of separation had taken an
emotional toll. They could never find time to be together
lately. Her schedule was tight. When she was free, he was
busy. Hurried meetings and frantic lovemaking left her more
frustrated than ever. Between their various commitments,
Sara was beginning to wonder if the separation would ever
end. When they did get back together, would they still feel
the same? Plagued by fears, she felt vulnerable and lonely.
Her family's interference only made matters worse. She
didn't want Roger. She wanted Leonardo. She missed the

sound of his voice and his low, gritty laughter. She longed for him to tell her of his day, sweep her into his arms, and kiss away her doubts. But for now, their relationship was on hold. Though she ignored her mother's comments, her insecurity grew with every passing day.

Even Sam had started seriously dating a woman named Susan, the daughter of one of Roger's investors. She'd come to dinner at the Carlyle house several times.

Blond and dimpled, Susan made a pretense of working in a boutique, but it was clear to Sara that her main job was that of being the daughter of a very wealthy man. It was Daddy this and Daddy that. "Daddy is so excited about the public offering," she said. "We'll all be rich. I just know it."

Sara forced a smile. Susan was like an animated doll who said, "Daddy," instead of "Mama." But a glance at her brother told her Sam was completely smitten.

Two weeks before Christmas, Kathryn announced that she'd arranged for the family to spend Christmas in Florida.

"We'll fly down to Orlando and stay at Club Med. I think the sun and warm weather will be good for your father."

Sara thought of Leonardo and how disappointed he would be if she were not here for Christmas. But the Carlyles hadn't had a family vacation in years. She imagined her father soaking up the warm sun.

"I think it's a wonderful idea," she said.

"Then it's settled," Kathryn said. "We leave the day before Christmas."

Sara thought about inviting Leonardo to come along, but she knew what her family would say. Ben didn't need the excitement. He needed to rest. Perhaps they were right, and the vacation would rejuvenate him. *If only it were true,* she thought.

A week before Christmas, she arranged to meet Leonardo for breakfast at a French bakery in Rice University Village. Exams were finally over, and she had just turned in final grades. She felt like celebrating, but Leonardo was immersed in his painting. With his show just months away, he was working around the clock.

"After my show, we will see each other more often," he promised.

Sara clung to the hope that his show would be successful. Once his career accelerated, they would be able to spend time together again. In another six months, everything would change. She had taken the summer off and would be free then. If only Leonardo was also free.

Seasonal decorations hung in the restaurant windows, and Christmas carols played in the background as she made her way to a vacant table. As usual, Leonardo was late.

Glancing around the small bistro, she recognized knots of students, a table of Rice professors and several local business owners. It was the kind of eclectic mix she loved. Living in Memorial set her apart from university life, she suddenly realized. Since her father's stroke, she'd been involved almost exclusively with her family. After teaching classes, she went home, never interacting at all with colleagues. That would soon change. She belonged here with people like herself discussing literature or art or anything other than Carlyle Chemical.

A few minutes later, Leonardo came rushing in. In blue work-shirt and jeans, he drew all eyes to him. Exuding masculine energy, he was handsome, vital, and he looked good. Better than good.

"Sorry I'm late, but I was working and forgot the time." He bent and kissed her. Immediately she warmed to his touch.

Each time they met, he was a little different. This time, she noticed a gold earring in his left earlobe when he sat opposite her. "You got your ears pierced," she commented.

"One ear," he corrected. "Dove told me I had to. He said investors actually expect artists to look like artists."

She raised an eyebrow, speculatively. "Whatever that means."

"An artist Dove knows had a show and dressed formally for the opening. Did you know, Sara, that he did not sell one painting? For his next show, he didn't comb his hair for a week and wore jeans and a dirty T-shirt. He sold out completely."

Sara broke out in laughter. "I can't believe it."

"Dove says it's PR. What's PR?"

"Public relations. In this case, it really means that people expect artists to be kind of wild and crazy."

Leonardo grinned. "That won't be hard for me."

She nodded. It was hard for her. All her life, she had done what was expected of her. She'd gone to school, studied hard, and excelled. Deep down, she always longed for the freedom to do as she pleased—to wear bright colors, to dance on tables. That was what attracted her to Leonardo. He personified the very qualities she desired.

The waiter brought them cappuccino and croissants. While they ate, they talked of his work and progress toward the show.

"It has taken longer than I expected to accumulate enough paintings for a show."

"Why? When we spoke last, you had already completed five."

"I know, but I sold two."

"Already?" Sara's eyes widened in amazement. *Roger was right,* she thought. *Things could happen quickly in the art world.* She was happy and a little sad at the same time, but she managed to hide her feelings.

"Yes. I had taken them by the gallery. Bryan said an investor from New York came by and bought them. Now I must paint more. And I only got a little bit of paper for them so I'm not sure it was worth it."

"How much did you get?"

"Here I'll show you what he gave me." He retrieved a rumpled check from his pocket and gave it to Sara.

Sara gasped. "Four thousand dollars. That is wonderful!"

"It is? I don't know what to do with it."

"You have to open a bank account," she instructed and proceeded to give him a short course in banking. He listened attentively, then was distracted by the flash of diamonds at her wrist.

"That is very beautiful," he remarked, catching her wrist.

"Thank you." She hadn't intended to wear the bracelet Roger had given her last year, but for some perverse reason, she did. Perhaps she wanted to make him jealous. Carefully she withdrew her hand from his and cast her eyes down to her plate.

"Roger gave it to you, didn't he?"

She couldn't very well deny it. "Yes, a long time ago," she replied.

Leonardo studied her, intently. "Sara, I know I have been busy lately, but I am trying hard to earn a living. I need to be able to provide for you. I have learned this is what men do in this age. Isn't it true?"

She had to agree. "But I fell in love with you because you weren't like other men."

Green eyes locked on hers. "You can't live on love," he said. "I read that in a book, I think."

She laughed. "I guess that's true."

He gazed at her solemnly. "I want to be able to give you things like this." He tapped her wrist. "But I have to work hard for enough paper to do that."

"I know."

"You aren't still seeing Roger, are you?"

"No, I . . . don't know why I wore it."

He frowned. "Your father hates Roger, you know."

Sara frowned. "You really think so?"

"I do."

"How do you know?"

"He told me."

Her gaze narrowed. "I didn't think you had been seeing my father."

Leonardo said nothing as he gazed at her steadily. But she could tell by his expression that he had been seeing Ben.

"Sam said the doctor doesn't want Dad getting excited, Leonardo. He thinks it might not be good for you to see him."

"Perhaps they're worried I might find out something."

Anger flashed in Sara's amber eyes. "What are you saying? That my brother is deliberately keeping you away from my father for some ulterior reason?"

He drew in a quick breath. "I don't know, but I plan to find out."

Sara's anger was full-blown now. Leonardo marveled at the attractive rise and fall of her breasts and the bright spots of color tingeing her cheeks. He wanted to take out his sketch pad.

"Leonardo, you may be right about Roger, but my brother only has the family's interests at heart," she said. "Until I figure this out, it might be best if you don't see Dad for a while. The doctors say he mustn't be excited."

"I know he likes to see me."

She exhaled quickly. "Perhaps, but it's not a good idea right now. It will just cause trouble."

He took her hand. "I'm doing it for your own good. I've told you that your father hates Roger, and I believe he has good reason."

She frowned. "Are you sure about that? Since you're the only one who understands him, you could put any interpretation you want on what he says. What if you are wrong?"

Her words hit home. At times, he wondered if he'd translated Ben's comments correctly. But his instincts told him Roger was not to be trusted. "I am only repeating what Ben said. He thinks Roger has ruined the company."

"Okay. If that's true, how has he done this, and what am I supposed to do about it?"

"I don't know how, but I'm going to find out."

Pursing her lips in thought, she shook her head. "I can't just charge in and accuse him of wrongdoing. There must be proof. Are you absolutely sure about all this?"

"Sara, I care too much about you to make up stories to win your love. I intend to win your love fairly by telling you how I feel, by telling you the truth."

Her expression softened then. Sometimes what he said touched her so deeply. He wanted to win her love as if there were a contest, as if anyone could compete with him. Was what she felt for him really love? Or was she only fascinated by someone who was her total opposite? She sighed. "Leonardo, I wanted to see you so I could give you a Christmas present."

He frowned. "But it isn't Christmas."

"Christmas is next week, and I'll be spending the holiday with my family." She withdrew a small box from her purse and handed it to him.

Tearing off the wrapping, he opened it and found a perfectly round amethyst ball. He held it in his hand and it captured the light in varying shades of purple.

"To recall the past," she said.

"And, perhaps, the future," he added, bending close to kiss her. "Thank you. I will treasure it always. Will I see you after Christmas?"

Her lips tightened. "We're all going to Florida. My mother thinks it will be good for my father."

"And is Roger going with you? He is part of the family, isn't he?"

"No, he is not," but she hesitated, wondering if her mother had some ulterior motive other than her father's health.

Leonardo saw her hesitation and the light in his green eyes frosted over.

"No, really. It's just my family," she tried to assure him.

"Your family is the most important thing in the world to you, Sara."

It was not a question; it was a statement. "I guess it seems so."

"Yes, it seems so. I'm not sure there is room for anyone else," he said, rising from the table.

"That's not true," she protested, following him to the cashier.

"It is true. Ultimately, it will be them or me, and you will have to choose."

Mechanically, he paid the bill and escorted her out to her car without speaking. When he opened her car door, she slipped into the driver's seat. His hand rested on the roof of her car as he gazed off into the distance. Then, with sudden resolve, he brought his hand down with a loud thump. "Well, I guess this is good-bye for a while, Sara. I have my work and you have your family."

After kissing her lightly on the cheek, he turned and walked away.

Sara was very aware that Leonardo had given her an ultimatum of sorts. But what were her choices? If she chose Leonardo, she would forsake her family. Right now, she wasn't sure she cared. Her mother and brother blindly followed Roger like a couple of sheep. But she did care about her father. After what Leonardo said, they were in the middle of a mystery she would have to unravel first.

Time and again, she had dreamed of their life together. Though she had her own money, Leonardo was adamant that he must earn a living. He refused to rely on her income. Although they hadn't talked about marriage, she knew he wouldn't want her to work, especially when they had children. His views were old-fashioned, but refreshing in a way. Her logical mind rebelled against her marrying an artist. Her head had always ruled her heart before. Now, as she approached her twenty-eighth year, her heart longed to be free.

Christmas brought the usual round of parties. The Carlyle company party, which in the past had always been a lavish catered affair, was relegated to a barbecue dinner at a local western restaurant. As a major stockholder, Sara was obligated to attend. She went with her mother.

Roger hurried to greet them the moment they arrived.

"I have you both seated at my table," he informed them, taking Sara's arm.

"I didn't think you liked barbecue," she remarked.

"I don't," Roger said, accepting a beer from a passing waiter, "but it's cheap, and we have to cut corners to ensure profits."

Sam and Susan showed up in matching western attire. They had been shopping together and had their names stenciled on the back of their belts.

"Daddy would love this," Susan said, wrinkling her nose when she smiled.

Sara nodded, thinking of Ben. Her father wouldn't love this. Not at all. Sam and Susan walked off, hand in hand.

She turned to her mother. "How's Dad?"

"Your father has not been himself lately," Kathryn lamented, shaking her head.

"But we're going to Florida. What did he say to that?"

"Nothing. He had no reaction at all," her mother said. "I'm not sure he understood."

Roger overheard the exchange. "Poor Ben. Seems like he's going downhill fast," Roger commented.

Not himself. Going downhill. Everything said about her father was negative. She cast a sidelong glance at Roger. If Leonardo was right, it would be in Roger's best interest to have Ben out of the way.

"You always say negative things about my father," she accused.

Roger looked as if she'd struck him. "You know I always tell the truth, Sara. I didn't mean anything by it."

They were the same words Leonardo had said. Sara turned away, thinking that Ben Carlyle would surely hate this affair. Each year, her father had donned a Santa outfit and took great pleasure in handing out gifts to employees' children. This year, there was no Santa. Santa had been replaced by a waitress in black leather shorts wearing a belt of tequila bottles. She walked up and down the long row of tables offering a shot of tequila and lime for five dollars. Her father might not be himself, but nothing else was the same either. Sara turned away in disgust.

She noticed other changes as the night wore on. The senior engineer who had been her father's right-hand man was conspicuously absent.

"Where is Mr. Weimer?" Sara asked.

"Didn't I tell you?" Roger responded innocently. "He took early retirement."

"Early retirement! I didn't think he was that old," Sara exclaimed.

Others were missing—the VP of Finance and the operations chief. Roger shrugged off their absence. "Lots of old people don't like barbecue. Too spicy, you know."

Was it really the food? Sara wondered, *or had they taken early retirement, too?*

As the restaurant filled, Sara realized she hardly recognized anyone. It was as if all the old guard had been replaced. Roger introduced her to each new employee, carefully explaining what happened to this person or that one. But in the end, when they finally sat at the head of the long table, Sara saw that Carlyle Chemical wore a completely new face. Even Sam was being displaced, she thought. But did her brother see what was happening? Too involved with Susan, Sam was oblivious to all else. Perhaps he didn't want to see. Perhaps he didn't care.

The change was apparent to Sara. She could feel the difference. Young, eager, and energetic, the company turned as one toward Roger and waited expectantly. Sara understood that there was only one face now. And that face was Roger's.

Consumed by doubt at the end of the party, she desperately wondered what she could do. She thought that after the holidays, she could persuade Sam to hire an auditor. Perhaps then they could get to the bottom of this.

Early on Christmas Eve, Sara brought her bag over to the Carlyle house. In a few hours, their plane would leave for Florida. She tiptoed into her father's study. Ben sat staring out of the window.

"Merry Christmas, Dad," she whispered, bending down to kiss him on the cheek.

A ghost of a smile flitted across Ben's features as he glanced up at his daughter, then he turned his attention back to the window.

"Dad, I have a present for you," Sara coaxed. "You can open it when we get to Florida."

Ben didn't respond.

"Mother, what's wrong with him?" Sara asked, tears welling in her eyes.

"Well, the doctor prescribed that new medication to calm him down. Roger brought it over two weeks ago. He's been sleeping well, but he acts depressed. Yesterday, I tried to talk to him and he started crying."

"Oh, no," Sara cried. "I can't believe it."

Kathryn sighed. "I know. Maybe Sam's right and he would be better off—"

"Don't say it, Mother," Sara ordered. "I don't want to talk about that. Especially not now. The fun and the fresh air will make him feel better."

Sam walked in and overheard their conversation. "Sara,

I don't want to spoil Christmas, but we will have to talk about this after the holidays. Mom can't go on like this."

Blinking away the tears, Kathryn stared at her folded hands. "Let's enjoy the holiday, dears. No more talk."

The doorbell rang and Susan appeared, two huge bags in tow. "I hope I brought enough clothes," she said.

Sara took her mother aside and Kathryn shrugged. "Sam wanted to invite Susan and I couldn't very well say 'no.' "

"I thought this was just a family vacation."

"It is," her mother pronounced. "But I have a feeling they may set a date soon."

Sara gave a deep sigh. Though she was happy for her brother, she felt left out, as if she didn't belong in this family anymore.

An hour later, the Carlyles and Susan took a taxi to the airport. All the freeways were jammed with traffic and they barely arrived in time to board. Just as they were seated on the plane, Roger rushed on at the last minute.

"I didn't think I would make it," he panted. "It's not easy to get away at Christmas." He slid into the vacant seat next to Sara.

Sara fixed her mother with an angry glare. Roger followed her gaze. "Did you not know I was coming? I was going to call another family meeting, but your mother said you were all going to Club Med in Florida. I thought that would be a great place to have a meeting. And," he whispered, conspiratorially, "we can write it all off."

Sara suddenly wanted to leave and be by herself. Had the doors not already closed, she would have left the plane. Her gaze rested on her father and she felt torn. For her family's sake, she would force herself to go through with this holiday, but no more. Leonardo was right. She was too dependent upon her family, and that dependence had to end now or she would never be free.

As the plane rose into the sunset, she wondered what Leonardo was doing at that moment.

On the other side of town, not far from the site of the Renaissance Festival, Leonardo stood looking at the property he intended to purchase: a vacant white-frame farmhouse wedged perfectly in the midst of a pine forest, as if it had dropped out of the sky aiming for that exact spot. Armed with a bottle of wine and a paper cup, he approached the house and sat on the porch. Dove and Stacy invited him to spend Christmas with them, but he'd declined in favor of spending the evening here alone.

"C'mon, man. Stacy's going to cook a vegetarian dinner," Dove had pleaded.

"Next year," Leonardo promised.

The chilly weather forced him to pull up the collar of his leather jacket, but he didn't mind. On this night, he wanted to be with the house.

In several weeks when the transaction was complete, a carpenter would replace the back windows with plate glass and add skylights to capture the late afternoon sun. Then it would be painted inside and out. Pouring himself a cup of wine, he saluted the house. His house.

The house responded with a gentle creak, which Leonardo interpreted as a positive response. He thought of Sara sitting on the beach in Florida. Would Roger be there with her? Somehow, he knew he would. Roger, the traitor. Unsuspecting, the Carlyles welcomed him into their midst, never imagining he might one day turn on them like a viper.

Sighing, Leonardo drained the cup. Often he'd tried to imagine himself in Roger's place, but he couldn't see it. Her family hated him, thought he was an ingrate, a troublemaker, a nuisance. Even if he were to obtain proof of Roger's duplicity, he was not entirely sure they would accept him.

He poured himself another glass and took the amethyst ball from his pocket. Turned this way and that, it captured the last rays of the setting sun. What did it all mean? Staring into the ball, he felt its pulsing energy radiate through his hand and he remembered.

He had only one purpose for coming into this life—Sara. She was the only woman he would ever love.

That is why he could not understand how he could have followed her through time into this life only to lose her.

Sixteen

Sara was furious. As the plane took them far away from Houston, she stewed. This time her family had gone too far. They wanted her to marry Roger and now were actively promoting their cause. All except Ben, who sat beside her mother and looked a little distracted, as though he didn't know where he was.

"I hope you don't mind that I came along," Roger said, reading her thoughts. "When your mother mentioned the family was going to Florida, I guess I invited myself. I thought we might have a business meeting, but the real truth was that I really didn't have any place to go for Christmas."

"Business meeting! This is supposed to be a vacation—a *family* vacation." Her voice rose and several people turned to stare at them.

"I had no intention of intruding. I spent Christmas with you last year so I thought you wouldn't mind."

"It's a little awkward, that's all," Sara remarked. His expression made her feel a little sorry for him. It was true that he had no place to go. His father left when he was ten, and his mother had died only recently. Since he spent last Christmas with the Carlyles, he had every reason to believe he would be included this year. But things had changed. *She* had changed.

"We'll all go our own way and have a good time," he assured her with a pat on her hand.

She withdrew her hand and looked away. Somehow she would get through all this. When they returned to Houston, she would put a stop to this togetherness. Leonardo's analysis was correct. In this tightly knit group, there was no room for him. That much was clear.

While Roger talked nonstop about business, Sara tuned him out. Doubts about his motives escalated. What did he really want? Was he a traitor as Leonardo said? If so, what had he done? Thoughts swirled through her head, and by the time they arrived at Club Med in Florida, she felt flushed and dizzy.

A cheerleading squad of Club Med workers in Hawaiian shirts and shorts greeted them with glasses of wine. Eschewing the wine, Sara went immediately to her room and threw up. Despite the balmy weather, she spent Christmas in bed.

The resort had a doctor on call. Finally, after three days, Sara consented to see him.

When he'd examined her, the doctor concluded she had a virus and gave her a prescription for antibiotics. Gradually, the fever abated. The following day, she felt well enough to sit outside with her father while the rest of her family and Roger set out for a day of water-skiing.

She'd purchased a leather case with pastels, water colors, brushes and a block of watercolor paper for her father's Christmas present. Opening the case, Ben seemed pleased and Sara hugged him.

"Merry Christmas, Dad," she said.

He smiled at her.

Then feeling tired, she returned to her room. Even the warm, bright sun had done little to lift her spirits. She realized she didn't want to be here. She wanted to be with Leonardo.

What was he doing? Did he miss her? It wasn't fair that her family had excluded him again, in favor of Roger. Of course he would be angry. All along, she had been torn between her obligations to her family and her desire to be with him. It seemed however she chose, she would lose. Now she knew the time had come to make a decision.

At noon, Roger, Sam, and Susan returned, exhausted and sunburned. Roger was openly attentive, genuinely concerned about her. She had to admit he had really changed in the past few months. *Too late,* she thought. *Too late.*

Sam and Susan were the perfect couple except for Susan's odd habit of talking about her father constantly. If Sara thought she was too dependent upon her own family, she had only to look at Susan. In many ways, Susan was still a little girl. She checked in with Daddy often and reported their conversations.

"Daddy's playing golf today," she exclaimed. "I told him all about Club Med. He said he might come next year."

They all smiled at her. What else could they do?

"I just know he would love it here," she giggled.

Totally in love, Sam didn't notice any of Susan's shortcomings. Sara had never seen her brother so happy and she was glad. Kathryn, too, was enjoying herself for the first time in months. Since Ben's stroke they had all been under a terrific strain, and it was good to get away. Only Ben was quiet and still seemed out of sorts.

On their fifth day at Club Med, Sara felt well enough to accompany her family to dinner. They followed the crowd to a sumptuous repast laid out in the Club Med dining room. Sara loaded her plate, but ate very little.

As usual, Roger and Sam talked about business.

"Once we take it public, we'll get the company on NASDAQ" Roger said. "Then we can play with the stock a little and cash out."

"What will happen to the company then?" Sara asked, concerned. Her stomach knotted as it did now every time they talked about business.

She glanced at her father who was chewing methodically.

There was no expression on his face, so she wasn't sure if he'd heard.

Roger smiled indulgently and patted her hand. "It'll be run with a skeleton crew. For all practical purposes, once we take our money out, we won't need the company anymore."

"But Dad worked all his life for this company, and you're just going to trash it?" She tried to keep her voice low so her father wouldn't be upset.

"Not trash it, Sara," Sam corrected. "Cash out. Don't you understand what that means? None of us will have to work anymore. We can come down here to Club Med two or three times a year if we want. I can tell you, I'm looking forward to it."

"It's just good business," Roger assured her. "I know some men have their egos so connected to their work that their companies become personal monuments, testimonies to life achievements. I don't like to get that involved. It clouds your judgment. After we cash out, we'll have so much money, we can go start a dozen little Carlyle Chemicals if we want."

Ben Carlyle laid his fork down and stared at Roger. He began talking unintelligibly and grew more agitated with each utterance.

"I believe Dad understands what you just said," Sara told Sam angrily. "He's not dead, you know."

Sam shrugged. "Sara, you know I'd include Dad in this if I could understand what he's saying."

Roger smiled. "Well, Ben, tell us what you think about all this."

Ben glared at him, belligerently.

Kathryn Carlyle patted her husband's arm. "Calm down, dear." She sighed and smiled. "This is a wonderful place," she said, attempting to change the subject. "I think we should come here every year."

"You should be able to when we cash out," Roger nodded.

Helpless fury welled in Sara. They acted as if Ben was incompetent just because they couldn't understand his words. His eyes told her intelligence was still there. Leonardo had said he did understand many things. She imagined what he might be thinking right now. He'd devoted much of his life to a cause that would soon be lost. His goal had been to build up a legacy for his family, and to that end, he'd succeeded. Now it seemed the company was to be sacrificed for financial security. Though she understood the reasoning, she didn't think Ben approved. Regardless of what she thought, they were going ahead with their plans.

Sara felt better with each passing day at Club Med. While they were there, she had a serious discussion with her mother about interfering in her life.

"I love you, but I must make my own decisions," she informed her mother.

"Of course, dear. I am sorry about Roger. But what could I say?" her mother asked. "He invited himself."

"You could have said 'no,' " Sara admonished. "I felt very strange about the whole thing, like I was being set up."

Kathryn smiled and nodded a little sadly. "It's definitely over between you two, isn't it?"

"Yes," Sara said firmly.

"And you plan to marry this Leonardo?" Her mother arched a delicate brow in obvious disapproval.

Sara sighed. "You better get used to this Leonardo, Mother. I think he's going to be around for a long time."

The moment Sara returned to her townhouse on the bayou, her fever returned. With it, she developed a rash, not unlike the rash that had covered Timothy Blanton's body a month earlier. There were several calls from Leonardo on her answering machine. Despite her illness, she tried to return his calls, but couldn't reach him.

Later, she learned that several other people with houses along the bayou near Carlyle Chemical developed fevers and rashes similar to Sara's. They were all told by doctors that they were experiencing an allergic reaction to something. Filled with antibiotics, they returned home and improved. Somewhat.

Laden with several toxic chemicals, the bayou seeped into the Memorial area surrounding Carlyle Chemical, killing birds and small animals at various intervals. But no one noticed. Except Ben Carlyle. His nurse reluctantly accompanied him on frequent trips down to the bayou.

"He's fascinated by nature and wildlife," Smitty confided to Leonardo. "At least once a week he makes me stop the car so he can walk down by the bayou."

In Italy there were canals, streams, and rivers. But Leonardo had never heard the word 'bayou' until he came to Houston. To his knowledge, the word did not have an equivalent in either Italian or Latin. Despite this stumbling block, he tried to question Ben about his excursions.

"Do you like the river?" he asked.

Ben did not reply.

"Do you like the stream?"

No response.

"Are you looking at the water?" he finally asked.

To this, Ben nodded affirmatively. He launched into a confused diatribe and ended by holding his nose.

"Is something wrong with the water?" Leonardo tried again.

Ben produced a jar of water.

Smitty shrugged. "He collected that this morning. I don't know what he wants with it."

The old man pushed it toward Leonardo. With some effort, the artist understood that Ben wanted him to have the water tested. He had no idea how to go about that.

"I can't imagine why he wants you to do this, but the

health department will test it for you at no charge," Smitty supplied.

With Smitty's directions, Leonardo found the health department and dutifully took the jar of water in to be tested.

"You say this water is from the bayou?" the lab technician asked. When Leonardo nodded, she wrote an identification tag and slapped it on the jar. "We're backed up here. I can't even tell you when we'll get around to it. If you'll leave me a telephone number, I'll call you when we get the results."

Leonardo left Dove's telephone number. He didn't have a phone in his new house and didn't want one. They were a nuisance. After thanking the woman, he stopped by Sara's townhouse, but no one was home. Later, he called and left another message on her answering machine. He hated little talking machines. He'd noticed several peculiarities about this age. People communicated through their machines and could go for long periods, perhaps their entire lives, without ever seeing another human being. They relied on their machines instead of one another. This, he felt, was not good.

He had been angry when he last saw Sara and had demanded that she choose between her family and their relationship. Now he realized that he had been unfair. He couldn't force her to make such a choice. She had to come to a decision on her own. The two weeks without her had been intolerable. But where was she?

Later, he drove out to inspect the construction on his house. He wondered what Sara would think of it and decided to wait until it was finished to show it to her.

Recent rains had left the shrubs and trees dripping with a silvery sheen, as if some painter had varnished the fading color to hold it fast. He rolled down the window to breathe in the crisp air, feeling a little nostalgic. Soon it would be spring again and he longed to be back home. But where was home? The Florence he knew no longer existed. If he returned to Italy, he wouldn't recognize it, and that might be even more painful. His mother and two younger brothers would have been dead for hundreds of years. In fact, the Brazzi family might have died out altogether, he thought wistfully. He was a man without a past. His past was gone.

When he drove through Magnolia, he always thought of Sara. He visualized her face, her creamy skin, and the molten amber of her eyes. Though they had known one another only a few months, his life had changed dramatically in that short interval. Often he had driven by the site of the Renaissance Festival. He had bought a house nearby because it was the only real tie he had to anything. The season had ended and everything was closed now. It gave him an odd feeling to think it was only a show. The Renaissance Festival wasn't real, and he wondered sometimes if he were real. He had no way of knowing for sure.

Turning right, he crossed the railroad tracks and then took 101 toward Navasota. A short distance away, he drove onto a gravel road leading up to a small farmhouse—his house. Though it would normally be hard to find, today there were dozens of vehicles parked outside.

The van coughed to a halt and Leonardo slowly alighted. A proud smile tilted up the corners of his mouth. It was finally coming together. A fresh coat of paint had completely revitalized the exterior. It was Taos blue as Dove had instructed— to ward off evil spirits. Though Leonardo wasn't sure what Taos was, he vaguely remembered something connected with an Eastern religion. Being superstitious, he felt he couldn't afford spirits at all, evil or otherwise. Obviously the house liked the color. It looked like a little piece of sky had dropped down between the trees. A surge of pleasure went through him as he gazed at it fondly.

He walked around back to see how the construction was progressing. Workmen were busily trimming out and painting a bank of windows that enclosed what had been a screened porch.

"You'll have plenty of light in here now," the foreman assured him.

Leonardo nodded. The work would all be finished by the middle of February. He was anxious to move. He had completed five canvases and would need many more for his show, scheduled for the last week in April. Already he had sold five of Henry's coins, and the rest were securely housed in a safety deposit box. They were his insurance for the future.

The gallery owner, Jasper Bryan, had promised he would make a good profit from his show, and Leonardo desperately hoped he was correct. But would it be enough to support Sara and their children? With a twinge of regret, he realized it would be a long time before he could afford to give her diamond bracelets. Still, as Dove said, if he established a reputation, he could slowly build a clientele. He interpreted this to mean that word of mouth would draw a steady stream of patrons to him. *If only that were true,* he thought. *If only it would happen soon.*

Sara was anxious to talk to Leonardo, not only because she missed him but because she had been haunted by her father's reaction to Roger's plan. But she continued to have intermittent bouts of fever and often couldn't get out of bed. Her doctor was baffled.

"Have you been around any toxic chemicals such as polyurethane?" he asked.

"Not that I'm aware of."

He shook his head. "I can give you another prescription for a different antibiotic. Let's hope this one works."

When she felt better, she tried to call Leonardo, but couldn't reach him. No one answered at Dove's studio, and Dove was not working at Texas Art Supply. Had Leonardo left town suddenly without telling her? she wondered. All sorts of terrible thoughts went through her mind that only made her feel worse.

Finally he called when she was at the doctor's and left a message that she could reach him at Dove's studio. Again she missed his call. Where was he? She had to talk to him. On impulse, she dropped by the studio one day only to find Leonardo had moved.

"He moved into a house," Dove informed her. "It's great. Way the hell out in the country, but he loves it."

"Please tell him to call me again," Sara pleaded.

"Will do," Dove promised.

A week later, he called again. This time she was there.

"I would like to invite you to my new house," Leonardo said formally.

"Why haven't you returned my calls? I didn't know you moved."

"Yes, I bought a house."

"You bought it? How did you do that?"

"It's very simple, Sara. I gave them the paper they wanted and they gave me the key."

She couldn't hide her astonishment. "I can't believe it. Soon you'll be wearing boots and a ten-gallon hat."

"I am wearing boots, but I don't like hats."

She laughed. She had missed hearing his voice. The low, gritty texture of his words soothed her soul and lifted her spirits. She agreed to drive out to his house the following day.

She arose an hour early to select just the right thing to wear. Since she had only one class to meet, she would go directly from the university on I-45. After some deliberation, she decided on a flowing honey-colored silk tunic and pants. It was a little dressy for class, but she didn't mind. She had a date.

Driving out to Magnolia brought back memories. It had been almost six months since the Renaissance Festival. The festival had occurred every year for more than a decade, yet last October it had changed her life. Had Leonardo not appeared, she would already be married to Roger. It was strange how a day, an hour, or a moment in time could instantly redirect your path.

She was a little amazed that Leonardo had bought a house, especially now when he had such a tight schedule. At the same time, the idea intrigued her. Undoubtedly, he was the most marvelously unpredictable man she had ever met.

As she turned off the freeway onto the Magnolia exit, she grew more excited. Just the prospect of seeing Leonardo again set her senses reeling and her heart beating fast. It had been too long this time.

Of course, he had never been far from her thoughts. Green eyes haunted dreams filled with her internal struggle. Once she saw him in a sword fight with Roger, about to run him through with his father's saber. On the sideline, she tried to pull them apart before it was too late. She never saw the outcome and still did not know how it would all end.

Constantly pulled between her family and Leonardo, she felt like she was on an emotional rollercoaster. Though her mother and brother disapproved, her heart had chosen Leonardo. Overriding her feelings for Leonardo was her desire to talk to him about her father. Instinctively, she knew her entire life was about to change dramatically.

Driving through the countryside, Sara again experienced that eerie feeling she'd felt at the Renaissance Festival. It was as if she were being drawn back again. *Could it happen twice?* she wondered.

Following her handwritten directions she turned off onto a gravel road. *My God,* she thought. *This is remote.*

Then she saw the small house sitting in the trees and her heart leaped to her throat. It was a fairytale cottage straight out of a childhood story book.

Leonardo's van was parked at the back of the house, and a truck was nearby. Probably a workman, she thought. She was an hour early, but didn't think he'd mind.

Alighting from her car, she breathed in the fresh, country air. Heaven. Pure heaven. Flowers and a few shrubs lined a small walkway, and Sara admired his choice. He was an amazing man.

She knocked on the door. When there was no answer, she tried it, found it unlocked and walked in. Not much furniture, she thought. But that would change. The sound of voices drew her to the back of the house where she supposed the studio was.

She paused in the doorway.

Light streamed in through dozens of open windows and two overhead fans circulated the air. These things escaped Sara's attention. Her gaze focused on the nude girl reclining on a settee before Leonardo's easel.

"Sara!" He sounded almost surprised to see her.

Sitting up, the girl quickly threw a robe around her shoulders.

"I guess I'm early." Sara's words sounded clipped and toneless.

"A little, but I'm glad you're here." He rose and wiped his brush.

Sara wrinkled her nose and her lips tightened into a straight line. "Looks like you're really busy. I'll come back another time." She turned on her heel and left the room abruptly.

"Sara," he called after her.

She didn't stop or turn around until he caught her shoulder. "Sara, what's wrong?"

"What's wrong? You have a nude woman reclining in your studio and you ask me what's wrong?"

"I'm just painting her."

"Just painting her?"

"I needed a model, and she was the only one I could find. I'd much rather paint you."

"You expect me to believe that?"

"Yes. Would you give up your job at the university to come be my model?"

"That's not fair and you know it."

"I'm sorry. I didn't mean to upset you. She was supposed to leave an hour ago. I forgot the time."

"I see. You weren't going to mention her at all."

He spread his hands. "Sara, I'm an artist. I'm very good at nudes and, occasionally, I have to have a model. There's nothing more to it than that."

Just then, the girl came out of the back door of the house fully dressed. She climbed in the truck and backed it out. When she arrived next to them, she rolled down the window. "You can mail me my check. I'll tell Stacy you said 'hi,' " she said, then waved as she drove away.

She couldn't have been more than twenty, Sara noted, ruefully. "She's a friend of Stacy's?"

He nodded. "Please Sara, she is only a model. Will you stay and have lunch?"

Sara softened. "I guess so. After all, I drove all the way out here."

He gave her a tour of the house. The only real furniture was a double bed and a nightstand. A card table and folding chairs were set up in an alcove off the tiny kitchen. He set wine, bread, and cheese on the table. Something about the repast reminded Sara of their time in England. Even the wine tasted familiar.

"This will just be my studio," he said, referring to the house. "I will buy another house when I sell more paintings."

"Another house?"

"For us, Sara."

"For us?" She liked the sound of his words.

"Yes, I like houses. I'm good with them, I think. I would like our house to be close by. What do you think?"

She frowned. It would be like living in another city—so

far away from her family and everything she'd known. She thought of her father and a sudden sadness enveloped her.

"You look troubled Sara. What's wrong?"

I wanted to talk to you about my father. Roger showed up at Club Med as you thought."

Leonardo smacked the table with his hand. "I knew it."

She nodded. "Well, I didn't. Anyway, Dad became very upset when Roger talked about plans for taking the company public then cashing out."

"Cashing out?"

"Roger wants to run up the stock and sell it quickly for a large profit. My father became livid when he heard this."

"Of course, your father does not trust Roger."

"But I don't know how to stop it all. Can you ask him what I can do? If only I could talk to him."

Sara's eyes filled with tears and Leonardo gathered her in his arms. "I will talk to him soon," he promised.

She didn't resist when he tenderly kissed her tears away. "Don't cry, my darling," he soothed.

Sara melted into his embrace, feeling secure and warm for the first time in weeks. Picking her up, he carried her into the bedroom. Slowly, he undressed her, kissing her hair, her neck, and her shoulders as the silk tunic melted away from her body.

"You are absolutely perfect," he said. His eyes were like emeralds, deep and clear.

Divesting him of his clothes, she traced the familiar lines of his muscled body. It had been too long. Far too long. She kissed his chest and ran her tongue along his shoulders. He groaned with pleasure. "Oh, Sara, I have missed you so," he whispered.

She glanced at the bathrobe lying on a chair. Little fingers of jealousy robbed her of the total joy she should have felt, when she suddenly remembered the model. Had he slept with her? "What was her name?" she asked as he led her to his bed.

"Whose name?"

"The girl who was here."

"I don't know. Something strange. Heather, I think."

Sara was not satisfied by his reply and he sensed the question she did not ask. "I did not make love with her," he said. "Sara, it is you I love. Only you."

Drawing her into his arms, he caressed her so tenderly that her nerves were instantly calmed into submission. From deep inside, she felt every fiber of her being gentled into compliancy. Soft, honeyed kisses drove away her doubts. His tongue probed and she answered. Yes. Yes. Instinctively, he knew where to touch, where to tease, how to arouse her deepest passion. It both frightened and pleased her that he knew her so well. Little by little her fears fled to a far away place and she gave herself to him totally.

The fiery explosion of pent-up emotions cascaded around them in dizzying lights and colors and feelings. The magic was still there, more intense now, more deeply felt. Finally, breathless and sated, they lay entwined listening to the combined throbbing of their hearts.

Later, they dressed and talked about Leonardo's show. It was almost dusk when Sara got in her car to leave.

"You will come back again soon?" he asked, his green eyes pleading.

"Yes," she answered. "I will come back soon."

The next few weeks flew by, and soon Sara had to devote herself to preparing midterms for her students. But on weekends, she hurried out to Leonardo's studio in the country.

Leonardo painted feverishly, possessed by a strong desire to prove himself to Sara. Desperately he wanted to buy her diamond bracelets, a new home, and a new car. It would not be easy, he knew. He would have to establish himself as a presence in the art world. Only then could he count on a measure of security.

Sara finally realized that no matter what, she loved Leonardo. Defying family and friends, she gave herself completely. Never had she been so happy. Never had she felt so free.

Leonardo wanted her to move in with him. When the spring semester ended, she thought she might consider putting her townhouse on the market. The country air had completely revitalized her, and she'd had no more bouts with fever.

On the Friday before Spring vacation, she sat in her office grading tests. Her mind kept wandering to Leonardo. She hadn't seen him in a week and she was looking forward to spending her entire vacation with him.

She heard someone in the outer office and looked up to find Roger framed in her doorway. His eyes were bloodshot and his face looked drawn. "I hoped you would be in today."

"What's wrong?" she asked. "You look terrible."

"I didn't sleep at all last night. And I doubt if it will get any better until this thing is resolved."

She frowned. "What are you talking about?" She'd begun to have serious doubts about Roger and wondered what he was up to now.

"You haven't talked to Sam?"

"No, I have been busy."

A slight sneer cut through his features. "With your artist friend?"

"I have midterms to grade. They've taken up all my time lately."

"Then I guess you haven't read the paper."

She shook her head, exasperated. "No. I rarely get a chance to read the paper. Why?"

"Your friend, Leonardo, is trying to ruin us. I told you he has ulterior motives."

"What!"

"It's all over the newspapers. He claims the bayou is being polluted."

"I don't understand. How would he know if the bayou were polluted or not?"

He threw a copy of the Houston paper down on her desk. Sara glanced at Leonardo's picture on the front page and gasped.

"I'm sure there's some explanation. This is not like Leonardo." But her thoughts were churning. Why hadn't he told her?

"Oh, I think it is very much like Leonardo. Doesn't he have a show coming up soon?"

"Yes, but what does that have to do with anything?"

"This is his way of gaining publicity at our expense. Carlyle Chemical is named as a possible polluter. Do you know what that means?" Roger's expression was livid.

"I'm sure he didn't mean to undermine us. He's not like that."

Roger's blue eyes narrowed into little slits of ice. At that moment, Sara was startled to see that he looked exactly like Guy Lemontaine.

"Just what do you expect me to do, Roger?"

"You can tell your friend he'd better retract his statement or he'll have a lawsuit on his hands. And, personally, Sara, I would take great pleasure in making sure he never works again."

Seventeen

After Roger stormed out, Sara immediately tried to call Leonardo. She got Dove's answering service. Damn! Why didn't Leonardo have his own phone? Why hadn't he told her about the lab report? Together, they could have come up with a plan of action. Instead, he'd gone public and now had the whole city of Houston up in arms. She felt a hard knot of fear form in the pit of her stomach.

Glancing at the paper, she noticed Leonardo's expression was a little surprised, as if the camera had caught him off guard. However, next to him was the head of the Houston health department, Dr. Walton Meigs, who held a small vial of water from Buffalo Bayou.

"If a responsible citizen such as Mr. Brazzi hadn't come forward and demanded action, our city's water supply might have been severely compromised. As it is, a massive cleanup will be underway immediately," Dr. Meigs said.

Carlyle Chemical was named as the major polluter. Little fingers of dread marched up her spine. The more she read, the worse it sounded. Though Leonardo was right in coming forward, the damage to the company might be irreparable. She knew her family would be outraged.

As if mirroring her thoughts, her brother called. "Mother is beside herself. With everything else, I don't think she can take anymore stress. I'd just like to know what Leonardo had in mind."

"Sam, he did what he had to do. If we've polluted the

bayou, we need to take responsibility for it. What I want to know is how this happened?"

Sam was in no mood to explain. "Look, it almost doesn't matter what happened. We have cut down our manpower. Apparently the system isn't working properly."

"Are you sure about that Sam? Is that what Roger told you? Dad's system was supposed to be the best in this part of the country. Roger has changed everything around. How do you know he didn't change that, too?"

Sam was suddenly defensive, and she heard fury in his voice. "Whose side are you on here? This is your money, too. I intend to get together with Roger and we'll look into these things. But all this adverse publicity is ruining us, don't you see that? Why didn't Leonardo come to us before he went public?"

"Obviously, he could not come to us. He knew no one would believe him. He had to take matters into his own hands."

"Sara, already our sales have fallen off, and customers are calling to complain," Sam shouted. "Don't you realize a scandal like this could stop us from taking the company public? We won't get a chance to find out what is wrong. In fact, we won't be able to do anything at all."

Sam's anxiety was contagious, and it was all she could do to keep her voice calm. "Settle down, Sam. Let's just tell them we'll clean it up," she suggested. "Then perhaps Leonardo will make another statement. Surely all this can be smoothed over somehow."

"I wish it were that simple. At this point, I doubt we can even afford to clean it up. Please, we don't need anymore statements from Leonardo. He's done enough damage already."

Sam's words cut into her like a knife. She tried to tell herself that he was overreacting. However, businesses had folded overnight due to a crisis like this. "Roger said he would file a lawsuit if Leonardo doesn't retract his statement," she informed him.

"It's too late for a retraction. The media is having a feeding frenzy. You know Sara," Sam's voice was deadly serious, "at some time, you'll have to make some hard choices. This man is ruining the family."

After hours of trying, she finally reached Dove and left an urgent message for Leonardo. However, the situation escalated overnight. The following day an article about the polluted bayou appeared in the newspaper. TV and radio shows constantly referred to the growing crisis of Buffalo Bayou.

Kathryn Carlyle was beside herself when Sara went by the house two days later.

"Leonardo may well have ruined us all," she commented.

"Mother, it isn't his fault the bayou is polluted," Sara countered defensively.

"Had he cared about this family, or you, for that matter, he could have told us about this before he called in the media," Kathryn replied, tersely.

"And that would have helped?"

"At least we would have been prepared," her mother said.

"Do you realize this is probably Roger's fault?"

"Roger's?"

"Yes, Sam said they'd had to cut down on manpower because of expenses. It's Roger's fault that the bayou is polluted, Mother."

"Oh well, I don't know what to say." Kathryn waved away her statement as if it were of no consequence. "I do know that whatever problems we have could have been handled privately. Now that they are public, I doubt we can salvage the company."

Sara approached her father who sat at his desk. "Do you know what's happened, Dad?" she asked.

Ben looked at her and smiled.

"I don't think he understands you, dear," Kathryn said.

"I've tried to talk to him, too. I'm at my wit's end." Tears filled her mother's eyes. Sara moved over and hugged her.

The truth had to come out, but why did it have to be so painful? She couldn't bear to see her mother so upset. Right or wrong, the company might be ruined and indirectly it would be Leonardo's fault. Though she defended Leonardo to her family, Sara had the sinking feeling that they would never allow him in their house, much less accept him as her husband.

Reports of toxic poisoning began to surface. That night, Sara watched an interview with the Blanton family who lived in the next subdivision. The Blantons claimed that their son, Timothy, had suffered a high fever and rash on and off for the last six months. After listening to his symptoms, Sara's spirits fell. She realized that she, too, had suffered from the same malady. The newscaster indicated that people living near Carlyle Chemical Company could have been exposed to toxic chemicals.

Kathryn Carlyle put her hands over her face and wept. "How can it get any worse?" she sobbed.

Leonardo's picture flashed on the screen.

"Were it not for this man," the newscaster said, "the situation could have become critical."

Leonardo had become a modern-day folk hero.

"Good heavens!" Kathryn said and turned away.

Sara checked her answering machine and there were several messages from Leonardo. He was sorry, he said. He needed to talk to her. She shook her head and sighed. Well, she certainly needed to talk to him.

Leonardo had left hundreds of messages on Sara's answering machine. He'd called her office so many times her secretary was tired of hearing his voice. In desperation, he drove by her townhouse, but she wasn't home. He wanted to explain that he had no idea that the newspaper would put his picture on the front page. After that, the press had hounded him every day. Everything he said had been twisted to appear as if he were on some sort of crusade. Now it seemed he was president of an environmental group. That he had never heard of such a group didn't make any difference.

Dove had called to say Sara was trying to reach him. "She sounded stressed out," Dove said.

Leonardo could only imagine what she thought of him and was, by now, a little afraid of what she might say. Finally he stationed himself in Sara's townhouse parking lot and waited for her to return. When he saw her drive up, he leaped out of the van to intercept her.

"Sara, where have you been?"

Her face was drawn and she looked as though she hadn't slept in some time. Pausing as if in a trance, she only stared at him without speaking.

"Sara, what's wrong?"

"What's wrong? My family is falling apart, the company is ruined. My parents and brother will probably be bankrupt and I am trying to understand how this whole thing came about. What did you have in mind when you went to the health department?"

"I? I just wanted to find out if the bayou was polluted."

Her eyes widened. "You were just curious?"

"Well, it was more than curiosity. I—"

"Did you think about the possible consequences of this?"

"Not really because—"

"Then I don't want to talk to you anymore. Please excuse me."

She turned to walk to her townhouse. Shoulders drooping, but head held high, she looked like a defeated soldier returning from a war. Leonardo's heart constricted in his chest. Every move he made was the wrong one.

"Sara! Do you think this was my idea?"

She stopped and cast him a sidelong glance. "If it wasn't your idea, please tell me who thought up this brilliant plan?"

"Your father. He's the one who collected the water and sent me to the health department with it."

She swiveled around. "Do you expect me to believe that? My father can't even talk. How did he tell you to do that? He certainly wouldn't want to sabotage his own company!"

"Oh? He's suspected for some time that the bayou was being polluted."

She frowned. *"He* collected the water?"

"Yes. I didn't know there was a health department. In my time, we don't have such things. The nurse told me where to go."

She had to acknowledge the truth of his words. He had learned many things, however he would not have known the procedure. "Even if my father provided you with the water and ordered you to have it tested, I really don't think he had this outcome in mind."

Leonardo closed the distance between them and stood looking down at her. Green eyes bored into hers. "He wanted to stop it—any way he could."

"I tried to talk to him about this yesterday, but he didn't understand."

"I've told you, he doesn't understand English. He has indicated that Roger is behind all this."

Sara put her hand over her eyes. Suddenly, she was very tired. "He may be right. But now it might be too late to do anything about it."

"What do you mean? You can fix it, Sara. Then everything will be all right."

She saw the innocence of childhood reflected in his green eyes. His motives had been pure and honest. He just didn't understand how American business worked. She shook her head and turned away. Methodically, she unlocked the townhouse door and walked in. He followed. Throwing down her purse and books, she collapsed on the couch and he joined her.

"I'm sorry it turned out like this," he told her softly.

She sighed. "I wish it could have been done differently so that everyone had a chance to react before the media got it."

Leonardo pursed his lips in thought. "I'm not pleased about the way they've handled it, but apparently, the media is the fastest way to get a message across. I think your father feared that the situation could become dangerous."

Sara turned, frowning. "How do you know what my father thinks? Do you really talk to him or do you only interpret what you think he means?"

"I do a little of both. I am hoping to find a way that you all can communicate with him as I do."

Sara looked away. She would give anything to be able to talk to her father again. Now she didn't know what she would say.

Leonardo took her hand and kissed it. "At moments like these, I think I should never have come back with you. Perhaps I would have been better off in my own time."

"You would have been killed."

"It seems I've encountered as much trouble here."

He was right, Sara thought. For some reason, he drew problems to him. Now his problems were hers as well and, at the moment, they seemed insurmountable.

Dropping her hand, he rose.

"Where are you going?"

"I have work to do. I have only a few weeks until my show."

Suddenly she realized how much time had elapsed. It was March, and Leonardo's show was scheduled for the middle of April. She forced a smile, but her heart wasn't in it.

"Tell me you will come, Sara."

The beseeching look in his green eyes left her with little

choice. Though her family might not like it, she was determined to go. "Yes, I'll be there."

Bending, he kissed her lightly on the cheek, then left. Sara stared after him. Her heart hurt from this tug of war between her family, Roger, and Leonardo. *How could things get any worse?* she wondered.

Things did get worse. When Carlyle Chemical was threatened with lawsuits, the media seized the information. Several more people came down with symptoms of toxic poisoning. Complications continued to pop up every day. After many complaints and phone calls, the Carlyles drew the drapes and dug in for a long siege. When a national news program focused on Houston's Plague, Roger called a family meeting.

Sara arrived to find her mother distraught and her brother fuming. Roger sat in their midst, plotting a counter strategy.

"I have written a press release stating we had no knowledge of any pollution stemming from our company," he announced. "We instigated pollution controls years ago and assumed they were still in good working order. We disclaim any liability. Other companies must be at fault."

"Roger, why would you say something so obviously untrue?" Sara asked, aghast. "We are at fault. Why not own up to the fact and get it behind us? Other companies have survived crises like this one."

"What makes you think the fault is all ours?" Roger snapped.

"According to Leonardo, Dad indicated—"

Everyone in the family stopped to look at Ben who stared straight ahead.

"I don't believe any of that," Roger barked. "I don't believe your dad gave Leonardo the water to test. It sounds like a made-up story to me. Ben hasn't uttered a single word we could understand in the past eighteen months, and we're supposed to accept as fact that he communicates with a foreign artist. If he was communicating, do you think he would instruct Leonardo to expose his own family as frauds and criminals? Ben wouldn't do that."

"Dad thinks you're the criminal," Sara countered.

"Well, that's great," Roger shouted. "Then why don't I just resign right now?"

"Wait a minute!" Sam ordered. "Sara, I think you've lost your mind! We don't know what Dad has said, if anything!"

Again, they turned as one and looked at Ben who stared at each of them, one by one.

Is there a trace of the old fire in his eyes? Sara wondered. When Ben turned away at last, she told herself she'd imagined it.

"You see?" Sam said. "If he confides in Leonardo, why wouldn't he confide in his own family?"

"Then ask the nurse," Sara pleaded. "What's her name, Smitty?"

"She's gone," her brother informed her. "We hired a new nurse with strict instructions that Dad is not to talk to Leonardo under any circumstances."

"But Dad wanted him to test the water—"

"Sara, darling," her mother chided, her voice tremulous, "we're all under a great deal of pressure. I feel we should cooperate or I'm afraid we'll lose everything. Sam and I have already heard Roger's proposal. Will you just sit and listen?" She turned away, dabbing at her eyes and Sara lapsed into silence while Roger outlined his game plan.

"If you give me power of attorney over the majority interest of the company's stock, I could still get something for the company. Regardless of the publicity."

At this, Ben suddenly left his chair and, pointing at Roger, spewed forth a stream of invectives.

"Dad's upset," Sara exclaimed. "He doesn't want this to happen."

"Dad?" Sam questioned him.

Ben continued gesturing excitedly until a stream of saliva

ran down the side of his mouth. With a loud sigh, Roger shot Sam a pointed look.

Kathryn rose and went to her husband. "Calm down, dear," she soothed, patting his arm.

Roger shook his head. "Your father never acted this way before . . ."

"Before Leonardo," Sara supplied.

"Well, yes. I have to say Leonardo has certainly made a mess of things."

"You all hate him, don't you?" Sara cried.

Kathryn had taken her husband to his room and returned to hear this last exchange. "He has caused a rift in the family, Sara." Her blue eyes were cold and unyielding as she stared down at her daughter.

Tears welled in Sara's eyes. If she wanted to marry Leonardo, she would surely have to forsake her family to do so.

Though he desperately wanted to see Sara, Leonardo kept his distance. Instead, he drove over to Memorial Park where a new nurse sat on the bench with Ben. Large and imposing, the woman wore a sour expression. Her frowning demeanor was positively threatening. As Leonardo approached, Ben smiled and waved a greeting.

"You're the artist." The nurse pursed her lips as though she'd just eaten something thoroughly distasteful. "I am under strict orders to prevent you from visiting Mr. Carlyle."

"But he likes my visits."

"That is no concern of mine. If you persist in harassing us, I'll call the guard."

Ben continued smiling hopefully, but Leonardo turned away. There was nothing he could do.

Perhaps, I've done enough already, he thought, discouraged. He drove back to his studio with a heavy heart.

Over the next few days, he concentrated on his work. He

had only three weeks left and much to do in that short amount of time. Dove showed up one day with paints, canvas, and a six pack of beer.

"I missed you, man," he said, offering Leonardo a beer. "You look like you could use this."

Nodding, Leonardo took it. "I guess you've seen the news."

"Who hasn't? Your stock has gone up. Bryan called yesterday to make sure you have enough paintings. He says he can sell every one on account of the publicity and all. He won't even have to advertise."

Leonardo shrugged.

What does it matter? he thought disconsolately.

He had turned Sara's family against him forever. She might love him, but in the end, she would have to make a choice between him and her family. He thought he knew what her choice would be. Right now, it looked as though Roger had won.

Dove clapped him on the shoulder. "It's Sara, isn't it? And it's your fault that the company is going down the tubes, right?"

Leonardo nodded. "They hate me."

"I can imagine."

"I only did what I had to do." Leonardo spread his hands, palms up.

"Maybe in Italy, heroes are still honored. Here, I'm not so sure. But for what it's worth, I think you did the right thing."

"Not if I've lost Sara."

Dove shrugged. "It's a sad thing, but the bottom line is always money."

Leonardo took a sip of beer as the words sank into his mind. If he were rich, perhaps he could replenish the family coffers. However, that wasn't the case. Yet.

Dove broke into his thoughts. "Somebody once told me to paint my pain out. You ever heard that?"

"No, I don't understand what you mean."

Dove smiled. "It means if you pour your feelings into your work, then it doesn't hurt so bad. I did some of my best work last summer when I broke up with Stacy. Since we got back together, things have been slower. Makes you wonder, doesn't it?"

Dove set up a canvas on another easel and opened a second beer. Following his friend's advice, Leonardo primed a large canvas with acrylic. After allowing it to dry under the ceiling fan, he began to paint. Broad strokes of sienna and umber covered the cobalt. While he worked, Sara's face haunted his thoughts. He tried to push her away, but there she was, insistent, demanding.

Finally he saw her features emerging on the canvas. Pale, alabaster skin glowed under his brush, russet hair fell over pearly shoulders. Slowly her perfect body came to life beneath his skilled fingers—every line, every detail of her flawless figure took form. She was a magical combination of ancient earth goddess and modern woman. He couldn't believe that he had captured the essence of her nubile curves, gently rounded hips, and full breasts. They were exactly as he remembered them. Surrounded by a leafy glade, she lay by a stream, her long fingers dipping into the water. At her feet were a fawn, a squirrel, and a rabbit.

After a while, he sat back to admire his composition. Dove strode over and gave a low whistle. "God, she is beautiful."

The figures of the animals were not complete, but Leonardo liked the grouping. Still, something was missing. Executed in his classical style, it was correct in every detail. It was almost too perfect. It needed something else.

Lost in thought, Leonardo pondered the problem. Then, Dove switched on his portable radio. And there was the solution: a jam box, the perfect modern addition to a classical painting. He would entitle his painting, *Reclining Nymph with Radio.*

Dove approved. "Super," he exclaimed.

Leonardo had no idea what "super" meant, but he thought it must be good.

Sara made the decision not to see Leonardo for a while. He was busy, and she was in turmoil right now. Ultimately, her world would right itself. Then they could reprise their relationship. But right now, she needed space. Even so, his absence took a toll on her and she walked around like a woman in a trance.

Though they talked on the phone frequently, there was a new distance between them. She spent her spring vacation at her parents' house lying by the pool, wishing things were different.

After several weeks, the controversy surrounding the bayou died down. A clean-up team was at work, and their efforts eased physical outbreaks as well as tension. Roger's press releases had the desired effect of deflecting the blame. Other companies pitched in, promoting a sense of neighborhood camaraderie.

One day, Sara received an invitation to Leonardo's show. The engraved card was impressive and the catered event was to be black tie. When he called to see if she'd received the invitation, his voice sounded as excited as a child's.

"I only hope I can find something appropriate to wear," she confessed.

He laughed heartily, and she realized how much she'd missed him.

"You would look good in anything," he told her. "Or even better in nothing at all."

It had been a long time since they'd made love, and his comment sent fires of passion surging through her. Now that business problems had stabilized, she began to hope she and Leonardo could work things out. It had been almost a month, and she could hardly wait to see him again.

* * *

Roger sat at his desk at Carlyle Chemical. Over the last six weeks, his anger at Leonardo had steadily increased. Several times, he'd had to restrain himself from driving over and blowing the artist away. Now he examined other options. "I want him ruined," he spat into his speaker phone.

"Look Latham, things don't work like that. Just two months ago, you asked me to make him a success. Well, I did my part, and it wasn't hard because he is a great talent. Then, the media played into our hands—"

"Sully his reputation, blackball him. I don't care what it takes—"

"The die is cast and I must say, you are responsible for much of this. The gallery won't hold the amount of people who want to attend. I cannot remember when we've had this kind of response to an opening."

"Cancel it!" Roger's face was beet red and the veins stood out at his temples. He looked as if he'd been standing on his head for an hour.

"I can't. Even if I could, I wouldn't risk it. Not at this point."

"You'll be sorry, Bryan. I have a lot of influence in this town. You'd better reflect on another line of work."

"You've turned surly, Latham, or perhaps you live too close to the bayou. They say toxicity eats into the brain and causes real problems."

Roger was so stunned, he didn't realize for several seconds that he was listening to a dial tone. Slamming down the phone, he balled his fists. Leonardo was not going to profit from all this. He wouldn't live that long.

Sara didn't know exactly what made her choose a flowing purple silk gown, except that she wanted to wear the amethyst earrings. Resting against her cheeks, the stones suffused her with an energy she had not felt in a long time. The warmth enveloped her in a violet haze as she drove over to the gallery on Kirby Avenue. She felt this would be a night she would always remember.

Bryan Gallery had long been a fixture in the Houston art community, and Sara was impressed when Jasper Bryan agreed to represent Leonardo. He was a very particular man who catered to the wealthy River Oaks Community. His reputation was impeccable and an invitation to a show at Bryan Gallery was, in itself, an honor.

The parking lot was already filled when Sara drove in. A valet hurried to assist her and apologized for having to park her car at a nearby supermarket, but promised there would be a guard on duty.

My God, Sara thought. *Everyone in town must be here.*

In fact, she had to elbow her way through the chandeliered entryway. With a little stab of fear, she wondered if she would even get to talk to Leonardo. How would he see her in this crowd?

Then she heard him call out her name from across the room.

"Sara!"

Immediately, he was at her side, more handsome than ever in a tuxedo coat, white linen shirt and paint-spotted jeans. There was a tie of sorts at his neck—black with splashes of outrageous color interspersed with Disney characters.

"You look beautiful," he said, kissing her on the cheek.

She blushed. "Thank you. So do you."

"Come." He ushered her through the crowd. "Let us mingle. I want you to meet Bryan and some of his investors."

A portly man with shrewd gray eyes, Bryan huddled with the museum director and several other men Sara didn't recognize.

"Oh, Leonardo. You know Peter Sussman, the museum director, and this is Reese Harden from the Chronicle."

"Peter, nice to see you again," Leonardo said, shaking hands with both men.

"Peter has told me about your work," the reporter said. "I haven't seen this much talent locally in some time."

Leonardo bowed. "Thank you. And may I present Sara Carlyle."

"Miss Carlyle, we've met before, though indirectly," Bryan said, exchanging a look with Leonardo.

Leonardo cleared his throat. "I . . . she hasn't seen the painting yet. I was about to show her."

"You must, indeed. She's likely to become as famous as you," Bryan quipped as they turned to leave.

"What did he mean by that?" Sara asked as Leonardo led her away. A moment later, she stopped short and her mouth dropped open in astonishment. There was her own body, displayed larger than life on canvas, and covering an entire wall.

"I hope you don't mind, Sara."

Several people moved by the painting and smiled knowingly at Sara.

"Mind! Do I mind having my body displayed like a . . . a . . ."

"Goddess," Leonardo supplied.

"Absolutely beautiful," someone muttered behind Sara.

"He paints with such feeling," another person commented.

Sara peered at the painting more closely. She could see the intricate brush strokes, the tiny details of her face, each individual hair on her head executed with loving care. She had to admit it was excellent. But there was so much of her—all of her there. "Why didn't you tell me you were painting this?"

"We haven't talked for a while, remember?"

She nodded. So much had happened. So much had come between them.

"Don't be angry, Sara. I don't intend to sell it."

"I hope not," she exclaimed, with righteous indignation.

After a glass or two of champagne, she felt better. However, she doubted that her family would approve of the painting. They didn't approve of anything she did. And, at the moment, she just didn't care.

It was a glorious night. She and Leonardo took delight in noticing the little red circles that indicated a painting had been sold. As the evening wore on, the circles accumulated until there were only two or three paintings left unsold.

"Don't worry," Bryan assured Leonardo. "We'll sell those, too. The show is a huge success. I only wish I'd extended the opening to Saturday. So many were turned away—"

Suddenly there was a burst of gunshot and the shrill sound of breaking glass. "Get down!" Bryan barked.

Leonardo fell over Sara, shielding her with his body. Other gallery patrons, plied with champagne, sank to the ground. Another round broke windows in front, then came the sound of a gunned motor as the perpetrator sped away.

"Drive-by shooting," Bryan whispered. "You all right?"

Leonardo moved away from Sara. She sat up and nodded.

The guests stayed frozen to the floor until a guard stuck his head in the door. "He's gone, Mr. Bryan."

Leonardo followed Bryan to the door. "Who was it? Did you get a license plate?" the gallery owner asked the guard.

"Probably a gang of kids," Leonardo commented, frowning.

"No, it wasn't kids. It was one man, driving a white sports car, but the license plates were covered."

"A sports car?" Bryan exclaimed.

"Yessir," the guard answered. "I think it might have been a Porsche."

Eighteen

Glass was everywhere, but none of the paintings were damaged. The police arrived, took all the details of the incident, and promised to investigate. Because of the area and the fact that no other galleries were hit, they concluded it wasn't a random drive-by shooting. Somebody wanted to make a statement.

What could have been a complete disaster proved to be nothing more than a sobering moment in the evening. Gallery patrons got up from the floor, brushed themselves off, and laughed nervously. Sara watched Leonardo as he gingerly walked across the broken glass. She thought the brief interval was a little like an air raid or a fire drill, only more exciting. Afterwards, waiters poured more champagne and, surprisingly, the festive mood resumed.

The frame of one unsold painting was nicked, but Leonardo said he could easily fix it. Just as Bryan was about to remove the painting, someone offered to buy it. The patron even wanted to keep the bullet hole in the frame. By the end of the evening, all the paintings except Sara's portrait were purchased, and there were orders for more.

"You would think clients would disperse after something like this," Bryan remarked. "Instead, it only stimulated interest. I'll never understand human nature."

"I am sorry about the damage to the gallery," Leonardo said, full of concern.

Bryan only smiled. "Insurance will take care of that. This

could be the best show I've ever had. I only wish I had a hundred more of your paintings."

A crowd gathered around Leonardo, following him wherever he went. He deserved the recognition, and Sara had never been so proud of him. He was truly a genius. She had known it all along. In this age, others appreciated his creativity. Perhaps that is why he came with her. That and the fact that they were meant to be together.

"I've rented a suite at the Ritz-Carlton for us," he whispered in her ear. "I wanted us to celebrate with champagne and caviar."

It was the most romantic idea she could ever have imagined. She forgot the past few weeks, forgot her family. Nothing seemed as important as the two of them.

At twelve o'clock, a long white limousine arrived and whisked them away to the hotel. There, more champagne and a late supper awaited them. The evening was perfect in every way.

"To us," Leonardo proposed, touching his glass to hers. "Tonight, I can honestly say, I have a career."

"To us," she echoed. "And to you. You are the most amazing man I've ever met."

"Am I?"

"Yes," she whispered.

Her sherry-colored eyes glistened in the dim light of a single candle. Taking her hand, he brought her fingers to his lips. She was so beautiful. Each time he saw her, he glimpsed a new angle of her face. Auburn hair caught and held the candle flame, and her skin was shimmering alabaster. He wanted to paint her this way with less light.

"I want to marry you, Sara," he said.

"You do?" Sara felt the intensity of his gaze boring into her, reaching deep inside. It was the first time he'd actually proposed marriage, and the thought filled her with happy anticipation.

"I do. But I want to make sure I can support you and our family."

Family. Of course, she wanted children. She took a moment to imagine what their children would be like. Smart, of course. And good-looking. With her pragmatism and his energy. *My God,* she thought, *they would be a handful.* She smiled at him. "We've never talked about a family."

"Then it's time we did."

She nodded.

"I want us to have children and live out in the country where the air is fresh and clean. First, I want to make enough money to buy you a beautiful ring. Before long, I can do that. Next week, I go to New York with Peter Sussman. He wants to introduce me to all his friends."

Sara's eyes widened. "That's wonderful." The museum director had many connections in New York. Peter Sussman had been at NYU before coming to Houston. A tiny doubt edged its way into her mind when she remembered Roger's warnings. She wondered if Leonardo would want to move to New York or Paris. But he'd just said he wanted to live in the country and have children. Brushing aside her fears, she vowed nothing would spoil tonight. Nothing.

A huge king-sized bed awaited them in an alcove that also housed an enormous hot tub.

Leonardo led her to the marble tub. "Should we take a little swim first?" he invited.

Stripping off their clothes, they sank into the warm water together. The swirling water bubbled around lulling them into a state of perfect bliss. In the womblike warmth, they glided together, aroused by the hypnotic magic of the water on their skin. The champagne and the success of the evening combined to elevate their spirits. Bubbles foamed around them drawing them closer in a playful dance. Then her breasts were against his hard chest, his lips on hers, and the water churned around them enticing each to the other. He entered her easily, pressing deeper when the waves pushed them together. He thrust far inside to the deepest part of her again and again.

She drew him in, willing him to take her completely. The blood pounded in her head as she rose to meet him in a spangled explosion. Then the waves spiraled out, rippling far into the night. Breathless, they clung together as the water rushed around them, but they heard only the sound of their two hearts beating.

Somewhere in the back of Sara's mind, she knew they would have to purchase a hot tub. First. Even before the house.

"Oh, Sara." He collapsed against her. "I will miss you so much when I go to New York."

"I already miss you," she whispered.

"Come with me."

For a moment, she caught a vision of the two of them there, far away from all their recent problems. She saw herself walking down Fifth Avenue with Leonardo, laughing and talking. Just to be alone with him for a few heavenly days would be a balm to her weary soul. Yes, she wanted to go. The words rose to her lips, but she bit them back and shook her head. "I can't. I have class. Perhaps after you return from New York, we can talk about moving in together."

He nodded and kissed the damp tendrils of her hair. Then wrapping a soft white towel around her, he carried her to bed.

The next morning, they arose late, and had breakfast in bed. Afterwards, they made love again.

"I think we should start every day this way," Leonardo said, smiling at her.

"Yes, I think so."

"Sara, what will your family say when you tell them we are going to be married? Will they accept me?"

"I don't care what they say."

"But they're still angry with me."

She shrugged. "They think there might have been some other way to handle the pollution problem. Especially since Roger still plans to take the company public and sell it."

"Would your father want this?" Leonardo reminded.

"I don't know. After all the bad publicity, Roger says we're in financial straits. If we sell the company, we won't have to worry anymore."

"What about the bayou?"

"I think he's made a deal with the EPA. He convinced them that Carlyle's problem is minor. With the purchase of a new company, Americana Petrochem, they will generate enough money to refurbish Carlyle's controls. They will also install controls in the new company to comply with EPA standards. It gets him off the hook and the EPA off him."

"I don't understand why it is Roger who makes all these decisions."

"I don't either, and I've told them how I feel. My mother and Sam will not listen. Both of them trust Roger implicitly."

"But," Leonardo argued, "I don't think Ben would want this."

Sara frowned. "Dad has gone into a depression."

"Depression? What is that?"

"It's when a person is sad all the time and doesn't respond well to anything. It can become a serious condition. Dad hasn't been himself. He just sits and stares out the window now."

"I should go see him," he said. "He is lonely."

She placed a restraining hand on his arm. "I know you mean well. After all that's happened, it's best if you don't see Dad for a while."

Leonardo was concerned. He hadn't seen Ben for some time, and he felt guilty for abandoning the old man. Of course, the family had forbade his visits. They even hired a new nurse. Still, he could have tried harder. He was Ben's only link to the outside world. Now that he had no one with whom to communicate, Sara's father must feel lost. That was why he felt so sad. Despite Sara's family, Leonardo knew he would be able to cheer Ben up, and he resolved to see him before he left for New York.

In his conversations with Peter Sussman over the past month, Leonardo had told him about Ben's strange method of communication. Peter was not surprised. He said he knew of a psychiatrist in New York who dealt with patients having similar characteristics. One man awoke from a car accident speaking fluent Swedish—a language he had never known before. Leonardo had been encouraged, but he hesitated to raise Sara's hopes before he talked with the doctor.

"Don't worry, Sara," he told her. "Your father is a very strong man. He will get over this depression."

"I hope so," she said. As always, his words reassured her.

On Sunday, they checked out of the hotel. They spent the day together, shopping and preparing for Leonardo's upcoming trip to New York. Later, they grabbed a quick sandwich and in his van, Leonardo followed Sara to her townhouse.

"I am sorry to say good-bye." He kissed her tenderly. "But I have much to do before Wednesday."

"Let's have lunch before you leave." She wound her arms around his neck, reluctant to let go.

"All right," he said. Resting his forehead against hers, he sighed. "I dislike being parted from you, Sara."

"Me, too."

She was surprised to find her eyes filling with tears as she watched him walk out to the van.

Is this love? she wondered.

Yes, her heart answered.

Her answering machine held messages from her mother and Sam, both wondering where she was. But she didn't care. Instead, she called a realtor and discussed putting her townhouse on the market. When Leonardo returned, they would be together. No more separations. No more family interference.

Leonardo spent Monday with a photographer, preparing a portfolio to take to New York. The museum director, Peter Sussman, had taken the artist under his wing. He'd arranged a number of interviews with gallery owners and a dinner party with potential investors. If he had anything to say about it, Leonardo would take New York City by storm, he promised.

Despite his preparations, Leonardo couldn't stop thinking about Ben. Now, hearing of Roger's plans, he understood why Ben was sad. But what could he do about it? Could anyone stop Roger? Only Ben would know, and Leonardo was the only one who could communicate with him.

Though Sara had stood up to her family and openly accused Roger of polluting the bayou, she'd had no effect on her mother or Sam. Roger still controlled Carlyle Chemical. Leonardo decided if he could just expose Roger as a fraud, then perhaps Sara's family would eventually accept him as Sara's husband.

Roger was firmly entrenched, and Leonardo determined to see if Ben had any other ideas. The fleeting thought crossed his mind that by now the old man might have given up.

When Leonardo arrived at Memorial Park, he saw Ben and his nurse on the park bench. He parked the van, then taking in a deep breath, he approached them.

The nurse stood, blocking his way. "You! I've already warned you."

"I'm leaving town for a while. I just wanted to say goodbye to Ben. Please let me speak to him for a moment."

The nurse held her ground. "I'm sorry. Mr. Carlyle is a very sick man. The doctors do not want him excited," she informed him, crisply.

"Just this once. I promise I will not stay long."

Her small blue eyes narrowed, reminding Leonardo of Henry's eyes. "I have my orders and I have an alarm button. Believe me, I will use it to call the police if necessary."

Behind the nurse, Ben gazed at Leonardo hopefully, then sighed when he walked away.

But Leonardo had no intention of giving up. The nurse settled beside Ben on the park bench. Leaning against a tree some distance away, Leonardo tried to think of a way to distract the woman. A few minutes later, he noticed a woman in a jogging outfit doing exercises.

"Would you please do me a favor?" he asked, stepping over to her.

She regarded him warily.

"I'm sorry. I didn't mean to startle you, but I don't have much time."

"Neither do I," she said. "I have to be at work soon."

"I need to talk to that man on the bench, but his nurse will not let me near him."

The jogger looked from Leonardo to Ben, then back again. "Your face looks familiar. Have I seen you somewhere before?"

"My name is Leonardo Brazzi, I—"

"I know, I saw your picture in the newspaper!"

"Yes, I'm afraid I've been in the newspaper often."

"You're the artist who said the bayou was polluted," she smiled."

Leonardo nodded. "It has brought me much trouble."

"I can imagine," she said sympathetically.

"I really need to talk to Ben Carlyle and tell him what's happened."

Her eyes widened in recognition. "That's Ben Carlyle? Gosh, what happened to him?"

"He's sick, and at this moment, a prisoner of his nurse."

"She looks tough."

"She is. I just need to talk to him a short time."

The woman thought a moment. "I could tell her she has a phone call in the clubhouse."

Leonardo grinned. "Yes! Tell her Mrs. Carlyle is calling."

"I'll offer to stay with her patient while she's gone."

"Oh, how can I ever thank you?"

She smiled and pressed a card into his palm. "Paint me a picture some time," she said, jogging toward the pair on the bench.

Leonardo watched her pause at her destination and, pointing toward the clubhouse, hold a short conversation with the nurse. He saw the nurse jump and set off in a fast trot. The jogger sat next to Ben.

Then she waved at Leonardo and jogged off. "He's all yours," she called over her shoulder.

He saluted her and sat next to the old man. "Ben! I'm so happy to see you," Leonardo hugged the older man.

Ben grinned like a child who'd just escaped from a smothering parent.

Immediately, Ben launched into a tirade that Leonardo couldn't understand. Patiently, he tried to get the old man to slow down. He took a small notepad from his pocket and wrote down a few words. Ben spewed out phrases he'd been holding back for weeks and, scribbling as quickly as he could, Leonardo could not keep up with the flow.

It was true, he thought. Ben was sad because he had no one to talk to. They talked about the water sample. The old man knew the test outcome already and had known for some time that the bayou was being polluted. What he didn't understand was what Roger planned to do about it.

Leonardo explained Roger's proposal to the EPA—that of buying Americana Petrochem and installing pollution controls. Painstakingly he translated the words into two different languages, hoping he would get through.

At the mention of Americana Petrochem, Ben flew into a rage. Leonardo feared that he'd said something wrong or left out details of the transaction. As he tried to explain what Sara had told him, Ben became more furious and kept repeating unintelligible expletives over and over. He repeated one name that Leonardo couldn't really understand. The way Ben shouted, it sounded more like a curse.

People walking or jogging by stopped to stare at the old man. Unmindful, Ben raved on. Leonardo tried to calm him down, but he continued. Finally, Leonardo realized it was Roger's name Ben repeated. Had Roger been present, Ben would have strangled him.

Nothing would calm the old man down and Leonardo grew frantic. He looked around for help, but now people were jogging away from his screeching cries as if they were an alarm that could not be silenced. Waving his hands in the air, Ben continued screaming and shouting, then suddenly sank to the ground. Horrified, Leonardo thought he might have had another apoplectic stroke. Picking him up, Leonardo tried to revive him, but his eyes glazed and spittle dripped from his mouth.

Oh God, Leonardo thought. *I have killed him.*

Just then, he saw the nurse approaching.

"What have you done?"

"Nothing, I—"

"I told you he was not to be excited!" She bent over and felt his pulse. Quickly withdrawing the alarm button from her pocket, she depressed a button to call an ambulance. Then the nurse returned her attention to Ben. Moments later, all her efforts to revive him had failed.

"Is he dead?"

"No, but he's very close to death, thanks to you," she snapped.

In a few minutes, they heard the whine of an ambulance approaching. The nurse turned to Leonardo. "I will lose my job, but you will have more on your conscience, young man."

Leonardo realized she was right. If he hadn't talked to Ben, this whole thing would not have occurred. He had acted impulsively, ignoring Sara's pleas and the doctors' orders. "I am so sorry," he said. "I like Ben very much. I never wanted this to happen."

The ambulance stopped a short distance away. Paramedics jumped out and carefully hoisted Ben onto a stretcher, then moved him into the vehicle. The nurse marched in behind them. Leonardo looked on helplessly. *What have I done?* he wondered as the ambulance pulled away.

Sara rushed to the hospital. In the waiting room, Sam paced nervously. Kathryn Carlyle sat in a chair, crying. Both looked up when she arrived.

"What happened?" Sara asked. "He was fine the last time I saw him."

"I told you to keep that artist away from him," Sam accused. "But no, he followed Dad to the park, just like some stalker. Then he got him all worked up again. Only this time, it may have killed him."

Sara's eyes flew open wide in shock. "What! You're saying this is Leonardo's fault?"

"Damn right I am," Sam gritted out.

Kathryn grabbed her son's sleeve. "Accusations aren't going to help now."

"I don't ever want to see that guy again," Sam turned and stalked down the hall.

Sara sank down in a chair next to her mother. She'd told Leonardo that Ben was depressed and must not be excited. She'd asked him not to see her father. And he had ignored her wishes. How could he have done such a thing? Why would he take a chance like that?

Of course, Leonardo wouldn't have anticipated this outcome. He was from another time, another planet almost. He did not understand how things worked here. Clenching her jaw, she shook her head. He had learned the hard way how his actions could affect others. He would certainly be sorry, deeply grieved. But this time that would not be enough to excuse him.

Now she stood to lose her father, and that she could not forgive.

And Leonardo had turned her family against him for good.

Roger appeared a few minutes later, his face full of concern. "I came as soon as I heard. How is he?"

"We don't know," Sam said. "The doctors are with him now."

Roger stepped over to Sara and her mother. "I'm so sorry," he said.

With a tight smile, Sara nodded.

In a short while, two doctors appeared in the waiting room. Kathryn rose.

"Your husband has a strong constitution, Mrs. Carlyle. Right now his left side is partially paralyzed," the doctor said.

Kathryn gasped. "Oh, no."

"That may improve with therapy. You can go in now; he's awake. But don't stay long. He doesn't need any excitement for a while."

Sam shot Sara a pointed look as if to say this was all her fault. Her shoulders sagged and tears seeped from her eyes.

Roger moved over to her and took her hand. "We'll get through this," he said.

Desperate to learn about Ben, Leonardo delayed his trip to New York. He called Sara's townhouse, but there was no answer. The hospital could give out no information on Ben's condition. In desperation, he drove over to Dove's and related the entire episode. His friend listened sympathetically, then made several calls, finally contacting the Carlyle's maid.

"The doctor said Mr. Carlyle goin' to live," the maid informed Dove. "But right now he's in bad shape. He's paralyzed."

Leonardo, listening on the extension, dropped the receiver. "Paralyzed? What does that mean?" he asked, green eyes misting with tears.

"He can't move," Dove explained.

"Oh," Leonardo said, as tears flowed freely down his cheeks.

Not knowing what else to do, Dove hugged him. "It's a tough break."

"But it's my fault that Sara's father will never walk again," Leonardo told him sadly.

Dove tried to console him, but Leonardo would not be appeased. Leaving Dove's, he drove out into the country and locked himself in his studio.

Finally, Peter Sussman sent a courier to inform Leonardo that they could delay the trip to New York no longer. Reluctantly, he left.

He knew that Sara would not return his calls now or ever. Now they could never marry. He had committed the unpardonable sin and, in so doing, had lost his only ally in the Carlyle family.

Roger had won. Now he would have the company and Sara, too.

Nineteen

In the hospital room, Sara gazed at the shriveled shell of her father. Once hardy and robust, Ben Carlyle was almost unrecognizable. There was little left of him—hardly enough to cover with a sheet.

This stroke had removed the expression on his face. Now he was like a ghost who came and went, only occupying his body on occasion. In those brief moments, blue eyes locked with hers and she thought she saw recognition there. That was it. He could not move or speak. From time to time, a stream of saliva dribbled from his mouth, and she wiped it away. It was as if he'd been shot full of Novocaine. She kept thinking it would wear off. But after five days, he was the same.

She thought of Leonardo and tears welled up again. It wasn't his fault. No one could have anticipated such a disaster. Yet she had asked him not to see her father, and he had ignored her wishes. Now this.

As much as she loved him, she could not come to terms with what he had done. He'd been so intent on proving his point—that he could communicate with Ben—and in so doing had disregarded all else. Now her father lay close to death, and she simply could not bear to lose him. Not this way. Perhaps it was the difference in their cultures or their times, but he had never fully adjusted to this age.

That night, when she finally returned to her townhouse, weary and distraught, her answering machine contained messages from Leonardo. She erased them all. Someday maybe she would talk to him again. Not today. Not for a long time.

Boarding the plane for New York, Leonardo knew how it felt to have a broken heart. Exquisite pain rent his internal organs as if he'd swallowed a knife that had carved him up completely. If he could have looked inside, he knew he'd see nothing but a hollow cave with his heart floating through his body in little pieces. The pieces had sharp edges that jabbed him here and there. Pain in his shoulder, pain in his head. He hurt all over.

The museum director, Peter Sussman, led the way to their first class seats. Leonardo sat beside him.

Ordinarily, the fact that he'd never been on a plane would have excited him. He would have been fascinated with the seat belts, craning his neck to see the big jet engines roar into life. But his response was rote and mechanical. Dead. He snapped on his seat belt as Peter did and stared out the window.

Vaguely, Leonardo heard the voice beside him.

"I have the itinerary here, if you'd like to go over it," Peter said.

Silence.

"Leonardo?"

He looked around and forced a smile. "Yes."

"I'll just go over a few things, okay?"

"Yes."

His voice operated on its own as if it had a motor. Bits of heart stuck there made it sound raspy, like it belonged to someone else. Listening to Peter talk, he nodded his head like a puppet. He smiled or frowned, appropriately. Perhaps he was dead after all. It made no difference now.

"How old did you say you are, Leonardo?" Peter asked.

The question caught him off guard, and he had to think

a moment. He thought he might be twenty-six although he didn't know for sure. "Twenty-six."

"Great," Peter said, adjusting his horn-rimmed glasses. "They'll love it that you're so young."

Young? Leonardo almost laughed at that. Chronologically speaking, he was almost five hundred years old. He didn't think Peter was ready for that news.

"I'm writing up your bio. You're twenty-six, from Florence, you said. And your teacher was . . . ?"

"da Vinci."

Peter laughed. "Well, of course. He was everyone's teacher, wasn't he?"

"Was he? I didn't know."

Peter shook his head, smiling. "Leonardo, they're going to love you in New York. They are so jaded, you know. Just tell them you studied with da Vinci and you paint in the nude."

"I do paint in the nude, especially when I forget to do the laundry."

"That's too wonderful. You'll blow them away."

"Okay," Leonardo said. But he didn't really care. He'd lost interest in going to New York. Lost interest in accumulating paper money. Sara had been his motivation and now she was gone.

Peter talked all the way, giving instructions, going over dinner parties and scheduled meetings, but Leonardo didn't hear a word he said. They stayed at the Helmsley Plaza, Peter's favorite hotel and, soon after they arrived, they went downstairs for high tea.

Leonardo went through the motions, drinking tea, smiling and talking. But he heard and saw nothing. Like an automobile, his mind was in the automatic position.

"I thought that went rather well," Peter commented on the way to their rooms.

"Yes," Leonardo said.

That night, they attended a dinner party given by a New

York socialite to introduce Leonardo to her friends. Lady Barclay, wife of a former British diplomat, had become a social fixture after her husband's death. At sixty, Tita, as a chosen few were entitled to address her, had literally made the careers of several artists. She had impeccable taste. Her Fifth Avenue penthouse displayed an eclectic mixture of art. Most of it was modern, but there was a fair representation of Impressionists, a van Eyck, a Vermeer, and a small panel by El Greco. Even Leonardo was astonished by her collection. He and Sara had been to the museum in Houston, but here was a private collector who had accumulated a history of art on the walls of her own home.

"This is magnificent," he exclaimed to Tita.

"Thank you, Leonardo." Tita's laugh was a low, throaty chuckle. "Peter told me about you over the phone. I had Jasper send me some slides. Now that I've seen your work, I believe you belong in my little gallery."

"She has decided to buy two of your paintings," Peter exclaimed excitedly.

"I am flattered," Leonardo bowed and kissed her hand.

"And, uh, your teacher was da Vinci, himself, I understand," Tita smiled.

"Yes."

"Well, I can certainly see the master's influence."

The evening was an enormous success, Peter declared in the taxi later. Leonardo sold two paintings to Tita and had orders for five more. He should have been overjoyed. Instead, he only wished he could tell Sara. Sitting alone in the hotel room, he finally called Dove and woke him up.

"That's wild, man," Dove commented, sleepily. "Are you coming back?"

"Not for a while," Leonardo said. "Tita has a house in Martha's Vineyard, and she has offered it to me for the summer. I said no at first, but then Peter said it wasn't really a vineyard, but a resort. So I may stay for a while. Tita has lots of friends who want to buy my paintings."

"Who's Tee-taw?" Dove drawled. "Is she good-looking?"

"She looks good for being sixty, I suppose, and she's very rich."

"Sounds great," Dove said. "I'll keep tabs on your house in Magnolia. By the way, I called over to the Carlyle house. Ben Carlyle is home from the hospital."

"How is he?" Leonardo was almost afraid to ask, but he had to know.

"He's still partially paralyzed, but the maid said he is talking some. Of course, she said that no one can understand him. But that's nothing new, right? At least he's not dead."

"At least he's not dead," Leonardo repeated. He hung up the receiver with a heavy heart. Ben was still paralyzed, and he had done this to Sara's father. It occurred to him to write Ben a note. But he didn't know how to say what he felt in any language—Italian, Latin, or English. Besides, the Carlyles would throw away the note. He couldn't blame them. He could never forgive himself and knew Sara never would.

Sighing, he thought how strange life was. His career was made, Peter had said. Tita, alone, had cinched it, the rest was garnish. Whatever that meant.

But he didn't care. It could all go away tomorrow. He could fade back into the past and no one would really notice.

The rest of the week was filled with more parties and meetings. Leonardo trudged wearily through it all, smiling, shaking hands, and telling his personal story, which Peter had carefully edited.

"I understand you began painting at an early age," one gallery owner said.

"Yes, I was just a boy when my father sent me to Florence."

"To study?"

"Yes, I was an apprentice."

"My goodness, I didn't think they still did that. And you were very poor, Peter said."

Leonardo nodded. "We had no cash at all."

The gallery owner laughed as if that were very funny. "You know, your bio reads like that of a Renaissance painter."

Leonardo laughed, too. "I guess it does. I've been told I am a Renaissance man."

"Oh, that's good, that's really good," the man clapped Leonardo on the shoulder. "The world needs more artists like you. Are there anymore where you came from?"

He thought for a moment. "Yes, but they may be dead by now," Leonardo answered honestly.

The gallery owner paused, briefly, then broke into loud laughter. "Peter, this man is a rare find. Have Bryan send me a brochure immediately. I know I can sell him."

On Friday, exhausted by the round of social activities, Leonardo took the day off. Earlier, when they had talked about Ben's condition, Peter had volunteered to introduce Leonardo to a psychiatrist who specialized in stroke victims. A meeting was arranged for Friday afternoon.

Dr. Howard Kraven was surprisingly young. Lively brown eyes magnified behind thick glasses studied Leonardo with intensity.

"Of course, I can't recommend treatment without seeing Mr. Carlyle," he told Leonardo after listening to his story.

"I had hoped there might be some way his family could communicate with him. So far, I'm the only one who can understand what he's saying. His family thinks I just made this whole thing up."

Dr. Kraven nodded. "It's an unusual phenomenon. It's almost like one part of the brain has short-circuited, and things are suddenly hooked up differently. In recent years, we've had to reassess our beliefs about how the brain functions. Cases like these are making us realize that the untapped portion or unused parts can suddenly be called into active duty. Apparently, Mr. Carlyle accesses information or communicates in a totally new way. These rare occurrences stymie most people.

"Even his doctors are saying he's lost his mind."

The doctor raked long fingers through dark, curly hair. "He may not have lost it; he may simply have stumbled into another hemisphere. You say he was a classical scholar."

"Yes."

"So he did have some knowledge of Italian and Latin."

"And Greek."

"And Greek," the doctor mused. "Yet many people still speak these languages today. Perhaps all you need is an interpreter."

Leonardo shook his head. "Ben is speaking an archaic form of these languages, words that few people would recognize. An interpreter would only know the modern language, isn't that correct?"

"That is correct," the doctor said, narrowing his eyes. "How is it that you recognized this? Why are you able to understand him when no one else can?"

Leonardo hedged, trying to gauge the best answer. "I am something of a classical scholar myself. I have read many sixteenth century manuscripts in both Italian and Latin. I assure you, that if an Italian man of the sixteenth century were to listen to conversation in modern-day Italian, he would have great difficulty understanding it. It is the reverse for Ben."

The doctor pondered this. "Yes, I suppose you are right."

"Can anything be done for my friend?"

Dr. Kraven smiled. "Let me show you a computer program I implemented for one of my patients who began to speak fluent Swedish after a serious head injury. He had never spoken Swedish before. Naturally, he had an American wife, American children, American relatives, none of whom had ever even been to Sweden. They came to me in desperation. I modified a language program and, ultimately, he was able to relearn English, although he does still have a little accent. His wife likes it," the doctor chuckled. "She thinks it's kind of cosmopolitan."

Leonardo worked with the doctor for several hours that day, then promised to come back when he next returned to New York.

"I'll be living in Martha's Vineyard over the summer," he told the doctor.

"Good. Leave your number with my secretary. I'll call you when I've made some progress with the program."

Leonardo moved into Tita's house at Martha's Vineyard. Amazingly, she had it all set up for him with brushes, canvases and two different easels. He had the feeling that he wasn't the first artist to summer here.

Inspired, he began to paint feverishly. Tita visited occasionally, always bringing a friend who immediately wanted one of Leonardo's paintings. Paper money rolled in, and he opened a bank account, not really caring that the figure grew every week. His only hope was that he could do something for Ben. Perhaps in some small way, he could undo the damage he had inflicted upon Sara and her family.

Soon after he arrived, Dr. Kraven called. He'd found three programs: one in Latin, one in Greek, and one in Italian. He was so excited; he couldn't wait to get to work on them.

"I've got three pieces of the puzzle," he explained, "now all we have to do is figure out how to make it work."

Leonardo took the train to New York the following week. Together, they made a compilation of the three programs. This composite would allow the user to choose a word in Italian, Latin, or Greek, then the choice was repeated using Leonardo's voice. A "yes" or "no" answer would signify whether the choice was correct. A summary of words selected followed with a positive or negative key-in at the end.

Over the summer, Leonardo devoted himself to painting and frequent trips to New York to see Dr. Kraven. Though his mind was occupied, his heart still ached for Sara. When he painted a woman's body, it was hers. He tried to put a different face on her, but thought any other face looked strange. At night, he saw her eyes imploring him not to talk to her father. He awoke each day to a feeling of dread, of knowing he would have to face another day without her.

His work with Dr. Kraven gave him some measure of comfort. He was doing something for Ben. After three months of preparation, they tried the program out. Leonardo brought his copious notes. He'd written down every word Ben had uttered, and they applied it to the text as if Ben were right there. And it worked.

"By God, it works," Dr. Kraven shouted happily. "I wish we could market this."

Leonardo frowned. He now knew enough about America to believe that a program such as this would have a limited audience. He was so grateful and didn't want to hurt the doctor's feelings. "It is a good program. I believe Ben will be able to speak to his family now."

Though she'd tried to exorcise him from her thoughts, Sara couldn't forget Leonardo. The anguish had dissipated; the angry words she'd thought of saying had flown away. Now she felt only loss. His words rang in her ears, his face haunted her dreams, and a growing sadness followed her wherever she went. All the arguments that had fortified her over these last few months had slowly deteriorated, especially when her father began to improve. Now what Leonardo had done didn't seem so bad. Now their relationship didn't seem irreparable. But since he never returned from New York, she couldn't tell him that. She'd called every number she knew, but could not reach him.

After hours of daily physical therapy, Ben gradually regained use of his arms and legs. He still had a limp, but overall, he was much improved. Sara came by once a day to walk with him, usually in the mornings before the heat became unbearable.

As they walked along the sidewalk, Ben spoke to her for the first time in two years. Looking directly at her, he said something. She noticed that he did not slur, but she had no idea what he said. It was as if he were speaking another language, a language that seemed vaguely familiar.

Elated, she could hardly wait to tell her mother.

"Dad spoke to me," she exclaimed.

"Really?" Kathryn said. "What did he say?"

"I don't know. I didn't understand the words, but he said something very clearly."

Her mother sighed and shook her head. "Well, he is much better, but I don't know if he'll be able to talk to us again."

Ben continued to improve and by the middle of August, he'd gained weight and strength. He looked better than he had in months. Sara was encouraged. Her father was much more responsive, and he continued to ask her several questions over and over again. If only Leonardo were here to help her.

One day a package arrived addressed to Ben Carlyle and Family. It had been sent by a Dr. Gerald Kraven in New York. For a long time, they all stared at the package as if it might explode. Finally, Sara opened it and immediately saw it was a computer program of some sort.

"I don't understand who sent this," Sam complained. "I hope this isn't some elaborate sales gimmick. We probably ought to send it back."

"Let's see what it is first," Sara urged.

Since Sara could not install the program, she persuaded a computer expert from the university to come over the following weekend. While he worked, they all stood around waiting expectantly.

"It looks like some sort of a language program," Sara proclaimed once it was up and running. It was like a sophisticated word game.

The unknown doctor had put his phone number on the label in case they needed help. Sara called him.

"I heard about your father's condition from a colleague," Dr. Kraven said. Leonardo had not wanted his name mentioned, but promised to work with Dr. Kraven again on other projects. "Since I have experience treating patients with communication problems arising from head injury or stroke," the doctor told Sara, "I had already developed a program and simply modified it to meet your father's needs."

Dr. Kraven explained how to use the program, and Sara couldn't wait to get started.

"How did the doctor find out about Dad?" Sam asked when Sara related the conversation.

"A colleague," she told him, frowning. A strange feeling crept over her, and she wondered if this colleague might be Leonardo. If so, where was he?

"Are you saying we can communicate with Dad by using this thing?" Sam was astonished. "I don't believe it."

"The doctor said there are no guarantees. It's worth a shot, don't you think?"

The fall semester did not begin until September 15th, so for the next few weeks, Sara worked with her father every day. At first, the going was slow. Having only a limited knowledge of word processing, Sara had to get used to the program. Finally she mastered it and in doing so, discovered how ingenious it was. With this discovery came the realization that it could only have been conceived by Leonardo. Then, when she heard his voice repeating the words, it was like having him in the room with her, and she began to cry. He had done this to help her father. How wonderful he was, and she had let him go away, perhaps for good. Now it was up to her to prove he had been right all along, and she forced herself to work with the program.

Ben was reluctant to take part. When Sara made it into a game, he relented. When she pieced together Ben's first sentence, she was completely astonished. She asked her fa-

ther to confirm the words, then translated them. Then she
sat staring at the screen, tears running down her cheeks.

"Where is Leonardo?" her father had asked.

"You say your father is communicating via a computer
program?" Roger asked Sam.

"It's the damndest thing. Apparently Dad *was* speaking
Italian and Latin or some kind of combination."

Roger drummed his fingers nervously on his desk. "Well,
what did he say?"

"Not much so far. Sara's been working with him every
day. It's a tedious process, taking the words and translating
them. She starts school tomorrow so things will slow down
a bit I imagine. But God, all this time, he really was speaking another language like Leonardo said."

Frowning, Roger shuffled papers on his desk. The public
offering was to take place in a matter of weeks. There had
been too many delays already. Now he was determined that
nothing would stand in the way of his success. Nothing.
With effort, he arranged his features into a pleasant smile.
"But what has he said, actually?"

Sam scratched his head and grinned. "You know the first
thing he said was, 'where is Leonardo?' I guess he got kind
of attached to the guy. I thought he was a flake, myself.
But maybe not."

You stupid fool! Roger wanted to scream. *You and your
ignorant family will ruin everything I've worked for. I'm the
only one who knows about business here.* Instead, Roger
smiled. "A computer program. Imagine that."

Leonardo. Where is he? Each day, Sara was plunged
deeper into despair. She had called and left messages, but
no one returned her calls. She phoned the gallery, but the
secretary could give no information on Leonardo's where-

abouts, except to say she believed he was still in New York. But where in New York? She called Dove at home and at Texas Art Supply. He no longer worked at Texas Art Supply, and a brief message on his answering machine said that he was in Santa Fe. She called Dr. Kraven in New York, but he was not available, and his receptionist had heard the name, but had no address or phone.

Everywhere she searched led to a dead end. She'd waited too long and now he was gone for good. If only she could talk to him, just hear his voice. But he had disappeared without a trace.

The summer was over and Sara sat at Ben's desk waiting for her father to finish breakfast. Tomorrow, she would have to return to school and would be unable to work with him for a while. She wanted to get an early start today. The more her father said, the lower her spirits sank. Leonardo was right, but no one had believed him, and even she had turned against him in the end.

Ben appeared in the door, smiling. He wore a jogging suit and white sneakers.

"Hi!" He waved.

Since they'd begun working together, he was a different person. He was relearning English, a few words at a time.

Today, Ben was in fine fettle. He sat next to her, ready to go. Yesterday, he had told her about the bayou. His words were still in the computer.

"I believe Carlyle Chemical has been polluting the bayou for some time."

Ben pointed toward the screen. He said a word or two, but she could find no equivalent in either English or Latin. She tried Greek. Ben tried another word. This one she managed to translate. The word was traitor.

"Roger?" she asked. Over the past few months, Sara had noticed a radical change in Roger. After Leonardo had convinced her that Roger was responsible for the pollution of the bayou, she'd taken a stand against his plan for taking the company public. Now her mother and brother were weary of arguing. They just wanted to cash out and pressured Sara to go along with them. To appease them and in part to assuage her guilt, she had signed the necessary papers. Now she had second thoughts.

"Are you saying that Roger is a traitor, Dad?"

Ben let out a stream of curses and nodded vigorously.

"What about the public offering?"

Again, her father talked so fast that Sara couldn't understand. When she finally calmed him down, she translated the message: "Not necessary."

Sara felt her stomach knot. They had been so willing to go along with Roger. All the while, her father had been trying to tell them that Roger was a traitor. Leonardo knew, but no one believed him. Perhaps they hadn't wanted to know the truth.

They worked far into the afternoon without taking a break. To her shock, Sara learned that her father had visited the plant several times, but Roger threw him out. He said Roger had hired new personnel and cut the pollution controls out. Since Sam was usually out in the field, he did not know. Besides, Ben said, Sam had turned everything over to Roger, believing he would do the right thing.

"I hate Roger," Ben said. "If you married him, I would have died before I attended your wedding."

Sara didn't know what to do. The paperwork on the public offering was completed, and the transaction would happen very soon. She didn't want to tell her father this, for fear it would upset him. But could she stop it? What should she do?

She called Sam, but he was out of the office so she left a message. Then she contacted a law professor at the university. She hardly knew the man, but his legal reputation was impeccable. She expressed doubts about going through with the public offering and he asked her to send him the prospectus. She faxed it to him.

Sam returned her call a few hours later. "What's up?" he asked.

"Dad said some things you need to know right away."

"I can't come over tonight. I'll be there first thing to-morrow morning."

"Make it early," Sara urged. "I have class at eleven."

Several hours later, the law professor called her back.

"Sara, do you understand what's happening here?"

"I don't know; I thought I did. Why?"

"Is this Roger Latham a member of your family?"

"No."

"It looks like he will get most of the money. He has set up an option program that kicks in at the completion of the offering. From what I can tell, he will then become the majority stockholder."

"What? That isn't possible!"

"I could be wrong. I'd like to run it by a merger and acquisitions lawyer."

"Yes, please do."

Sara's head throbbed. How could this have happened? Why didn't Sam see it? Why didn't she?

When Kathryn came in to announce dinner, Sara showed her what Ben had said. Her mother's face blanched and she had to sit down.

"Your father said all that?"

"Every word of it."

"I knew he went over to the plant, but of course, I couldn't understand what he said. I remember that he was upset. I assumed it was because Roger had taken over the company."

"Dad says Roger has used us all for his own personal gain."

Kathryn closed her eyes. "Are you sure about all this Sara? Everything is riding on this public offering. Roger says we'll all be rich."

"He's lying, Mother. I had a U of H law professor look

over the prospectus. Did you know that when the public offering takes place, Roger will become the majority stockholder?"

"Oh my God! How could that be?"

"Easily. He throws a little money our way, then steps in and takes over. Not only will he own the company, but he'll get the lion's share of the profits."

"Are you sure?"

"I asked the law professor to look this over as a favor. He's sending it on to a merger and acquisitions lawyer. But yes, I'm sure about it."

"What should we do? Call Sam!"

"He'll be by tomorrow morning. I'm going to save all this so he can see it."

In order to meet with Sam, Sara spent the night at the Carlyle house. Sara, her mother, and Ben had dinner. Ben was exhausted and retired early, leaving Sara and her mother to talk.

"Leonardo was right, Mother," she said.

"I suspect we've treated him badly," her mother agreed.

"Yes, and I'm not sure I'll ever see him again."

Sara went to bed in her old room. Stacked on shelves were scrapbooks from high school, plaques for achievement, her diploma, framed. Everything chronicled the life of a model child. Even her doll sat neatly on the rocker, dressed in school clothes, her dark hair braided. She'd always followed the injunctions of her family—study hard, excel, be good. Now at twenty-eight, she realized that they could be wrong. Relying on them to have all the answers, she'd never really trusted her own instincts. The one time when she'd followed her heart and gone against her family, she'd been right. Then when the first major obstacle blocked the path, she'd thrown it all away.

Tears trickled down her cheeks. Would she ever find Leonardo? Could he ever forgive her? The future looked black and uncertain. For a long time, she tossed and turned, unable to sleep. Then she thought she heard a sound. Dismissing it, she turned over. Then she heard it again.

Slipping from her bed, she drew on a robe and slippers and very carefully opened her bedroom door. There it was again. Someone was in the house. Retreating into her room, she picked up the phone and dialed 911.

"We have an intruder," she told the operator and gave the address. "Please hurry," she urged.

Replacing the receiver, she tiptoed down the steps. If she caught a glimpse of him, she might be able to identify him to the police when they arrived. She thought of her mother's silver in the dining room and started in that direction. Another sound drew her to Ben's study. Peeking around the door, she saw a shadowy figure bending over the computer. With a deep breath, she switched on the light.

Roger whirled around, his blue eyes ablaze.

"Roger! What are you doing here?"

"Go back to bed, Sara. I'm getting something I need for work."

Sara approached cautiously. "In the middle of the night? You're taking Dad's laptop! Put it down!"

Disconnecting the printer, he ignored her. "I'll bring it back."

"I said *put it down!*" she shouted.

"I'm taking this and you can't stop me," Roger stated coldly.

When Roger turned to face her, she saw something that sent a chill straight through her.

He looked crazed, insane. Exactly like Guy Lemontaine. *Oh my God,* she thought. He *is* Guy Lemontaine.

Twenty

The police arrived almost immediately. Sara stood dispassionately by while they pushed Roger up against the wall and frisked him.

The sirens awakened Ben and Kathryn, who hurried into the study.

"Tell them who I am, Kathryn. Sara, tell them!" Roger ordered.

Kathryn gasped and Sara waved her mother away. "Actually, Roger, I don't know who you are anymore. I think you're a criminal."

"Officer, I was just getting some information I needed—"

"He broke into our house and was attempting to take that computer," Sara interrupted.

"Do you intend to press charges, ma'am?" the police officer asked.

"I certainly do."

"Sara, I can't believe this," Roger sputtered.

"Believe it," Sara turned away and joined her parents in the entry hall.

"Sara, come back here!" Roger shouted.

He was still shouting when the policemen escorted him out the door. Ben had a smile on his face.

"We got rid of him, Dad," Sara told her father. "You don't have to worry about him anymore."

"What was he doing with your father's computer?" Kathryn wanted to know.

"I guess he wanted to know what Dad had said. He thought he could sneak in here and take it away. I don't imagine he realized I was spending the night."

At the family meeting the following morning, the Carlyles decided to press charges against Roger. Reluctantly, Sam went along with Sara and Kathryn.

"I still can't believe this." Sam shook his head. "Are you absolutely positive, Sara?"

"I talked to the attorney again this morning. He said Roger has been very clever, but he is the only one who will benefit from the public offering. That's why he's been pushing so hard. Bert suggested that we hire an auditor. And the lawyer he recommended will be calling us very soon. We have to take control of this thing now," Sara said.

Ben resounded with an Italian expression that sounded like "echo."

The Carlyles stood together, united at last, and to Roger's astonishment, they pressed charges against him. When his lawyer bailed him out, he continued to call and try to explain. No one returned his calls.

Two weeks later, the merger and acquisitions lawyer met with the Carlyles and outlined a strategy.

"The public offering was initially based on the supposition that Ben Carlyle was incompetent," he explained. "As trustees, Sara and Sam then signed on behalf of the family. But you now tell me that Mr. Carlyle is not mentally incompetent and that he has been communicating with you through a computer program."

"That's right," Sara said. "He is not incompetent and we can prove it."

While they hooked up the computer, Sam began to pace. His friend had betrayed him and played him for a fool. "This is my fault. I should have seen it coming. Dad counted on me to carry on and I let him down." The expression on his face was heart-rending. "I've always been a good salesman, not a manager. Roger stepped in and took over. Honestly, I was glad to turn the management over to somebody else. But, God, I never expected this!" He ground his teeth. "Roger kept urging me to put Dad in a home. I was at the point of believing that might be the best thing to do." He shook his head sadly. "I just hope Dad will forgive me."

"We all made the same mistake," Sara told him. "Leonardo was the only person who realized the truth."

The thought of Leonardo brought a lump to her throat. She had no idea where he was or if she would ever see him again. They had been wrong and he had been right all along.

A short time later, the Carlyle family and their lawyer went before a judge to prove that Ben Carlyle was not mentally incompetent. They hooked up the computer program and Ben related the complicated operation of the pollution control system. The judge was very impressed. Quite obviously, Ben Carlyle was in full possession of his mental faculties, and therefore, the stock transfer was invalid.

There could be no public offering. Since public offerings would not proceed with pending litigation, there would be no contest to the judge's ruling.

The backlash was intense for the few days after the announcement, and Sam was caught in the middle—between Roger and the investors. But he stood his ground. Carlyle Chemical would remain a private company. Roger was out and the investors would have to be satisfied with a long-term payout.

The final straw for Sam came when his girlfriend, Susan, called.

"I don't think we can see each other for a while," she told him. "Daddy is very upset by this whole thing."

"Then you better take care of Daddy," Sam replied.

Overhearing the conversation, Sara realized her brother had grown up quickly. *Perhaps the crisis changed us all,* Sara thought.

Slowly, Ben began speaking English again and advised Sam to rehire Carlyle's former management team. Eventually, Sara's father felt well enough to take a trip with Kathryn. Sam started dating someone else—an independent divorcee with her own business.

Throughout the ordeal, Sara continued thinking about Leonardo. The same questions filled her mind. Where was he? Would he ever return?

One afternoon after class, she dropped by Bryan's gallery. Bryan was in his office, working on a brochure. Bryan looked up and smiled at her.

"I understand you've been looking for Leonardo," he said. "I just returned and was about to instruct my secretary to call you. He's been at Martha's Vineyard and has done some fabulous work. A patron lent him a house for the summer. My God, the man has talent."

Sara's heart sank. Of course he would have a rich female patron who catered to his every need. Determined to speak with him, she took the number.

That evening she phoned, and a woman answered. "Leonardo? Such a darling man. But no, he left yesterday. I loved having him here and tried to get him to stay, but he was anxious to get on the road, I guess. The creative spirit doesn't stay in one place long."

"Do you know where he went?" Sara asked.

"He didn't leave a forwarding address, but he did say he'd call," the woman said.

Sara hung up. *Leonardo probably had a relationship with the woman,* she thought. Disheartened, she knew he had every right to pursue his life without her. She would have liked to talk to him one more time, if only to say she was sorry.

Multi-colored leaves and chilly air reminded Leonardo that it was again October. Had it been only a year since he'd traveled through time with Sara? He had purchased a new car in New York and decided to drive back to Texas. The beautiful, bright red Lexus was a far cry from the van. He thought it a little staid with its air bags and leather seats, not to mention the fact that it was all one color. But Dove could take care of that. A few flowers might break up the monotony. This time, he'd have Dove paint a portrait of the Grateful Dead on the door instead of the Beatles.

He drew in a deep breath and thought about Texas. Once there, he would take care of business with Bryan and eventually join Dove in a place called Santa Fe, New Mexico. Dove raved about the perfect desert light.

"You have to come, man," Dove pleaded. "It's a real art community. My parents have a guest house with an extra bedroom."

"Sounds good," Leonardo said. But he didn't care. One place was as good as another.

His thoughts turned again to Sara. Dr. Kraven relayed their initial conversation, but had no further word after that. He didn't know if they'd even figured out the program. Leonardo sighed. Ben was still partially paralyzed, and he would never forgive himself for that. He had done his best to make up for it. That was all he could do. One day Sara might find it in her heart to forgive him. But he didn't know when that would be. In any case, the rest of her family hated him. He knew Sara well enough to know that she would never go against their wishes.

Many times he had replayed the scene with Ben in his mind. It always came out the same. He loved the old man and regretted the outcome of their last meeting. But he knew that if he had it to do over again, he would probably act in the same way. That was the reason he and Sara could never be married. They were truly opposites. She preferred a stalwart, predictable man—the kind he would never be. Not in this life or any other.

But losing her was a wound from which he would not

recover. He saw the remainder of his life stretching out before him like a long highway without an end. He would continue traveling down it, stopping here or there, but never staying long. He would go to Santa Fe, then California. Someone said that during certain seasons in Alaska, there was continuous light. Great. He could go there and paint forever without sleeping. He didn't sleep anyway.

Three days of driving brought him back to Houston. But he was not prepared for the overwhelming sadness he experienced upon returning to the little blue house in Magnolia. Everywhere he looked, there were traces of Sara. Her book lay on the table; dried flowers they had picked last spring were in a vase nearby. He picked up her coffee cup that said, "I'm not hyper, I just like things my way." Whatever that meant. Her jacket was in the closet. She'd bought it because it was reversible, she said. Taking the jacket off the hanger, he hugged it to his chest. It still bore her sweet, spicy smell. Perhaps he should call her and tell her he had it. Soon it would be cold again. She might need it. But he couldn't bear the thought that she might not want to see him. Replacing the coat in the closet, he shut the door.

He busied himself with setting up his studio again, stretching canvases, buying new paints and brushes. Yet the weight of the memories grew heavier with each passing day. At night he dreamed of Sara. During the day, her face was constantly in his mind. He painted another portrait of her from memory, but was dissatisfied with it. Eventually, her face would fade from his memory. Then he would no longer be able to recall the color of her eyes, the exact tilt of her lashes, or the way her auburn hair fell across her shoulders. This thought filled him with renewed sadness.

One evening, he sat drinking a glass of Chianti while the sun set. For some reason, he remembered that the Renaissance Festival had begun. He'd seen an advertisement somewhere. On impulse, he retrieved the amethyst ball from his bedside table. As he held it in his hand, he felt the energy flow through his palm and up his arm. A strange warm current seemed to course through his blood.

Holding the amethyst up to the fading light, he pondered the possibilities. Such a strange stone.

If it could bring him here, couldn't it also take him back?

Sara had almost given up hope of ever seeing Leonardo again. Almost. She thought if she gave up hope completely she might die. She couldn't blame him for leaving. He had every reason to believe he would never be welcome in her parents' home. Then she had made it clear that she did not want to see him again. So he had managed to disappear.

She thought he might still be in New York or he might be in Santa Fe with Dove. He could be anywhere. But as the days stretched into weeks, she began to despair. Could a person just disappear and never be heard from again?

October came with a blast of chilly air and the leaves had begun to turn early this year. When she realized it was time again for the Renaissance Festival, Sara's heart skipped a beat. She thought back on last year. Had it only been a year? So much had happened in such a short time. But the Renaissance Festival! *Would he go? Would she find him there?* she wondered. Probably not.

Had it been a dream after all? Had she mentally fabricated a lover from the past who embodied all the qualities she desired? Then had this Renaissance Man just faded back into the pages of a history book? She didn't know anything for sure, except that she had to return to the festival and find out.

It was a Saturday morning the first week in October. The irony of that coincidence filled her with anticipation. Then, when she drove out into the countryside, the same, eerie feeling came over her. A slight mist hung over the still-green fields and the dewdrops were strung like pearls through the bushes along the road. It was just as she remembered it—like a pastoral painting of some earlier time.

Her hands on the steering wheel began to sweat, and she opened a window. Even the smell! The scent, too, had been imprinted on her memory. Her nerves were now on edge, and she could scarcely breathe when she came across the sign that announced "Todd Mission."

"Oh, God. There it is," she said aloud.

She turned into the parking lot and stopped. Prying her hands loose from the wheel, she left the car. Doubts flooded her mind. What if he isn't here? What if he went back in time without telling her? What would she do then?

But she knew what she would do. In her pocket were the amethyst earrings. Retrieving them, she slipped them into her ears. Instantly, she felt the heated energy go straight through her. She was a little frightened to think it might happen all over again.

She didn't care. Filled with resolve, she trudged to the gate. Rain had beaten down the marigolds and they lay askew in yellow clumps. Mud filled the ruts in the dirt road just as before. Taking note of this and of the dark clouds overhead, Sara sighed.

If Leonardo wasn't here, she would just go back in time and find him.

Though it was early, the Black Boar was crowded with patrons. Jodie was back again this year, sporting a tattoo on her right shoulder—a little mushroom with some grass growing around it.

"You look familiar," she said to Leonardo, delivering a flagon of mead.

"I was here last year," he told her, smiling.

"I thought so," Jodie nodded. "I never forget a face."

"Well, the face is the same, but I was wearing tights. And I had a sword."

"Isn't it fun to dress up? That's why I like to work here. It's like really being back in the olden days."

He wanted to tell her she didn't know what it was like, but he nodded instead and took a drink of mead. The mead tasted weird. But it was wet and cool.

Outside, he heard a rumble of thunder. Taking the amethyst ball from his pocket, he thought it was just about time.

After returning to Houston, he'd lost the creative energy that had driven him through the summer. Sadness overwhelmed him. Being this close to Sara without having her was pure torture. He no longer wanted to go to Santa Fe. He didn't care to tour the west coast. Alaska held no allure, because he couldn't paint. Every time he picked up a brush, he wanted to paint Sara, and painting Sara, only made him sad.

Often, he caught himself staring at his father's sword, wondering if he should end it all. Then he thought there might be another way.

During the last week, he'd gotten his affairs in order, even drawn up a will, leaving all his worldly possessions to Sara. It was as if he did plan to die.

The truth was, he didn't know what would happen. Then when he heard the weekend forecast, he decided to try to go back to his own time. Here he was, back in the Black Boar, waiting for God knows what.

Thunder crashed outside and he knew it was now or never. He signaled Jodie and paid his check, as if she could really collect where he was going. Still, he liked to leave things in neat order.

Rising from the table he walked outside. There was the tree, sprawled out in different directions. Walking over to it, he thought it looked larger. The amethyst ball was in his hand, sending vital energy through his veins. Gripping it tightly, he took a deep breath.

Again, thunder cracked over his head and a flash of lightning seared the sky.

Slightly out of breath, Sara rushed into the Black Boar. A quick glance around the room told her he wasn't there. She sank down on a bench.

"Damn," she said under her breath.

"I swear, you look familiar, too," Jodie said. "Were you here last year?"

Sara nodded. "Have you seen a tall man, long reddish-blond hair, pulled back in a pony tail?"

Jodie thought. "Yeah, there was a guy just here. He paid his bill, but I didn't see him leave. He might have gone to the bathroom."

A loud thunderclap resounded through the bar. "The bathroom! Damn!"

Sara raced to the back of the bar.

"Wait a minute, you can't go in the men's," Jodie called after her.

Bolting out the back door, Sara ran straight into Leonardo, who was coming back inside. They fell into each other's arms.

"Oh, thank God!"

"Sara. I can't believe it. I thought I would never see you again."

Tears ran down her cheeks and he kissed them away. Lightning flashed and energy swirled around them in a dizzying spiral. Throwing her arms around his neck, Sara kissed him passionately, then when they saw they had an audience inside the bar, they closed the door. He returned her kiss and let her go only when both were out of breath.

"I thought you had gone back in time," she panted. "I was so afraid."

He shook his head. "I wanted to. I decided I couldn't

stay in this life without you. You're the reason I came here in the first place, you know."

"But you didn't go back. You're still here."

"I tried to will myself back, but nothing happened," he said, turning the amethyst ball in his hand. "Are you sure this is pure amethyst?"

"Oh, damn. I hope it isn't. Remind me to give you a clear crystal."

He touched her earrings. "You're wearing the earrings. Why?"

"Oh, Leonardo, don't you know? I was going to go back and get you."

His eyes filled with tears. "You would have done that for me?"

She nodded.

"Sara, I'm so glad you came, but what of your family? How is your father?"

"He's better. He's talking, in English sometimes. Thanks to you. We all appreciate your sending the program."

"I'm so happy he is better."

"He wants to see you."

His green eyes widened. "He does?"

"That's right, and so does my mother."

He smiled broadly. "They do?"

Sara nodded.

Leonardo frowned. "What about Roger?"

"Roger is history.

His eyes were like saucers now. "History?"

Sara shook her head and laughed. "Never mind, I'll explain later. Let's just say, Roger is out of the picture."

Hand in hand, they walked back into the Black Boar. Another woman was at the bar and they stopped to stare. She looked exactly like Sophie Winborn.

"Oh, no," Sara said. "Not again."

The woman smiled. "You looking for Jodie? she just stepped outside for a minute."

"Your name isn't Sophie?" Leonardo asked.

She shook her head. "I wish it was. My name is Gidget, and I've tried to rename myself a hundred times, but they never stick."

Jodie was smoking a cigarette outside the front door.

"You found him, I see," she smiled at Sara. "You didn't have to go into the men's room, I hope."

"No," Sara said, smiling at Leonardo, "but if I told you where I had to go to find this man, you wouldn't believe it."

DANGEROUS GAMES   (0-7860-0270-0, $4.99)
by Amanda Scott

When Nicholas Barrington, eldest son of the Earl of Ulcombe, first met Melissa Seacort, the desperation he sensed beneath her well-bred beauty haunted him. He didn't realize how desperate Melissa really was . . . until he found her again at a Newmarket gambling club—being auctioned off by her father to the highest bidder. So, Nick bought himself a wife. With a villain hot on their heels, and a fortune and their lives at stake, they would gamble everything on the most dangerous game of all: love.

A TOUCH OF PARADISE   (0-7860-0271-9, $4.99)
by Alexa Smart

As a confidence man and scam runner in 1880s America, Malcolm Northrup has amassed a fortune. Now, posing as the eminent Sir John Abbot—scholar, and possible discoverer of the lost continent of Atlantis—he's taking his act on the road with a lecture tour, seeking funds for a scientific experiment he has no intention of making. But scholar Halia Davenport is determined to accompany Malcolm on his "expedition" . . . even if she must kidnap him!

Available wherever paperbacks are sold, or order direct from the Publisher. Send cover price plus 50¢ per copy for mailing and handling to Penguin USA, P.O. Box 999, c/o Dept. 17109, Bergenfield, NJ 07621. Residents of New York and Tennessee must include sales tax. DO NOT SEND CASH.

ROMANCE FROM JO BEVERLY

DANGEROUS JOY   (0-8217-5129-8, $5.99)

FORBIDDEN   (0-8217-4488-7, $4.99)

THE SHATTERED ROSE   (0-8217-5310-X, $5.99)

TEMPTING FORTUNE   (0-8217-4858-0, $4.99)

ROMANCE FROM FERN MICHAELS

DEAR EMILY   (0-8217-4952-8, $5.99)

WISH LIST   (0-8217-5228-6, $6.99)

AND IN HARDCOVER:

VEGAS RICH   (1-57566-057-1, $25.00)